LITTLE WOLVES

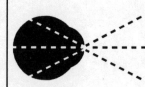

This Large Print Book carries the
Seal of Approval of N.A.V.H.

LITTLE WOLVES

THOMAS MALTMAN

THORNDIKE PRESS
A part of Gale, Cengage Learning

GALE
CENGAGE Learning®

Detroit • New York • San Francisco • New Haven, Conn • Waterville, Maine • London

GALE
CENGAGE Learning®

Copyright © 2012 by Thomas Maltman.
Thorndike Press, a part of Gale, Cengage Learning.

Thorndike Press® Large Print Peer Picks.
The text of this Large Print edition is unabridged.
Other aspects of the book may vary from the original edition.
Set in 16 pt. Plantin.

LIBRARY OF CONGRESS CATALOGING-IN-PUBLICATION DATA

Maltman, Thomas James, 1971–
    Little wolves / by Thomas Maltman. — Large print edition.
        pages ; cm. — (Thorndike Press large print peer picks)
    ISBN 978-1-4104-6452-1 (hardcover) — ISBN 1-4104-6452-0 (hardcover)
    1. Fathers and sons—Fiction. 2. Murder—Fiction. 3. Spouses of clergy—Fiction. 4. Family secrets—Fiction. 5. Minnesota—Fiction. 6. Psychological fiction. 7. Large type books. I. Title.
PS3613.A524L58 2013
813'.6—dc23   2013032227

Published in 2013 by arrangement with Soho Press, Inc.

Printed in the United States of America
1 2 3 4 5 6 7 17 16 15 14 13

For my parents, Ruby and Doug, who instilled in me a love of places and of the stories those places hold

And ever and anon the wolf would steal
The Children and devour but now
and then
Her own brood lost or dead, lent her
fierce teat
To human sucklings . . .
— Alfred Lord Tennyson,
"The Coming of Arthur"

Beauty is a terrible and awful thing! It
is terrible because it has not been
fathomed, and never can be fathomed,
for God sets us nothing but riddles.
Here the boundaries meet and all
contradictions exist side by side.
— Fyodor Dostoevsky,
The Brothers Karamazov

"We've been waiting for you, Judas,"
Jesus said.
"We couldn't begin till you came."
— Madeleine L'Engle,
"Waiting for Judas"

■ ■ ■ ■

BOOK ONE

■ ■ ■ ■

THE WOLFLING

She heard him from the mountain, a voice high and thin, breaking the night's quiet. The cry was such as her own children made when she was gone too long searching for food to bring back to the den. It was the cry of something blind and helpless, a cry of hunger. She heard it and she could do no other thing but go toward it.

How it came to be alone in the tallgrass is a story for another time. She heard it with her sharp pointed ears and smelled it with her sharp black nose. Her nose told her the truth. It was not a wolf pup but a human baby, alone on a bed of prairie grass under the starry dark. She smelled on the breeze the horses that had come and gone, running hard. They had run away pulling a wagon that scarred deep ruts in the grass.

Her paws stepped in these ruts, found the gouges the horses had torn from the prairie. She paused, suspicious, and sniffed the ground and raised her nose and sniffed the wind. They had been here, but they were gone, except the baby. In the torn grass she smelled the fear on the horses and in the air she smelled something burning. She knew the ways of the wind and fire out on the prairie. The fire was a breathing thing, ever hungry. The fire would be here soon and find where the baby lay in his nest of grass.

She could not resist his crying because she was a First Mother who had birthed many children, and there were no others like her in this valley that smelled of smoke and terror. Her children had grown fat and happy until the coming of the Trapper the past moon, the Trapper who had killed her Mate, scattering the others, and then found the den where she had hidden her pups away.

The cries of the human baby traveled through the night and found her ears and went into her ears and into her blood. The cries opened up places inside her that had not yet gone dry, where milk recently flowed from her nipples to feed her pups and make them strong. It hurt to make milk again.

The coyote was skinny and mangy, her ribs poking from her pelt, and she needed food for herself, a plump mouse or jackrabbit. Here was this thing wrapped in a white cloth under the night sky. It had fallen from the running horses but the soft grasses had broken the fall. The running horses had not stopped for it. The child might as well have come from the stars themselves. And now it was alone here as she was alone. She did not think what to do, even if the baby bore the same tainted smell as the Trapper. Her body had told her when the milk rinsed out of her. She went toward it, sniffing tentatively at the corner of the cloth, and then touched the baby's soft skin with her wet black nose. The baby quit crying. It gurgled, shocked.

The coyote licked it with her tongue and tasted the salty skin. If she had not been a First Mother, if another of her kind had found this pink bundle in the grass, the story might have been different. She stood over the child and crouched down so that it might reach her nipples and suckle. Yes, it hurt to make milk again. Her milk flowed out of her, emptying her of all she had to give, but her heart was full, as full as the night sky above.

When the child was done feeding she opened her jaws, clenched the white cloth, and lifted the child from the grass. She carried him away from the smell of burning where the prairie grasses would soon blossom with flames. The child rocked to and fro in his hammock of cloth. She took him in this manner to the place she called home, the mountain from which she had first heard his cries, the mountain where she had been alone for a time, but not any longer.

Her father had told her many stories, and this was just one, the one that reached furthest back into history, when settlers had gone to war with the Indians, and after the massacre, one child was saved by a feral mother. Her father told stories of a giant who lived inside a mountain, of wolves and lost children and the monsters they later became. The stories he told were the only answer he had for the absence of her mother. Though he never said so outright, they were about a childhood place he would never see again. She did not set them down on paper until after her father died and she herself was six months pregnant, a pastor's wife, a stranger living in a small town.

Her hand shook as she wrote the words. She was in the room that was to be the nursery, and it was bare except for a small desk she planned to use as a changing table and the rocking chair where she sat with a spiral notebook spread open on her lap. Aqua-colored light soaked the room from blue curtains drawn across the window.

Yesterday, one of her students had rung the doorbell while she was down in the basement. She had looked up through a grimy basement window and beheld tennis shoes and the ragged edge of a coat. She saw the legs of this scarecrow figure and nothing more. He rang and rang that bell, and she just stood rooted there. A cold hand touched her shoulder, bidding her to stay. Even the baby she carried inside her was still and waiting. The bell kept ringing in her brain a long time after the figure in the coat went away.

And now the bells were ringing at church next door, as though this were any other Sunday, but she would not be joining her husband in the sanctuary. As pastor's wife she did not want to face the congregation after what had happened. Her husband's parishioners would greet her and smile. They desperately needed good news, and she was it. *How are you? The baby?* They would lay hands on her. The child was not hers alone; it belonged to them as well. They would touch her hair as though she had returned from the dead. They would speak once more of angels.

No. She needed to be alone here. She opened her notebook and began to write, balancing it on one knee. She could hear organ music and recognized the strains of "This Is My Father's World" as the service began. Quaking voices. Such a gift, this murmur in her blood. The rocking soothed her, as did the words she scratched on the page with a fountain pen, a Montblanc Meisterstrück her father had given her when she graduated from high school.

Late last night she had seen the coyotes, three of them emerging from the cornfield late after dark. They did not howl at first but entered the cemetery behind the church with a short series of yips and barks, one and then the other, their calls braiding into a chorus, until eventually one howled in a language that was part of the great outer darkness. The coyotes weren't supposed to be here; they were searching for something. They had come from the lone mountain like a storybook curse and roused the town with their plaintive singing, vanishing by daylight.

Clara Warren's hand shook as she marked the words on the page because she knew she was trapped inside of one of her father's stories, and the only way out was to write it down. She wrote as if her life depended on it, and maybe it did.

THE BOY

The day before, Seth Fallon limped toward town under a boiled-blue sky, a dry wind trailing him from the fields. Despite the heat he wore a long, oilcloth coat he'd taken from the mudroom, and inside the coat he had the twelve gauge his father had given him last Christmas, with the promise they would hunt whitetail in the swamp come fall.

Earlier that morning he had taken the shotgun into the shop, clasped it in a vice, and sawed off precisely seven inches. Then he sanded down the bore, oiled the barrel, shined it with a rag, and leaned the gun against the door, so he could tidy what mess he had made, discarding the sawn barrel in the trash and sweeping steel scrapings from the concrete floor. He hung the saw back on its hook, folded the cloth in a neat square, and stored it with the gun oil in a metal cabinet. When he left everything was in its place, just as his father had raised him to do.

Barely a scratch of rain had fallen in two months the Saturday afternoon he set out for town. A summer of drought baked the crop in the furrows, leaving whole rows sere and stunted, so that the wind gnawed at what remained and lifted a fine scrim of topsoil from the fields and flung it against the outbuildings. He walked with this wind under a sun that was a cinder in a vacant sky, the gun cool against his ribs.

The farthest he had ever traveled from this valley was across the state border to Sioux Falls. This was the only home he had ever known. The town of Lone Mountain perched along terraced streets overlooking the surrounding valley, a half mile wide and thickly wooded on either side. For aeons the Minnesota River had been at work eating through topsoil toward the earth's core, carving out this place from vast prairie farmlands stretching hundreds of miles all around.

The valley had been a place of both shadow and shelter for generations of Indians — the Cheyenne, the Fox and Sauk, the Dakotas — all who came to hide from the winter winds on the prairie. Only the ghosts of the Indians remained, but these

18

were potent ghosts with no love for the Germans who had stolen their land following a summer of war a hundred years before, and when a little girl drowned in the river, the old-timers crossed themselves and thought of the brown hands that surely pulled her under. They later said such a ghost moved in the boy, an angry spirit urging him on. Such darkness could not have come from one of their own.

They had lived here for generations after traveling across the Atlantic but still felt like sojourners. When the hail came, when the river bucked and broke its banks, when the children lay awake in the late hours fevered and coughing — they knew this place belonged to the devil, had always belonged to him. Prince of the broken world, broken now more than ever with the last family farms going under. The Torvicks. The Kantors. Jerry Kroger and his tribe of daughters. All gone.

And now this wickedness.

The boy stopped at the parsonage first, where the pastor and his wife Clara lived next to the church. Clara was his substitute English teacher at Lone Mountain High. Her husband was off visiting a homebound couple when the boy rang the bell. Alone down in the basement, Clara wasn't able to explain later to authorities why she didn't answer the door.

Next, he went down the main drag, moving toward a downtown that bustled with weekend traffic, so many people parked outside the pool hall and Jurgen's Corner Grocery. No one later remembered seeing him on the sidewalk or could recall phoning the sheriff, Will Gunderson. It might just have been that Will was driving past at that very moment and what he saw — a school-age boy hunched into a coat in the fullness of Indian summer — troubled him. Will was a survivor of two tours in Vietnam, a decorated veteran, and he was a known hard-ass who had taken the boy into custody several times before this day.

He pulled over beside Seth Fallon and rolled down his window to say something. What passed between them is a mystery. Seth flung open his coat and brought out the gun. No one remembered seeing Seth come down the sidewalk, but that shotgun blast echoed all over Lone Mountain.

NAMESAKE

He came home from driving a seed truck to find his farmyard swimming with lights from four or five squad cars parked out on his lawn. His Christian name was also Seth, like his son, but most in town still called him Grizz from his days playing nose tackle for the Lone Mountain Braves. Grizz felt as sapped as the yellow leaves clinging to the trees out in the yard, and he wanted nothing more than a Steak-umm sandwich on rye bread, to wash it down with Seagram's and Seven and sleep until the ache in his back woke him. As soon as he saw those lights, he knew it was something to do with Seth. The cars had decals from Brown and Lyon Counties, sheriffs and deputies from miles around. Dark was just beginning to spread long shadows through the yard and surrounding fields where a couple of the deputies fanned out, their Maglites carving trails through the blond corn.

Grizz stayed in the cab of his semi, watching it all from far away, his radio tuned to Lone Mountain's only station, KLKR, where long-dead country singers like Patsy Cline crooned above the stir of static. Lights were on in the outbuildings, both the barn and the machinery shed, and his house blazed in the falling dark. He didn't know how long he stayed in his seat, but eventually he felt eyes on him and saw a man waving from the porch. Grizz climbed out of the cab, his legs stiff from sitting all day, and limped across the lawn to greet him. The waving hand belonged to Steve Krieger, who had cut back to part-time in the sheriff's office, a semi-retirement. Grizz had known Steve since they were boys. Their families went way back to the founding of town, tributaries of bad blood branching between them over generations, and he didn't care to find the man out on his porch, leaning against the banister.

"What'd he do now?" he said. From the very beginning it had been hard raising Seth alone, without a mother. Grizz was sure this new trouble had to do with drugs. It explained everything, the boy's moody behavior, his frequent absences and trouble in school. The last time he found pot in Seth's sock drawer he'd called the head sheriff,

Will Gunderson, hoping to put a scare into Seth before it got more serious. When he saw all those squad cars on his lawn he figured Seth had gotten mixed up with dealers, Mexicans and the like, rumored to be planting marijuana in the thickly wooded river valleys and ravines, the very worst trouble he imagined a boy could find out here.

"You'd better come inside," Steve told him in a thick voice. Steve still had black hair in his sixties and his mustache glistened with oil. He looked like he hadn't aged a day in the decades Grizz had known him.

From upstairs rumbled the sound of boots on hardwood where a few men tromped through Seth's room. It sounded like the house was coming apart, as if these men were set to rip right through the plaster, looking for Seth.

"Go ahead and tell me." Grizz intended to stay standing, wanting to be at eye level when Steve said what he had to say.

"Seth shot Will Gunderson in the face," Steve said flatly.

"What?" Grizz braced himself against the table. "No," he said, but it was a muted protest. His mouth had gone dry and wouldn't form the words.

"Will didn't die right away. I want you to

23

know that."

"Jesus." Grizz had grown up with Will; they had played on the same nine-man football team. When he hadn't known what else to do with his son, Will was the one he called. Their boys were the same age, both troubled.

Steve's ruddy face flushed a deeper red, as though the news were bleeding inside him. He kept his rheumy eyes fixed on Grizz. "The slug tore away his jaw; blew out the window. By the time people reached him Will had drowned in his own blood, and Seth was gone."

Steve spoke in a monotone, even though the dead man he described was married to his own oldest daughter, because everyone in this place was tangled by blood in one way or the other. Grizz saw he laid stock in such gory detail and that he was angry and wanted to paint a full picture of the horror and so hurt him with it. Steve's heavy fists, hanging at his belt, clenched and un-clenched. He looked to be measuring him now, watching his face to see what he knew.

Then Grizz did sit down because his body gave him no choice. He didn't question any of this or think to ask for a warrant. Another parent might have doubted, but he knew Seth was capable of such a thing and had in fact done it. A gap opened up inside him where the air whistled thin and tight in his lungs. "Where is Seth?" he asked when he found his voice.

"We were hoping you might tell us," Steve said. "When did you last see him? Did anything seem unusual this morning?"

Grizz shook his head, explaining he'd left before dawn. He hadn't spoken to his son in two days, not since Seth overturned a table in his biology lab, shattering a twenty-five-gallon aquarium filled with channel cats, bullheads, and crawdads. Seth was suspended for it, and the principal had promised to send Grizz a bill for the aquarium and dead fish, a bill he knew the Fallons couldn't afford. This morning when he left to drive a seed truck for the co-op, Grizz had seen a light on under his boy's door and wondered why Seth was awake so early or if he had even slept. He had paused at the door but had not gone inside, fearing another fight.

"Found part of the sawed-off barrel in the trash out in the machinery shed," Steve continued. "He planned this and maybe worse. Grizz, we got to find him before he hurts someone else. Tell us where he might have gone."

The mountain. He would go to the mountain. There were caves there that only the boy knew. There were the little wolves Seth had raised from pups. He kept his head down and twisted his hands in his lap while the hope took shape.

Don't you know your own son? was what Steve was asking. Grizz started to explain about the twelve gauge, how it was a gift meant to reward the boy for staying in school to finish out his junior year, when another man walked in the door and drew Steve aside. They whispered together, Steve watching Grizz over his shoulder.

He put his face into his hands. The mountain wasn't big enough. They'd send dogs and find him. He hoped that Seth had run, that he had stolen a car and made for the Northwoods and was even now nearing Canada and that the awful thing he had done had scared all the evil out of him. Wild thoughts. *Get as far from here as you can,* he prayed. *Be gone; then don't you ever come back.* Even as he thought these things, he knew on some level his only child was dead.

Steve walked over to him. "They found Seth," he said. "He went into Miller's cornfield and shot himself."

The emptiness in his gut seared up into his throat, but Grizz swallowed it and felt it burn all the way down. When he held out his hand it trembled, but he was determined not to show any sorrow before these men. "Good," he said, raising his gaze to Steve's. "I'm glad he can't hurt no one else."

"He was carrying a bandolier of ammunition," Steve continued, his voice rising in pitch, "and the pockets of his coat were filled with lead slugs. . . . If Will hadn't stopped him earlier, there's no telling."

Grizz took this in. "Seth stopped himself."

"Seth didn't say anything to you? What was the last conversation you had?"

He tried to answer, but the words drained away. Steve kept after him, badgering him with questions. Grizz swallowed several times, and his breath wheezed in his lungs. *Don't you cry,* he commanded himself. *Goddamn you. Don't you give them any kind of satisfaction.* "I need a glass of water," he said in a parched whisper, "please."

Steve walked into the kitchen and slammed around the cabinets before he found a glass he filled with tap water and carried it to the table. He didn't hand it to Grizz. With his man looking on, the one who had brought the news about Seth, he made a noise in his throat and hocked into the water, so Grizz would know how things were going to be for him here on out, a Fallon with a criminal history of his own in a valley settled by law-abiding Germans, the father of a cop-killer. Steve set the glass down with a thunk, the water Grizz longed for sloshing up the sides and the yellow phlegm riding the surface. Steve leaned in, his small eyes black as beetles, and said, "Sin as ugly as yours won't stay down."

Grizz hesitated. His son had been right all along. Seth had come to Grizz for help, but he turned his back on him because he had to learn how this town was and his place within it. *Child, where you have gone, I will follow. Yes, even there if it means I might see you once more.*

He lifted the glass and drained it to the dregs. Then with them looking on he held the empty glass in his palm and squeezed. It was one of those old-fashioned ones his wife Jo had liked, with *Drink Coca-Cola* in red letters on the sides. It shattered in his grasp, and he kept squeezing until the shards bit into his palm, and only then did he let it drop. There wasn't as much blood as he hoped for, his skin too leathery and cracked. He looked up at Steve, and his eyes had cleared, and he had his voice again. And he knew this was the terrible clarity that must have come over his son when he went into the fields after murdering Will. "There isn't any reason for you to be here," he said.

"I want you out of my house."

They didn't leave right away, despite his words, but dark had fallen, and as news about Seth spread among the searchers one by one the cruisers pulled away.

Steve was still worked up. His son-in-law was dead and he wanted justice, but what justice could be wrung from such a situation?

Grizz wanted Steve here now. His oldest nemesis. He wanted Steve here because he was terrified of the quiet, and he felt his son's death like a sharp stone he had swallowed that was only now wedging into his chest.

"I want to know if you put him up to this," Steve said, his bitter coffee breath washing over Grizz.

"That's enough," said the other man. "He's just lost his son."

"Stay out of this. You don't know these people like I do."

"C'mon," the deputy insisted, laying a hand on Steve's shoulder. "It's late. Let's go."

Steve shrugged away the hand but didn't say anything more. Grizz thought they might ask him to come identify the body and dreaded the moment, but they didn't. There wasn't any need. There was no mystery to be solved, or so it seemed. Seth himself was a mystery, but not to them.

He didn't speak or look up as the men left. Few people know you so well as those who hate you. He was imagining his boy out in the corn. A child where no child should have been. Did that barrel taste of hot powder when he put it in his mouth? Did it clack against his teeth, sear his tongue? *Tell me why, Seth. Tell me if I am to blame. Tell me what I am to do now. Speak, boy.*

GAST

Clara Warren went into the kitchen when she heard him fumbling with his keys at the back door. A moment later her husband stepped into the entryway and slipped out of his loafers. She drew in a deep breath and folded her hands over her stomach, smelling from the staleness on his skin how awful his day had been. She knew the stray cat busy lapping up milk from a saucer on the floor was about to add to his unhappiness. Clara had been hoping to get rid of it before he returned.

"Clara?" Logan said after he climbed the stairs to the kitchen. "Is that the same tomcat I asked you not to let in the house?"

"It might be," she said. "It bears a certain resemblance."

He put his hands around his face and then he sneezed. Logan was twenty-seven years old, two years older than Clara, but still the age of many of his parishioner's grandchildren. He had ash-blond hair and a thin, mousy beard he'd grown to try and look older and wiser for their benefit. After expelling the sneeze, he rubbed his sinuses and peered at her with his glacial blue eyes. "Is that my mother's good china?" he asked, noticing the saucer. "That's been passed down in my family since the Warrens came over from Lancashire?"

"Next time I'll use the Tupperware." Clara went to him, touching his arm. "Logan, I know you don't need any more stress, but the cat was crying up a storm outside. It must have belonged to someone who lived here before. I'm sorry."

Logan wore a black clerical shirt called a Friar Tuck he special ordered from Augsburg Fortress. He had a closet full of them in varying shades, from lilac to midnight, which he always wore with khaki trousers. "I'm going to go upstairs and change," he said, tugging at his collar. "And when I come back downstairs that cat is going to be gone. Vamoose. Adios. No pets allowed in the parsonage, understand? Especially not a tomcat. It's not how things are done *out here.*"

Clara bit her tongue. She didn't like his authoritarian tone, but it was understandable after the day he must have had. While he spoke, the cat swirled around her ankles, purring. She had already named it Soren, hoping that calling the cat after Logan's favorite philosopher might endear him to it in some way. "Yes," Clara said, trying a hesitant smile, "I understand."

He paused. Logan had an aquiline nose and an imperious way of staring a person down, even though Clara was the same height. "You are going to be okay, aren't you?" She heard the weariness in his voice and knew he wasn't trying to be mean.

Clara tried to read what else might be in his eyes. Disappointment, surely. This was his first pastoral assignment, his first big test. His congregation had been stricken, and he hadn't found the words he needed to offer succor, and she wasn't helping him any.

They had been married less than a year when Clara discovered her pregnancy. And now they were here, serving a congregation way out on the southwestern Minnesota prairies, strangers to the small town of Lone Mountain and strangers to each other. Lone Mountain: the name of the place like a pebble dropped into a well somewhere inside Clara, some deep pool she couldn't see yet, where ripples were spreading. But Logan had told her he didn't want children.

Hadn't he made himself clear? She had forgotten a pill or maybe two; she was always forgetting things.

Their talk at dinner at first only circled the murder and suicide, like blackbirds blown hither on a windy day, unable to find rest. Over a beef roast she'd cooked so dry it stuck to the roofs of their mouths, they discussed funeral arrangements, the way the church would fill because Sheriff Will Gunderson had been deeply feared and respected. Both the victim and the killer were members of Logan's church. Would Seth's father want his boy's funeral to be held the day after, and if so, would anyone come? They didn't talk about how close Clara had come to being murdered. *Did he daydream about my death?* she wondered. *Would it have made his life simpler?*

Eventually the quiet between them became oppressive, and her throat thickened. When she looked over at Logan, his face was blurry.

"Why are you crying?" he said.

"Me?" She touched her face, surprised to find tears there. "I don't really know," she said softly, and then it became more difficult to breathe. In her second trimester sudden tempers bloomed up in her like cumuli over open plains. Once the tears started, she couldn't stop them, and they built and built until she bent over there at the table with her face in her hands, weeping.

Logan came around the table and leaned over her chair. He cupped his hands over the fullness of her belly, pressed his chin to the top of her forehead. How she had longed for him to hold her like this. Underneath the bitterness of his sweat she smelled a hint of his true grassy scent, at once faint and sweet. An earthy smell that made her feel safe from the moment she met him. "Don't be sad," he said. "There isn't anyone who can hurt you. Not anymore. Isn't any reason to be frightened."

She shook her head. She interlaced her fingers with his and drank down her tears. He didn't know. He didn't know how a monster story was supposed to work.

Logan patted her hair and gathered up their dishes to take to the sink, leaving Clara alone at the table. The conversation was over.

Why do people do the things they do? Of course, the first thing Clara did after Logan climbed the stairs for bed was let Soren back inside. She would not leave something to suffer.

Late that night Clara woke to an eerie calling. Only two days after Seth shot himself, she heard his ghost crying out under the stairwell and the sound of it shook her to the core.

"Help me," cried a child's voice, a whispery echo in the hollow drum of so much space, a sound that plucked her from sleep with little icy fingers along her neck and spine. Over and over those two words climbed the stairs and glided under the door to find her in the bed. And it was not his voice exactly she thought she was hearing, not the rasp of a boy nearing manhood, but the child inside him, still recoiling from what he had done. This was the voice of a murderer's ghost, some otherworldly summons. *Help me.*

No good comes from hearing such a thing when you live in an old stone parsonage at the edge of town. Clara reached over and jabbed Logan in the kidneys, but he only grumbled in his sleep and turned over. In the newness of her marriage it shocked her how alone she felt most nights with another human being lying so close beside her. The view out her window showed a steep hill freckled with rimed tombstones the color of polished bone under the moon.

She burrowed into her sheets, pretending she wasn't hearing anything at all. Six months pregnant, she was surprised how well her body took to it. Her thighs clenched a body-length pillow; her gown dampened with sweat. She squeezed her eyes shut and imagined she was elsewhere, but still she went on hearing the crying child.

"*Gast,*" she said, naming him aloud in Old English. *A lich, a feond.* Such words usually soothed her. They are the root of our language, our mother tongue. They are heavy with a thousand years of history and tether us to earth. Clara needed such words to hold her down when she thought about madness or escape. Hearing the ghost child, she searched her mind for other words, an Anglo-Saxon *galdor* to drive off elves and wicked spirits that she had written down in a notebook using a runic script Irish monks called the Insular hand, but she couldn't remember how the words went.

As she did this, she stroked the nubs of her missing ring finger and pinkie, where the skin was worn smooth as river-tossed stones, with her good hand. The left hand was her ghost hand. Two of the fingers, blackened by frostbite, were sliced off in an emergency room when she was only a baby. But ever since Clara could remember, at night when she dreamed the hand became whole again, played through her hair, ran along her skin with a spider's weightlessness. She dreamed of the hand writing things down in a book, things the good hand would never imagine. She had come to think of it as a gift, her own private absence, a reminder to go on searching for what was not there. Her body taught her every living day that such things as ghosts were possible, so it shouldn't have surprised her that the boy would show up two nights after the murder. There was no denying the voice under the stairs.

The voice rose from the basement, the place she had been standing on the day the boy came to her door. There was a tortured tenor to its vibration. The skin around her belly went taut as the baby pressed a hand or foot to the surface, testing the watery limit of its cell, urging her to rise. Whatever cried down there was in pain. Sweat beaded her upper lip; she tasted it with the tip of her tongue.

Why did you come here first with your gun? I was down in the basement on Saturday because that was where I kept a pack of Old Golds hidden and I needed a smoke and a slug of Widow Larsen's rhubarb wine if I was to make it through the tedium of another lonely afternoon. There, now you know it. Damaging my baby before it can even draw breath.

The sound of your gun sent a shudder right through me. It echoes even now. I wished I'd had the courage to climb the stairs and look you in the eye and talk you out of what you were about to do. Would your rage have dissipated if I took you in my arms? Or did you mean to murder me so that my blood and my baby's blood might be some terrible stain on the town, a nightmare story to be told for a generation? Have you come to haunt me to remind me of my cowardice?

The crying lulled for a moment, and Clara became aware of other sounds. September had arrived after a dry summer, and even after sundown the heat pressed on the countryside. Cicadas sang in an electric hum in the cemetery trees at the edge of the yard. *Rain birds,* her husband called them, a sweet name for a spiny insect. They droned in the dark, but if the cicadas promised relief, the way Logan had prayed for a rain the week before, they lied. *Stupid to pray for rain,* he'd come home mumbling; *it wasn't in my notes, but there the words were in my mouth. The wrong thing to pray for,* he'd said again without explaining why.

The sound scraped up the stairwell. *Help me.* Clara lay atop the sheets, wondering over it. She wanted to forget Seth. She wasn't even going to his funeral, and she resigned her long-term substitute position with the district the day after the shootings.

She pulled up the pillow around her ears, and still the cries came to her. The palpable heat beyond the window and the sound of the wind hummed in her blood. Clara gathered up her courage and climbed out of bed. Moonlight illuminated her room, scattered with cardboard boxes, the lids peeled open. From one she hefted out her *Shorter Oxford English Dictionary,* which she figured a suitable weapon for doing battle with ghosts trying to take up residence under the stairwell. She held the substantial bulk of the alphabet in her hands, a word for every reality. Madness was for when words failed.

Her bare feet felt cool against the floorboards. A hot breeze through an open window rustled her gown. The heavy dictionary hooked under one arm, she opened the door and advanced into the hallway. The parsonage was a two-story built of German red brick, an aging home with many empty rooms where the air had long gone stale and undisturbed. The bones of the house creaked in the night but then went still when her footfalls sounded in the hall. In this breathless quiet the boy's crying magnified. His *help me* throbbed in her ears.

Before she could lose courage she hurried along the hallway and crept downstairs. On the lower level the child's sorrowing continued to reverberate through the kitchen and dining room.

She felt the pull of that voice tugging her onward, a coiling rope of sound to bind her. She let it lead her to the lip of the stairwell and waiting basement. Here she paused, threw on the light switch, and went down, step by step, to meet the boy's ghost. The light did not comfort her because the stairs were painted nail-polish red and glistened like the inside of a sick person's throat. A waft of sour breath exhaled from the basement. This had once been a root cellar, and it retained a smell of rotting potatoes and onions, even though it was paved over with concrete when they put the washroom down here. At the base of the stairs shadows formed a tarry pool.

By the time she reached the bottom of the stairs and fumbled for a cord, she smelled the oil from the old furnace and under that a sharper scent of musk and blood. Every tiny hair along the back of her bare legs stood on end. Her nightgown stirred against her shoulder, as though a hand touched her there, but she did not scream or go back up the stairs. Shivering, she held the dictionary to her chest like a shield. The sound garbled here, an eerie whimpering no longer amplified by the empty space in the stairwell.

Clara found the cord and was momentarily blinded when a bulb swinging from a metal chain blinked to life. She waited for her eyes to adjust, her breathing tight and tense. Beneath the stairwell a shredded box lay on concrete, and here shapes writhed and cried out. As shadows retreated and spots quit dancing in her vision, she saw four tabby kittens squirming on the cardboard next to their mother.

"Oh," she said aloud. "Oh." *What a fool you are, Clara Warren. Your husband told you it was a tomcat and you took his word for things without checking yourself. You made a monster where none existed.* Laughter rippled inside her until she quaked with it. She set the dictionary down on the bottom stair and knelt beside the kittens. They sounded so very human in their distress. They had exchanged the warm seas of their mother for this cold ground, this blinding light. The cries they made were the cries of any newborn thing. This is what she discovered two nights after the murder: In birth all things are kindred, the sounds we make universal to any species. We enter wailing of a lost world.

The mother cat licked her fluids from the kittens, purring in her pride.

One of the kittens was slick and still. Clara picked it up and massaged it. A runt, born too small. She toweled it with the edge of her nightgown until it gave one soft mewl. A familiar warmth touched her cheeks, and she held the kitten there, trembling now, but when it mewled again for its mother she set it back with the others. She hated the thickness that welled up in her chest. There wasn't any reason for it, was there? She had been saved, too, hadn't she?

And yet something scratched at the corner of her brain, a lingering presence just below the trapdoor of her consciousness. Somewhere from the land of the dead, Seth Fallon was still crying out for help. Clara shook the thought away.

"Why, Herr Soren," she said, "you sly, sly minx. We shall have to give you a new name, fräulein. Sorena?" She smoothed the fabric of her gown with both hands against the solidity of her belly, whispering, "When the time comes I must think of you." Her voice was as soft as midnight itself. "Then I won't be so afraid."

THESE THINGS TO BE DONE

Grizz woke to a sound that made him sit up in the recliner where he'd last fallen asleep — hoofs click-clattering on wood. "The hell," he said. The sagging porch outside his open window groaned under an immense weight.

His head throbbed from downing an entire bottle of Seagram's. Sometime in the night he'd torn kitchen towels into strips and wrapped his wounded hands in these rags. The muscles in his legs felt watery when he stood to work the kink out of his neck.

Staring him eye to eye through the living room window was the bull, named Ferdinand by the boy, though he'd warned Seth time and again about naming livestock. The bull's huge head filled up the frame, one dark eye milky with cataracts, as he leaned inside the open window and sniffed at the sun-faded curtains Jo had handmade years ago. "You son of a bitch," Grizz shouted hoarsely, thinking the bull meant to eat his wife's curtains.

At the sound of his voice the bull snorted "Whuff," blowing mucus from his nostrils before ambling down the creaking porch stairs.

Grizz kicked the empty bottle of whiskey and sent it spinning across the hardwood floor. He was barefoot, and his feet were dirty, as if he'd been wandering all night long, and God knows he felt like he'd been on a long journey. Before he even reached the window he knew what he would see.

The fifty-odd head of Belted Galloway cattle the Fallons kept pastured behind electric fences were spread out on the front lawn and in the far alfalfa fields where they would gorge themselves sick unto death if he let them. They milled in the apple orchard, eating the small brown fruit that had fallen early. They lazed in the shade under the big oak where Seth had built his fort. The boy had not been there to feed them these last few nights, and Grizz had lacked the strength and will, so the cattle had busted down the fence to reach what grass remained in the yard.

The bull must have sensed him eyeing them because he turned toward Grizz now.

45

He stood bandy-legged, a great mop top of clownish curly hair on his head. Long past his prime, almost half a head shorter than the heifers, the bull was kept because he was a pure-bred Beltie and because Grizz loved the spunk in him. The bull turned his rump toward him and lifted his tail to drop some steaming turds on the lawn.

Grizz's blood went hot and all the aches in his body burned away when he spotted the ax he used to cut kindling for the stove. He picked it up and felt in his bones the thunk it would make cracking open the bull's skull. He walked out on the porch, all raw inside, like someone had scraped out his guts with a spoon, and he looked at the chaos the cattle had wrought in the night, how they spread out all over creation. Some might wander toward the county road and be killed by the semis passing there. They were senseless, stupid beasts, and they had made a mess of his yard, and he was going to kill the bull for it and leave his carcass for the rendering truck.

He let the porch door slap shut behind him. A few of the cows and calves lifted their heads when they saw him coming, but the bull kept his back to him. It would be a hell of a time getting them back inside the fence. One man couldn't do it alone. Seth.

He was remembering now, and it stopped him in his tracks. Grizz had been on a bender the last couple of days. Every few hours the phone would ring, an angry buzz in his ears that he ignored, knowing it was the pastor or the funeral home or the sheriff or some goddamn newspaper calling for a statement. Finally, after a night of it, he ripped the jack from the wall and pulped the phone on the floor, blue wires spilling out like innards.

Wild thoughts moved in him when he was liquored. He had not seen the body, and as long as he had not he could believe whatever he wanted. Seth, his clever child. When he had been coming through the corn it was to the mountain he had been running. There were secret limestone caves that only the boy knew, places so deep beneath the earth that had he gone there maybe even men with hounds would not have been able to track him. Seth, who studied survival magazines and planned on joining the army when he graduated, could live out there a long time, until even the story of the man he murdered bled into daylight and was forgotten. If there was anything Seth knew and loved it was the wild. Grizz tended this idea of his boy, a guttering flame cupped in his hands. Seth living in a cave, hunting geese and pheasants in the fall, tracking deer with thin, bony ribs through birchwood bogs in winter. Seth alone, no longer troubled by his demons. Seth alive, knowing his dad had not failed him.

He gripped the ax as he approached the bull. The bull did not run; a Beltie bull is not as aggressive as other breeds and maybe not as clever as Grizz had given him credit for. The bull lowered his head and kept cropping the lawn, watching Grizz with his doleful eye.

They both looked up when they heard the sound of tires crunching on gravel. A long tongue of dust billowed up from the half-mile driveway as a gleaming red sedan rolled closer. Whoever was approaching now was someone Grizz did not want to see. As his anger against the bull ebbed, he became aware of how he hurt and resented whoever was approaching for making him feel anything again.

The long driveway was lined by ancient bur-oak trees and cottonwoods, so the car passed in and out of the sun. The driver kept slowing, either to stare at the mossy concrete statues underneath the trees or because they were afraid. They must not have been from around here, because everyone in town knew this stretch of woods along the Fallon driveway and had named it the Frozen Garden.

Most of the statues were figures from Henry Wadsworth Longfellow's *The Song of Hiawatha* that Grizz had fashioned from river stones, concrete, and mesh wire over the years. The forms were layered with cowrie shells and old glass bottles so that they caught and held what light made it through the trees. They crouched behind hewn stumps and were half hidden by bramble. Wenonah, impregnated and then abandoned by the West-Wind, lifted her arms to the branches above her. Megissogwon, the magician, a caped figure with a long beard, craned his neck as though watching the road. Close by, the beaver king, Ahmeek, squatted atop a weedy knoll.

Keeping one eye on the bull, Grizz walked over to the machinery shed, opened the door, leaned the ax against the wall, and shut it behind him. He would wait out the stranger here. He watched through a greasy window as the sedan coasted in. The windows were tinted, but he could see the driver was young and female, her straw-colored hair tied back in a ponytail. She stepped out, dressed in a long burgundy skirt and creamy blouse, her uniform from the pool hall, and eyed the cattle milling on the lawn nervously.

He knew who she was, though he had never met her. Leah. Leah Meyers, Seth's girlfriend. Seth was secretive about such things, but Grizz knew he'd been taking her down to Aden's Landing, where all the teenagers went to drink and make mischief, because he'd come back late one night when Grizz was waiting up for him, and the smell of the river had been on Seth's skin. He had forgiven his boy the worry he caused, because it'd been a long time since he'd seen him so happy.

"Tell me about her," he had said that night, and Seth did. She was a niece of the sheriff's. She had come from the Cities and didn't know enough to avoid a boy with a reputation like Seth's. Her family was trying to make a go of it in town, her dad keeping books at the co-op. She didn't like talking about what had brought them here to the "boondocks," but there'd been some trouble, both with her and her father. She was entranced by the stretch of woods where the statues were, by the Longfellow lore, and the curse Seth told her the family was living under, the bloody history of the property. And yet she had broken up with Seth a couple of weeks ago, so Grizz sure as hell didn't want her on his land now.

Leah went up to the porch and knocked on the door and then peeked in the same open window the bull had looked in. Then she came out to the edge of the porch and surveyed the property. He moved away from his window and immediately felt ashamed. Moments before he'd been ready to crack the bull's skull with an ax, and now here he was hiding from a girl.

Though the room was swept bare, he noticed a faint musky odor. The smell of gun oil, of a boy sweating in the heat while he sawed down the shotgun barrel. Like his son had just come and gone a few minutes before and if he rushed out he might catch him in time on the road to town and stop him from what he was about to do.

Seth. *There are these things to be done.* Grizz busied himself gathering his tools, the wire for the fence, a few staves, an old shovel. He repeated his mantra. *There are these things.* Seth was dead. He could not deny it. He was going to have to bury his boy and do so honorably. *To be done.* With a church service, because his mother would have wanted it that way. Jo. He would bury the boy beside his wife, in the plot he had purchased for himself at Eden Acres. This thought loosened some tightness in his chest. Even if Grizz had stopped going to church a long time ago he couldn't shake loose from his childhood faith, its attendant hopes and fears. Then he hurried out into the sunshine before the smell could conjure Seth's ghost fully. Before he lost himself once more.

With fence wire looped around his shoulder, shovel and staves in one hand, he opened the door. Only a few minutes had passed, but the girl was still waiting for him next to her car, keeping her distance from the cattle. "Mr. Fallon?" she said in a soft but firm voice. "I knew you'd be around here somewhere."

"What do you want?" His voice had a harsher edge than he meant to give it. If there were forces that unsettled Seth, she was one of them. Grizz set his tools on the ground before he approached her.

"I haven't been able to sleep," she said. "I had to come see you." She glanced up at him, her chin trembling. "Today's the first day I've been back to work. I quit in the middle of my shift. I couldn't stand the way they were all looking at me, the gossiping."

"This what you came to tell me?" It seemed she had come here hoping for some kind of absolution, and he'd be damned if he was going to give it to her. Grizz glanced toward the plain white clapboard house

52

where Seth had spent most of his life. "They didn't know him. Nobody knew him."

Leah smelled of fried grease from the pool hall, a faint odor of cigarettes in her hair. She stepped back as if suddenly conscious of where she was. Her mascara was a black smear under her eyes. She looked almost as much of a wreck as him, but now she was wary of her situation, way out in the middle of nowhere with a man who had done time over in Sauk County. Still, she asked, "Do you think it was my fault, because I broke up with him?"

Grizz felt so tired, undone by her wariness. He didn't know what to do with such questions. "No. You aren't to blame." *There. Now go away.*

"I didn't want to break up with him. Will Gunderson came to see my daddy and told him how he'd seen Seth and me down at the landing, swimming together." She fidgeted, reaching down into the purse she carried and fumbling out a cigarette and lighter. Her hand shook as she lit it. She was clear eyed now, any tears gone. "He made it sound dirty. He told my dad all about your son."

He didn't want to hear any of this. What was he supposed to do with this information? Had Seth died a virgin? The girl drew on her cigarette, and the end flared red, and she tapped out her ash into the dry grass.

"There's things you don't know," she said.

Now the air was going thin in his chest and down in his belly as though a hot wind blew inside him. *There are these things to be done. Bury the boy. Get on with what must be.* The sound of a car passing on the county road above drew both their attention, Leah turning nervously to take it in. It was the sheriff's car, the lights dormant on top, the vehicle slowing to make out who was in the yard.

"Oh shit," Leah said. "I shouldn't have come."

She stepped toward her sedan, and he knew when she left again his thoughts would turn wild once more, trying to fill the space between her words. Before she could climb inside, he closed the distance and took hold of her arm.

"Not yet. You were about to say something."

"Let go. You're hurting me."

The sheriff's car pulled into the driveway, heading down between the oaks and statues. His hand tightened hard enough around her arm to paint a bruise, but she stopped trying to pull away. "Please," she begged.

He did as she asked, embarrassed by his

own desperation. She turned toward him, her head lowered, and spoke in a low breath. "That day Seth got in trouble for busting the aquarium, Mr. Berman had been egging him on. He didn't like it when he caught Seth flirting with me out in the hallways. He called him 'Seth Felon,' said some other things. Said the apple doesn't fall far from the tree. I've never seen Seth so angry. That's when he turned over the aquarium."

He shook his head. That was it? The sheriff's car pulled into the last stretch.

Leah dropped her cigarette in the gravel and held herself, one hand kneading the place he had hurt. "I hadn't stopped seeing your son, even though my daddy made me promise. I think I caused Seth to get punished that way. You know that Will Gunderson kept a hunting shack back in those woods near the landing?"

The sheriff's car rolled to a rest.

Leah rushed on before he could climb out, her voice barely above a whisper. "Kids at school say he took people there to punish them. Burnouts and stoners. He cuffs you to a chair and does things to put a scare into you. After school, that's where I think he took Seth."

Steve was walking toward them, his hands

on his hips. "Everything all right here? Horace Greeley called to say your cattle were loose near the county road."

Leah didn't look back as she went to her car. "I was only here to pay my respects," she said to Steve in a shaky voice. She opened the door and ducked inside. Safe behind tinted windows, she didn't look at either man as she drove away.

When she was gone, he told Steve everything was about as fine as expected. "Unless the sheriff has gotten into the fence-repair business."

Behind him, Grizz heard the cattle calling to one another as the bull led his harem and calves back inside the fence he'd wrecked. He turned in wonder. It didn't make sense, and Grizz had never seen such a thing in all his life, but with the sun burning off the clouds, it was hot and already dry by early afternoon, the land drinking in what modest rain had fallen in the night. The pond in the lower pasture had dried up during the summer drought, but with fresh rain there'd be mud where the cows could cool themselves awhile. His cattle, which could have run free all day, were leading themselves back into captivity.

"I'll help," Steve said, surprising him. The two men fanned out on either side and

56

raised their arms and shouted at the stragglers in the yard, "Get along, girl," and "move along, Bessie," until the rest were inside the damaged fence.

Grizz went to get his tools, the girl's words churning in his head. Seth had been hurt. He had been scared, but he hadn't come to his father for help.

Steve touched his mustache, ran his hands over his chin. Beads of sweat stood out on the fat man's forehead from the little effort it had taken to corral the cattle. "Look, Grizz," he began, "the other night I said some terrible things."

Grizz picked up his shovel and the staves and wire clamps he'd left lying in the grass. "There's things I have to do," he told him as he went to the barn to shut off the fence's electricity so he could make repairs. This new Steve, his voice slick with concern, scared him. He preferred the one who came to his house two nights before and spit in his drink. If he said anything else, if he said what he was truly feeling in that moment, it would reveal all Leah had confided. Because if Will Gunderson kept a shack in those woods, then Steve, his predecessor, surely knew about it. Seemed like everyone knew but Grizz.

"You're a hard man to reach," Steve said

when Grizz came back outside. He licked his lips. "Church council met last night. It was decided your son would be buried in the suicide corner of the cemetery."

"No," Grizz said. How could he have forgotten? This town and its sick traditions. "You wait just a goddamn minute. I want him buried next to his mother. I own the plot."

"And you signed a contract that spells out what happens in the event of a suicide. The rules are very clear on this. He'll have to be buried in the corner with the other suicides."

Grizz felt the heat of the sun on the back of his neck, filling him up. His fists tightened around the shovel. "I intend to speak to the pastor about all of this."

"Pastor Logan has already been informed of the council's decision."

Was it his imagination, or did Steve's mouth curve in a small smile under the mustache? He turned his back on the sheriff and headed for the broken fence. Steve followed just as he knew he would. When Grizz heard his footsteps behind him, he turned and swung the shovel with all his might. He pivoted, planting his feet and throwing his entire body into the swing. The clamps and staves fell away in a clatter. In his mind's eye, he saw the fanged edge of that old shovel cleave into Steve's neck, saw the first bright geyser of red erupt, saw him fall, his mouth opening in surprise.

But Steve was a cunning man and knew what Grizz was about, so where he thought the man's head or neck might be instead there was only air, and the violence of that swing twisted him badly on his hips, and he felt something tear inside when he fell.

Steve stood over him. "It's not a good idea to try assaulting an officer of the law," he said. "But I'm going to forget this happened. I don't know what that girl told you. I can understand your anger, why you might try to hurt me in the heat of the moment." He paused, made a sound in his throat, and spit to the side. "What I don't understand is your boy. I mean his pockets were full of ammunition, Grizz. Took his time sawing down that shotgun. I can't imagine such coldness."

Even if Grizz wanted to rise, he couldn't. It felt like there was a saw working in his gut, an old hernia tear he had torn again. He breathed in the dust where he had fallen and tried not to cry. How had he not seen this moment coming? Of course they would do this. They couldn't just let Seth be dead. They had to find some further way to punish him, send him on to hell.

"This town's had a terrible shock. They don't feel safe. The world is changing, and they don't know their place in it. Let go of your anger. If you want to be angry, be angry with your son."

Grizz put one hand over his eyes. It was good advice. He should have been furious with Seth, but when he searched himself all he felt was the shock of his boy's death. An emptiness, chaff in his palm.

Grizz didn't answer. He didn't trust his voice. Steve knelt in the grass beside him. "A group of us will come this fall and combine your crop. No charge."

"I'll pay for it."

"We both know you don't have the money. Probably don't have enough for Seth's funeral services. You're going to need help to get through this." Steve extended his hand, but Grizz didn't take it.

Grunting, Grizz climbed to his feet and picked up his shovel and the rest of his things. Steve shrugged and walked away. A moment later his car started. Only after the sheriff's car disappeared up the driveway did Grizz allow himself to lean over and vomit up what he'd drank last night. He let the sick come up, all liquid and no solids, until he was scoured out.

Then he walked to the broken place in the fence line where one post had been shattered in half. The bull must have been shocked by the electricity, enraged. The fence repelled him once, but the next time he charged it he must have hit the old post at full speed, splintering it. Grizz admired how the bent wires twisted and curled into space.

Grizz drove the staves into the ground and wound wire around the makeshift post, clamping it in place. The bull lifted his head from the dusty grazing pasture and studied his work. It was a jerry-rigged operation, and they both knew it. Just this small effort sapped Grizz's remaining energy, and he had to sit for a moment in the waving grasses to catch his breath. And even as the work drained him, it also renewed him, quenched his ache for a spell.

A boisterous cloud of blackbirds burst from the oaks as the sheriff drove away. The flock gathered into a swirling pinwheel that carried them high above the pasture, the line breaking and re-forming before arrowing toward the mountain, where they landed in the waving grasses and went silent as though they had never been. Grizz was left alone again in the hot sun with the cows chewing their cud.

In this year of drought the leaves fell early, small and brown and skeletal. The canary grasses were tawny in the light, bending under a hot wind, and the woods stretched toward town, dry as kindling.

LONE MOUNTAIN

Once there was a mountain, a bald grassy place that looked like the skull of a man, all brow and crown, because long ago a giant had trampled the valley before sinking up to his eyeballs and drowning. The little ponds around it were his footsteps, the mounds beside it his shoulders as he shrugged underground. Maybe he was not dead. Maybe he was only sleeping. The wind off the river was his breath. Night in the valley was sentient with his dreaming. Cows that escaped pasture fences went to the mountain and vanished. He slept his sleep of a thousand years and waited and no oaks or maples grew from the grasses over his head.

"Is the giant mean? I don't want him to wake up." She never tired of hearing such stories, imagining the hatchet-faced mountain rising above the fields.

"Don't you worry. He's old and sleepy, but he watches and waits. He only wakes in times of trouble. There are wolves that live in his caves, and he sends them forth to help those in need."

"His emis— ?"

"Emissaries. They do his bidding."

"Like the ones who came for the woman. To keep her from hurting the baby. Like the coyote who found the baby after all those people died in the war?"

"Yes, the very ones."

"Why did the woman want to hurt the baby?"

The giant in the mountain was as old as the moon or stars, as ancient as a stone left by the seashore. Things fastened to him like lichen or mollusks so the rocks found on the mountain were like nothing on the earth. The last tallgrass prairie became the giant's beard and eyebrows. Nowhere else in the valley could you find the Great Plains prickly pear cactus, green and bristling, among the cedar trees and prairie bush clover thick with bees.

Granodiorite. Gabbro. The rocks were living things the Indians said flew about the stars at night. The boulders were witnesses to creation. A hundred years before, the mountain was holy to the Dakotas. The sick went there to drink from a limestone spring; infertile women ate the dirt. Where red rock showed through the grass, pink as skin, the young

64

men painted their visions. Thunderbeings and black bears and buffalo. Sometimes just a hand etched into the stone to say *I was here,* if only for a single heartbeat of the one who lives within the mountain.

"Will you take me there, Daddy?"

"Maybe when spring comes again. When I'm feeling more peppy and can make the climb. Then we'll pack a picnic and sit on the mountaintop and feel the wind in the grass."

"When?"

"Someday."

There was no mountain near the town of Lone Mountain so far as Clara could tell, the streets as quiet as a secret on Sunday morning. The competing spires of Trinity Lutheran and Our Lady of the Sorrows peeked above leafy treetops. Silt laden, the Minnesota River wound like a thick ribbon of caramel in the valley below.

It was a pretty enough town at first glance, the women sweeping their porches, the men cutting precise patterns on riding lawnmowers. Victorian houses with gables and wide porches surrounded Hiawatha Park, a green space where the town enacted the annual Longfellow Pageant. Black iron lampposts lined the main street where buildings of dun-colored brick bore the mark of previous decades, advertisements for Lee's overalls and mugs of Sanka. Farmers wearing seed caps parked their trucks along the curb. At the pool hall, they passed rainy mornings playing a card game called sheepshead to determine who would have to pay for coffee. Know the price of beans or the weather forecast, and you might find your way into a conversation. Logan had told her that people lived in this town for twenty-five years and were still counted as strangers.

There was the grocery store, Jurgen's Corner, and a bait shop, the Bookworm, which sold yellowing paperbacks and comic books along with supplies for fishermen wishing to ply the brown river. The town movie theater had shut down, but the marquee still advertised *Red Dawn* with Patrick Swayze and Charlie Sheen. Downtown also held a hardware store, two bars, and a Chinese restaurant, the Golden Dragon. Two bars and two churches made for an even balance of liquid spirits and holy spirits in Clara's estimation. The high school and nursing home were across town from where Clara lived. On either end of the valley, where County Road 29 dropped from the prairie tableland as it sliced through town, big billboards had been erected, each featuring smiling babies meant to represent fetuses. I HAD A HEARTBEAT AT TWO MONTHS, read one, while the other, in stark black and white, admonished THOU SHALT NOT KILL.

The entire town clung to the south face of a steeply sloping hill overlooking the river lowlands, prone to flooding, where the Harvestland silos loomed over taverns and railroad tracks and mobile homes occupied by migrant workers during the pea and corn harvest at the Del Monte plant in nearby Amroy.

The town had all of these things by her accounting, but no sign of the mountain for which it was named, and this troubled her. During Clara's first few weeks here she made a habit of bumping over county roads in Logan's '69 Nova in search of one. She spotted a few low green hills knobbed by granite outcroppings and spindly cedars, but nothing like the vision of the mountain she held in her imagination. The locals she interrogated proved evasive.

"Oh, the mountain," said one codger when she asked about it during social hour in the church basement. "It's just east of town a little ways."

Clara nodded as if this made sense, wondering if the mountain could be little more than a glorified hill named by the homesick Germans who settled this valley.

"No, no," the man's brother interrupted, his mouth full of half-chewed chocolate-chip cookie. "You want to get there, you hook a left at the granite pit, head southeast down the gravel road 'bout a quarter mile. You can't miss it."

Clara knew who these men were because Logan had given her a church directory from a few years back with pictures from the congregation. The Hendriks brothers, Abel and Abram, were Dutch bachelor farmers who lived a few miles outside town.

Both men had bald, sunburned heads and bulbous frog eyes and puffy mouths. They wore western-style long-sleeved shirts and suede dress coats with patches on the elbows. Both sat up in the balcony along with a group of senior citizens Logan had already identified as malcontents after he roped off the balcony one Sunday, hoping they would sit closer to the front. Without a word they tore down his barrier, their sisters and wives leading the way, and climbed the steep winding stairs to sit where they had sat for generations. Gloating, triumphant. "Stiff necked as the Israelites in Canaan," Logan groused after the service. These Ger-

68

man Americans had endured Indian uprisings, locust plagues, two worlds wars, the Depression, a hail storm that destroyed most of the windows of the church, and an ongoing farming crisis killing their way of life. They would survive one upstart pastor fresh out of seminary trying to get them to change their ways.

So Clara wasn't surprised these men were directing her according to landmarks they took for granted, guided by a compass she was not born with. Neither of the Hendriks brothers offered to shake her hand or introduced himself, partly because she was a young female and partly because some residents here expected her to know who they were without being told.

The Hendriks brother with his mouth full of food was also staring at Clara's breasts, swollen because of the pregnancy, while he licked a crumb from his lip. Clara held up her left hand to her chin, as though contemplating something, to show her missing fingers. The old man swallowed hard and coughed. He gulped boiling coffee from a Styrofoam cup and, wincing, looked away. Most men didn't ask about the hand; they shuddered to imagine it touching them. She was damaged goods, and that's all they needed to know. Clara leaned forward, pressing her advantage. "Which granite pit do you mean?"

So many of her father's stories featured this missing mountain, a sacred, healing place. If she could find it, she would find the place where she was from. Knowing this would root her. A part of Clara felt as if she *had* opened the door that day and received the obliterating blast from Seth's shotgun, scattering bits and pieces of her true self all about where they could never possibly be gathered together again. She needed to get right before this baby came.

Welcome to the Country

Logan had already been up for an hour by the time Clara came downstairs. He sat alone at the dining room table, leaning on his elbows, his blond hair dark with sweat. He was wearing a T-shirt, skimpy Lycra shorts, and tube socks pulled up nearly to his knees. Logan didn't turn his head to wish her good morning when she entered the room, but he kept his attention fixed on the rain outside, muttering something — a prayer? — under his breath.

She had come downstairs wearing only a blue terry-cloth robe. She wanted to get a cup of coffee and then head upstairs to soak in a bath and write some more, but spotting Logan changed her plans. "I'm going to fry some eggs," she told him. "Want any?"

Logan startled at the sound of her voice. Then he shook his head without turning her way. "I can't eat so early in the morning, especially not after a run."

Clara crossed the room and touched his damp face with the back of her hand, feeling the Braille of his boyish beard. "You need to eat something," she said. Above his hollow cheeks, his eyes sank into their sockets. Day by day, Clara was growing rounder while her husband shrank, as if she were one of those spiders who feeds on her mate, drinking in his juices until he's only a sack to lay the eggs in. What a terrible thought. She was having such thoughts these days. Clara knew Logan was fasting in the mornings again, heading straight over to church and starting his day by kneeling before the altar, his hunger a punishment for not having the answers his congregation required. Perhaps it was wrong of her to tempt him with fried eggs, but looking at him now — her pale, handsome husband with his knobby knees and receding hairline — a motherly tenderness welled in her. "What were you thinking about here, sitting in the dark?"

"Satan," he said, glancing her way and smiling ruefully.

"Oh, is that all?" She pulled over a chair so she could sit beside him.

"Feels strange to say aloud. Sort of foolish."

Was it? She knew Logan loved the story

of Martin Luther battling the devil in his last days, flinging a book across the room and reminding Lucifer of his baptism. What was God without the devil, heaven without hell? Though he considered himself a modern seminarian, quick to point out that accounts of demon possession in the Gospels were likely manifestations of mental illness, Clara knew that he also believed in the devil. That the devil was active in this world made Logan's work urgent.

Clara put her hand over his. "Tell me what you saw."

"I don't know exactly," he said, squirming in his chair, edging deeper into the cushioned seat, "except that I was up in the pulpit looking out over my parishioners when I spotted him. He was ordinary looking, just a guy in a dark suit, but with his eyes he took away my voice. I tried to speak, but it was like there were hands" — Logan paused and massaged his throat with his free hand — "choking the words. The congregation knew something was wrong, but I was alone up there. No one even noticed him there except for me. The devil there, smiling."

"How awful." His hand beneath hers was cold, as if the rain had soaked straight through him on his morning jog. She wondered if Logan's telling of the dream was also meant to rebuke her for not being in church last Sunday. She knew exactly the rational reason behind what he'd seen, and that it was called the Hag's Dream, or sleep paralysis. While you sleep your body locks down your muscles to keep you from acting out your dreams. But sometimes you wake up partially; you rise to a conscious state and realize your body is paralyzed and in that moment you panic and see the thing you most fear. In the Middle Ages it was a mare, a black horse, which is how the word "nightmare," comes down to us through the ages.

Clara knew what Logan's dream was because she knew her etymology, like any good linguist. But she said nothing to her husband, because it wouldn't help him feel any better. She also had trouble sleeping, her dreams restless and furtive, as if she had tuned in to the voices scattered about town, where the story of what happened went on and on, a psychic echo. Writing in her notebook, telling her father's stories, soothed the voices and let her rest. Writing was her prayer.

The only language she spoke for a time was her hand on his. Nightmares aside, it felt good to be with him in the gloomy morning, touching. The next words slipped out of her without thinking. "Was it a mistake to come here?" When Logan flinched she wished she could take it back.

Logan withdrew his hand. "Doesn't do any good to think about that. We're here."

The room next to them was still cluttered with unpacked boxes a couple of months after their arrival. "We could go," Clara said, her voice barely a whisper. "You could tell the synod bishop it wasn't a good fit, ask for reassignment."

A faint flush crept into Logan's cheeks as he studied her. "Three years, Clara. If you spend less than that in your first call, it looks bad on your record. We waited two months for this assignment. How would I get another call?"

There was nothing kind in his blue eyes so she looked away from him.

"We can't leave them in the lurch. Not after this." Logan continued when she didn't say anything, "Besides, coming here was your idea, remember?"

"People make mistakes all the time. There's no shame in admitting it."

Logan rose from his chair, closing off the conversation. He was moving away from her once more, going off to shower and then to the church next door. "I've found a home for those kittens," he said, surprising her. "Last Sunday, after the service."

"What?"

"I think that's part of what's bothering me, my allergies, just having them in the basement. The Nelson family said they would take them. All their cats died from the distemper. Now they have rats in the barn again."

Clara couldn't bear to look at him. "I want to come with you when you take them."

"No. The Nelsons are very private people." Logan averted his gaze. Had she caught him in a lie? Was he planning on dumping those kittens by the side of the road or worse? It occurred to her that she didn't know what he was capable of doing. If Clara saw the Nelsons in church she would ask them about the kittens, but she had no idea whom he was talking about. Most of Logan's congregation were still strangers to her.

"They'll all die. They're too small. They were born too late in the fall."

"Welcome to the country," Logan said.

"I didn't know when I married you that you had a mean streak."

Logan touched her hair, patting it. This should have bothered her even more, but his touch took away the other words she was going to say, and she let his fingers linger there. It surprised her how much she wanted him to touch her, when she had just been ready to spit in his eye. She shut her eyes while he massaged her scalp. "You feel things too keenly," he said.

His voice was lower, calming. His fingers found the ridges in her skull, pressed gently at the tension. "I'm not trying to be mean," he said. "You knew from the night you found them you couldn't keep them."

"Just let me keep them one more day."

Logan kissed the top of her head. "A few more days. I'll take them on Friday. The Nelsons are good people, Clara."

By "good people" it was clear what he meant. His kind of people. Church people. She let the comment pass because she could feel the baby stirring inside her. She let it pass because her husband who had been avoiding her was touching her, his hands moving from her hair to her shoulders. "The baby," she told him. "It's kicking. Do you want to feel it?"

Logan's hands went still.

She opened her robe. Her breasts were heavy and full. Beneath them the globe of her belly stretched, blue veins wending over the surface. Something, a hand or a foot, thrust outward from the skin.

"Clara," he said. "The curtains are open."

The world outside was gauzy with rain. "I don't care." She guided Logan's hand to her stomach, closing her own over the top. They didn't have to wait more than a minute. Feeling Logan's cold hand, the baby thumped once more and then sank back into the depths within her.

"Weird, huh?" she said to fill the silence. Clara knew he was studying the curve of her breasts. She had seen the longing and loneliness in him from the very first time she met him. Now, she wanted him to stay. She wanted him to keep touching her. And shouldn't he want her even more, since she almost died? Shouldn't he affirm this life, hers, his, the mystery inside her? They hadn't made love since finding out about the baby.

Clara's conversion to Lutheranism was inextricably bound up in the physicality of her husband. Logan had been her father's pastor. A few weeks after her father died, Clara attended services at Logan's church one gray Sunday and was surprised when Logan asked her to brunch at the café down the street. They would meet again for coffee in a few days, then dinner out, followed by dinner at his place. He needed her, she saw, just as much as she needed him. In his quietness she read depth; in his shy touch, innocence. The first time she undressed for him, undid the buttons on her blouse, she had watched the pupils in his light blue eyes darken with desire. "I knew I would love you before I ever met you," he told her later in her bedroom that night. "It was the sound of your name in the stories your father told about you. Clara, clear as running water. Clara, like clarity. Clean like the sky. I knew you before I ever saw you."

Behind them the phone jostled on the receiver.

Logan's hand was still on her stomach, tracing slow circles. Her hand on his.

Don't. *Stay.*

Logan went to get the phone.

Was it only a few months earlier she had spread out the map on the kitchen table, her index finger tracing the black road that raveled along the river? She remembered tasting the name silently with her tongue against her teeth: Lone Mountain. The pull of something dark and sweet wafted inside her, a scent like burning sugar. Childhood whispers.

"I'm not sure this is a good idea," Logan said.

She touched the tiny dot, measuring. It

looked to be about two hundred miles west of the Twin Cities. She imagined endless cornfields, a flat prairie expanse, and then that cleft in the land where the road vanished into the valley. The big woods, sudden escape, shade. Her voice sounded tinny when she responded. "I think we should go."

Logan sipped from his tea. His cheeks were ruddy from a fever, the steam of his drink. "After two months of dead-end interviews in this synod, it comes down to this."

Clara sat down so they were at eye level. The sky outside held pewter-colored clouds, and a few fat raindrops rinsed down the window. "Ever since you told me the name of that town, I've known we should go there."

Logan shifted in his seat. "It's a dying church, Clara. Every year three times more funerals than baptisms. The whole region is dying, that way of life. They can barely afford to pay me synod guidelines."

"We have each other," Clara assured him. Baptisms and deaths and the numbers of baptized members versus the average worship attendance on Sunday. Numbers and facts and figures as he debated each open position in the synod. For a spiritual man, Logan obsessed over such things. And she knew why else he was afraid. In his last year at seminary, Logan had suffered a severe series of anxiety attacks during finals week. Clara had been the one to find him, rigid on his bed, paralyzed with some nameless terror. She had been the one to talk him out of the spell. He had gone to see a private therapist, afraid that if the news reached the board, they would make him undergo a new battery of psychological tests, and he would not be able to graduate.

She folded her arms across her chest. She wanted to tell him that she felt like she had to do this, now that she was going to be a mother herself. She wanted to tell him how badly she had wanted a mother growing up, someone to explain the mysteries of womanhood, how she had run away in search of her mother, how she needed her mother more than ever with a baby growing inside her. Instead she said, "How many interviews have you gone to?"

Logan frowned. "They're used to getting experienced pastors at these places, even if they no longer have the budget for it. And the answer is five."

"Only one of the five has called you."

Logan had been raised in the swank Lincoln Park neighborhood in Chicago, the only child of two agnostic psychotherapists

who later divorced. When his parents bick-
ered, he would sneak out of the house, walk
to the Lutheran church down the street, and
climb into the balcony where he napped on
the padded pew, light from a stained-glass
window pouring over him.

Against his parents' wishes he started at-
tending services every Sunday, befriended
the pastor, and would go on to study religion at Concordia in Moorhead, Minnesota,
before finishing his master of divinity at
Luther Seminary in St. Paul. It was a rebel-
lion in reverse, their only child choosing
what his father termed "the ultimate delu-
sion." Relations between Logan and his
parents remained chilly to this day. They
had not seen them since the wedding.

Logan held her ghost hand, the nubs
where the fingers were missing. He was
drawn by a wound that repulsed others.
"Those stories your father told you. You
think this might be the place?"

"I don't know," Clara admitted. "I don't
know if it's the place she was going or where
she died or maybe none of these things. But
he used to speak of a mountain in his
stories. How many places are there in that
part of the world with the word 'mountain'
in the name?"

"Where was she going with a baby in the

backseat in the middle of a blizzard?"

"My dad only said she was crazy."

Logan tensed. "Like postpartum?"

"They didn't have a name for it then. And he didn't keep any pictures of her, wouldn't even tell me her name. You saw when we went through his things. He didn't even have my birth certificate in his record files." Her fingers traced circles on the kitchen table before she looked into his eyes again. "We need to go there. You've been called. They'll have archives in the courthouse or even at the local newspaper. Someone will remember the story. I just have a gut feeling about this, okay?"

Logan blew his nose in a napkin. "Help me understand, Clara, because it sounds crazy. Why would you want to live in the place where your mother died?"

After he left that morning, Clara sat at the dining room table drinking coffee and lingering over her old textbooks. She would have to give them back now that she wasn't going to be teaching there anymore. In the background the local radio station, KLKR, quoted from Reagan's secretary of agriculture, who had said earlier that day in his press conference that farmers should "Get big or get out." Stormy Gayle, the an-

83

nouncer, hissed into the microphone in response, "This is what we've come to in this country. What will happen to the land when it is no longer worked by families who know the soil? What will happen to families when there is no longer land to anchor them?" Clara shut the radio off, saw from the clock that it was 9:45, second period for her on a normal day, sophomore English.

She needed to go the grocery store because the refrigerator was bare, but she didn't want to face people in town yet. She needed time. While paging through one of the English literature textbooks she would no longer be teaching from, Clara heard a wet whump sound, the sound of a body or some heavy object leaning against the back door.

She set her book down and went through the kitchen. She opened the back door and found a piece of paper had been slid under the jamb. She unfolded it. In her hands she held a pencil drawing of a wolf, jaws stretching wide to swallow the whole world. A single tree letting down its leaves upheld the earth, but even this was being squeezed by a serpent. She knew exactly what it was, a drawing of Ragnarok. She had been teaching Seth's class of juniors about Norse mythology so they could understand the pagan darkness in *Beowulf* better, where lives were ruled by *wyrd.* The wolf was Fenrir, who devours middle earth at the end of time. Under the drawing someone had written a note in runic letters: *There is no one who will be spared.*

And on the back of the page someone had neatly printed out a riddle:

A man tries to speak
with his throat torn
One woman shrieks
blood in the corn
Man in a pit
her without sleep
one drowns in shit
the other weeps
Wolves under moon
child in her skin
the end comes soon
she will suffer for her sin.

Someone knew. Someone knew about the notes she had been keeping.

The first note she discovered near the overhead projector, pleated in a neat square with her full name printed on the outside. It was Clara's third day as a long-term substitute, and she needed to get the journals written out on the transparencies for

85

first period. She unfolded the note, wondering who had left it there:

You have such a nice laugh, it makes me warm inside. But even when you are laughing your eyes look sad. You look like the loneliest person in the world.

Clara didn't know what to do with it. She searched her mind for the faces of those who sat near the overhead, who might have slipped this note here. Part of her wanted to throw it away. Keeping it invited an intimacy. Keeping it meant the words printed there were true in ways she wasn't ready to think about. She put it in her desk drawer, telling herself she would throw it away after school. But she never did, and every other day when she came in the notes were waiting for her in the same place, tucked carefully under the big bulky overhead.

He's always gone at night. Where does your husband go? Where could he go with such a pretty wife at home? If you were mine, I wouldn't leave you alone like that.

He was watching her. She was being watched even after school. But she always had that feeling, living in a small town for the first time in her life, like everything she did or said was being measured and judged. The handwriting of the notes was blocky, printed in all caps, and in places the ink

86

smudged. Someone worked on these in the late hours.

She thought she knew the writer, even though there was never a name. She thought she caught it in the glint of his eye when he watched her up in front of the room. And as deeply as they disturbed her, a small part of her was flattered. She was pregnant, after all, a married woman. Any day, any time, she only had to turn the letters in to the principal. To tell him her hunch, but then so what? It's not like she could prove anything.

The thing that troubled her most was why she held on to the letters afterward, why she had them still downstairs in a kitchen drawer under the hand towels, the pages folded and refolded so many times that some of the words blurred. She had wanted to turn them in when the sheriff came to interview her. She needed to show her husband. But by now it would have made her look guilty as well, and she hadn't done anything, had she? She hadn't encouraged him in any way. Or was it enough, sometimes to simply return his look in class, to stand talking as though there weren't anyone in the room but the two of them?

I don't know what to do anymore. Sometimes I watch you. Late at night. You keep a light on even after your husband has come home again. Do you feel me out there in the dark? I love you, dumb as that sounds. It's what I wanted to tell you. One day I will find the guts to tell you with more than these words. I will tell them all in a way no one can forget.

Her hands trembled as she smoothed the edges of the paper she held now. Seth. She had seen him working on this very same drawing the week before the shooting, and now someone had brought it here to her door. Seth Allis Fallon. There had been nothing between them. The only thing between them was that she had wanted to mother him, a student all the other teachers loathed and feared. Had he misread how she wanted to keep him safe, even from himself? How stupid, how arrogant of her to think that she had tamed him.

The drawing was a cover for the story he never bothered to turn in, the riddle some dark and bloody parody of the ones she had taught his class, but seemed to refer to both Seth's and the sheriff's death. It spooked her, especially the parts about the woman with "a child in her skin." This could only be Clara, could only mean that she was being hunted, but there was no reason for her to feel any danger, not anymore, and what was her sin?

We are all born into Adam's sin, her husband Logan had said to her once, each of us tasting exile in our mutual fall. Out of this grows our longing for the lost garden, for the paradise we might know again. It's what he told her the first time they talked about faith, holding her damaged hand in his, speaking of a place where they might be whole inside and out. And if she doubted anything, she did not doubt this man's goodness, even if she feared him doubting hers.

She scanned the yard, but there was no one there, just the winding gravel path that led to Logan's church and, beyond the empty graveyard, the blond field of corn and the encroaching woods.

WERGILD

As the day went on, the sun cooked up a heat so cloying even the wind lay still before it. His empty house droned like a dead phone line. Like Grizz was some kind of dog whose ears peeled back when he heard a faint calling from someone loved and gone.

There's things you don't know, the girl had said. Will Gunderson had kept a shack in the woods and he had taken his son there if she spoke true. He believed her, but he was going to have to see with his own eyes. Grizz only believed in what he could lay his hands on. That's why he needed to go to town, talk to the pastor. He was going to have to see the body.

After the cattle were gathered in and the fence fixed, Grizz went into the house to get cleaned up. He washed his face in the sink, rinsed out his mouth, and then eased his bladder. He paused when he went into the kitchen because Seth's mother was ever present in this room. The kitchen table and walls and cabinets were still the same matching lime-green color that she'd painted them before Seth's birth. Framed watercolor vistas of sugary sand beaches and glowing seas hung on the wall. Jo had hated the cold, and in the wintertime she'd sit in this room with the gas stove open, drinking chamomile tea while she worked on transcribing notes for Dr. Salverson's office.

Someone had been here and gone; he saw right away from the cleanliness of the floor. The visitor had come while he was sleeping and whoever she was had also taken the time to sweep up dirt the sheriff's men had tracked in from the fields and broken glass from the floor. A note on the kitchen table waited for him. He picked it up:

Do not ~~dispair~~ give up,
Your not alone.
Hotdish in the fridge,
Cook thirty minutes at 350.

The handwriting was unsteady, arthritic. One of the women from the Naomi Circle at church, the meddlesome old biddies. The world wasn't ready to leave him alone; he couldn't hide from it anymore. He crumpled the note in his fist. Grizz needed something in him to soak up the acids in his stomach, and hotdish, the food of solace in these parts, wasn't it. He got out some saltine crackers from the cabinets and forced these down with tap water.

When he was done he threw away the note, finding that whoever had come here had also discarded the weekly paper in the trash so Grizz wouldn't have to look at it. The lead article carried the story about his son and featured a yearbook photo from Seth's freshman year when he still wore his hair short, the bangs chopped unevenly, his eyes slitted like he was looking into the sun. It was the year they discovered Seth had the same systemic lupus that had killed his mother at age forty, the year little wolves had come to the Fallons. Grizz couldn't bear to look at the photo long.

Numbly, he read for the first time how the boy had stopped at the parsonage and how the pastor's wife had not come to the door. "I was scared," she told Edna Drooge, the coeditor of the *Lone Mountain Courier*. "I couldn't see who was there, but I just felt sure something bad was about to happen."

Grizz folded the paper and stuffed it again into the garbage. He felt a cramping along his left side and massaged the muscle. He had torn something for sure trying to take off Steve's head with that shovel. But was it possible that what Steve said was true and that he was a friend, not an enemy? Steve served on the church council and the board of directors at the local co-op. He was the sort of man Grizz needed to keep close if he was going to understand his son's death.

Seth's suicide had been Grizz's worst fear; he was such a melancholy boy, a daydreamer who sulked instead of doing his chores, but as he got older that sulking turned to anger, the anger to desperation. Grizz could almost wrap his mind around the suicide but not the sawed-off shotgun, the pockets filled with lead slugs.

He had kept Seth's bedroom door shut since that night. A shut door meant anything could still be inside there. Seth hadn't left any note or any clues so far as he knew, but maybe the men hadn't known where to look.

Grizz climbed the stairs and opened the door to a chaotic scene. The sheriff's men had torn open the drawers of Seth's desk and dresser and left them askew. On the floor his T-shirts and jeans pooled in piles, and his bed sheets were still dimpled with the outline of his body, a faint dark impression. It felt like trespassing.

Deer antlers, polished by years of sun, were embedded along the inlaid shelves of one south-facing wall. Seth had gathered the antlers as a boy, when he was a wanderer, when Grizz had hounded him about landmarks, keeping the house in sight, and avoiding the deep limestone crevices up in the hills where a body might fall inside and never be found again.

That boy kept him up at nights. And sometimes when Grizz did sleep, his jaw ached in the morning from grinding teeth, worrying on him. Once Seth had left a collection of women's bras and panties dangling from the antlers as a taunt, some with rust-colored stains lining the silk. All the sizes had been different, though Grizz had tried not to look too closely. Women's things, delicate and lace fringed, maybe some from girls at the high school. Only way the boy could have had them was if he had stolen them from houses in town. A creep.

"Where'd you get these?" Grizz asked that evening. He sat in his recliner, the offending articles piled on the floor below him.

Seth just looked away. He was not a handsome boy, tall and slump shouldered, as though apologizing to the world for being made so big. This had been a few weeks after Grizz had found the pot in his sock drawer and called Will Gunderson to arrest his own child. He didn't know what to do with him anymore, couldn't control Seth.

"I need to know I can trust you. Tell me the truth, now. Whose are these?"

"I see you've been in my room."

"Where did you get these?"

"Found 'em," Seth said, shrugging. He met Grizz's gaze. "You going to turn them over to the sheriff, too?"

"Should I?"

Seth swallowed his grin. "No." A shadow passing over his features.

"Why would you keep such things?"

His eyes had gone back to mapping the floorboards. "It was a dare."

"A dare? To do what? Who dared you? Did Kelan put you up to this?"

Seth raised his head, his eyes blazing. "Fuck you," he said. When Grizz stood he was still bigger than his son, but if they fought the outcome was no longer sure. Seth lowered his head and came toward him but turned at the last second, only brushing past him as he went up the stairs. A moment later his door slammed, and then his stereo came on: electric guitars, a blast of drums, a voice wailing from the speakers.

A dare? His best friend had been Kelan

Gunderson, the sheriff's older boy. Kelan was a lanky, handsome child, black haired with long-lashed gray eyes the girls all swooned over. Unlike Seth, Kelan was well liked, a congenial kid who put on a smiling face for all the adults, but Grizz always had the feeling he had egged Seth on. Kelan had a tagalong little brother, too, a boy with what the unkind called mongoloid features. The brother was always practicing spastic karate moves while trying to defend himself from the bigger boys and so they took to calling him Odd Lee instead of his given name of Bruce and the name stuck. Now he thought of Kelan and his little brother out there grieving their father, likely as mystified as Grizz, and he regretted thinking meanly of them. His son had murdered his best friend's father. His only friend.

He stood looking at Seth's closet door, hung with a poster of the Four Horseman charging out of red clouds, a city below them in flames, the words JUDAS PRIEST at the top and NOSTRADAMUS at the bottom. He tore the poster from its Scotch-tape moorings, picked up the scattered cassette tapes and survival magazines, because these things were not his son. As he gathered them in a garbage bag for the burn pile, his eyes were drawn to papers scattered on the desk. They were drawings mostly, wolves and strange giants in a far, frozen country. The boy had a fine hand for sketching. A creature with its arm torn off howled in the woods. In another, a child looked into a pond, but his watery reflection turned monstrous and fanged. A final one showed a hallway clotted with bloody bodies, a woman's severed head lolling on the floor. The sheriff's men hadn't taken these papers; there was no need with Seth dead.

When Grizz picked them up, he saw something that caught his breath. Seth had gouged a single word into the desk: WERGILD. The wounds in the wood were fresh, dark walnut surface peeled to show blond wood underneath. Seth had worked at this recently with a knife, prying up the slivers carefully. Grizz didn't know what the word meant but knew someone who did. It was time he got ready to head into town.

He ripped the bandages from his palms, scrubbed the wounds clean, then put on fresh blue jeans, a long-sleeved shirt, steel-toed boots he favored while driving loads for the co-op or taking trips to town, and then pulled his cap low to shade his eyes before setting out.

He drove the winding stretch of road between his farm and town, his hands light on the wheel. He'd driven past the church for many years without stopping, but today he parked out front. Grizz checked the office down the hall for the pastor, his hollow greeting echoing. It figured. He went into the sanctuary, where it was so quiet he could hear a few pigeons cooing up in the bell tower.

On a hunch he stepped through a side door, saw the path that went over to the parsonage, and almost ran right into a woman standing in the grass in her bare feet. She was staring off toward the cemetery, a single piece of paper in her hand. She had long auburn hair and was wearing a billowy blouse and skirt that could not disguise her pregnancy. She startled when she heard the door clamp shut and saw him come toward her.

He took off his cap as he approached. The way she stood, on the balls of her feet, it was as if she was preparing to run. Like she thought he was going to hurt her.

"You're the pastor's wife."

She nodded, her face ashen. The wind whipped her curly hair in front of her face.

"He around?"

She shook her head, no. The same relentless wind snatched the paper from her grasp and sent it tumbling across the lawn and into the cemetery where it was lost among the graves. "Fuck," she said, the very first word he'd heard her speak, and then brought up her hands over her mouth as though to cover the profanity.

At that moment he also noticed the missing fingers on her left hand. It had bothered Seth, he remembered. His boy had come home telling about the new teacher, a mystery. "When is he coming back?"

Her eyes darted between Grizz and the place where the paper had vanished. What had she been holding? "He has a service at the nursing home. I think. Probably return in an hour, unless he has visits."

"You know who I am?"

She met his gaze. "You're Seth Fallon's dad. Logan's been trying to reach you."

"I wasn't ready to talk before now. Are you okay? You look about ready to puke."

"That paper I was holding? Someone left it at my door." She wrapped her arms around herself and shivered. "It was a drawing your son made for my class. Did you see anyone else around here?"

The look he gave her must have showed his confusion. She shut her eyes briefly and drew in a heavy breath. "I'm Clara Warren. Seth's English teacher." Tentatively, she held out her hand, and he took it. "I'm sorry for your loss, Mr. Fallon." Her hand felt smooth and hot within his own. She held on a moment too long, maybe feeling the wounds in his palm and reading some story from the touch. He jerked his hand away and then felt embarrassed of his foolishness. Her eyes were bright and amber colored. She had sharp features, her small nose twitching as if scenting something troubling in the air. A petite woman, despite her pregnancy. Grizz loomed over her.

"What was on the drawing?" He thought of the ones on the boy's desk. The monster in the woods. The woman's severed head.

"A wolf," she said. "He'd written something in runes on the bottom about no one being spared." She rushed on, nervous. "We were studying *Beowulf* in class, just finishing up a unit. It might not have meant anything."

Grizz fanned the air with his cap. "He liked your class." It was the only class Seth had spoken about once school started.

She smiled faintly, and her eyes filled. "I know."

They were alone, the cemetery behind them, hidden from any traffic on the street by the big two-story parsonage. "Why didn't you go to the door, then?"

"I didn't know it was him. I didn't know

who was there."

"Had he threatened you before this?"

"It was only a feeling," she said.

"The same feeling you have now?" He was tired of it, the way people looked at him, shrank from his size. Tired of being feared. A weariness Seth must have felt as well.

She raised her chin and studied Grizz. "No. I know you're not going to hurt me, Mr. Fallon." Then she wiped her hands along her skirt and peered into his eyes.

Grizz stepped back. It was the expression on her face, open, expectant. He was afraid she was going to hug him, and he didn't want her to do any such thing. He needed to hold on to his anger, see this to the end. "There's something else," he said. "He carved a word in his desk. It doesn't look like English. 'Wergild,' or something. You know what it means?"

After a moment, she nodded. "It's Old English. A blood debt, that's what it means. It's a price a family paid to keep others from taking revenge. Gold for blood spilled."

"Why would he write that, then do what he did?"

She was quiet while she thought about it. He saw this and knew he would trust her. Her hands were around her stomach, as though to soothe the baby inside her.

"Maybe he wanted someone to stop him."

He set his cap on his head, not wanting her to see his eyes. It was clear to him what she had to offer. This woman had liked his son. She had not hated him the way the rest of the town had. Even now she was not judging him. "Do you think he really meant to kill a whole bunch of people like they're saying?"

"I don't know," she said. "Only Seth knows."

He turned and walked to his truck.

"Mr. Fallon," she called after him.

"It's Grizz," he said, facing her once more. "What everyone calls me."

"Grizz, would you like to come inside the parsonage and wait for my husband there? I'll make tea. Maple tea. It's a secret recipe my father taught me."

"No," he said. "I'll come another time."

THE CORNFIELD

After his truck passed on the road, Clara was alone in the fading day. She thought of Seth with his desk all the way in the back of the room, a circle of space around him. A kid with a face so gaunt he almost looked cadaverous. *Steorfan.* The word flashed inside her the first time she looked into his eyes, an Old English word for "starving," a word that once simply meant "death." She didn't know why it popped into her brain. Seth's eyes were slanted and golden brown, and the way his dark clothing draped on him made him appear tall and lean and dangerous.

He had been tracked along with the kids not in precalculus and college chemistry, the ones who didn't expect anything more out of life than to head up to Bowden Technical College for a year to study plumbing or electrical maintenance before returning to Lone Mountain. His class was hell on teachers, and they came to Clara during her fifth period, right after lunch, a riot of noise and distraction. Her first day they continued talking after the bell while she paced in front of the room, deeply regretting wearing heels because she wasn't used to being on her feet all day long.

The boys sprawled in their desks while the girls gaggled. Clara went over to the doorway and switched the lights off and on to get their attention, but this just made them ooh and aah. They were going to make an example of her to set the tone. Clara's blood pressure spiked when she realized she had lost control of them before she even got started. A young teacher who didn't know what she was doing. A mistake to take this job. Logan had argued against the long-term-substitute position when it was offered, reminding her that she was supposed to be finishing her dissertation, an investigation of the remaining Old English texts that described the massacre of St. Brice's Day under the reign of King Aethelred the Unready. Clara raised her voice again to tell them about *Beowulf,* which they had just started reading before their last teacher, Mr. Gleason, had a stroke.

Then Seth rose from his place at the back of the room, holding one of the heavy

English literature textbooks. In a single, smooth gesture he let it drop from chin height to the floor. The book whipcracked the linoleum. The entire room hushed and turned in his direction, the quiet kids up front tensing and hunkering down in their seats. "Shut the hell up," Seth told them, "and let the lady talk."

Clara didn't say anything right away. Her mouth felt coated with paste, and her eyes watered because her feet were killing her. In the new silence, she took off her heels and tossed them into a corner and let her swollen feet kiss the cold floor. She sipped from her water, drew in her breath, and shut her eyes. Then she began to sing them the story in Anglo-Saxon as it was meant to be told, her voice starting low and then rising in pitch, a lilting soprano that drew in all the cadences of Old English alliteration and bound it together in a weave of sound. Clara, a music minor at the U, had sung in the choir but never soloed before this. She felt all their eyes on her. She hadn't done this for the earlier class, the smart kids who bent to their reading and the questions at the end of the section without giving her trouble.

"Do you know what language that was?" she asked the silent room. "What story I was telling?" A few mouths gaped; she had their attention. She walked the room and began to speak of it, a kingdom under siege, the nightly terror in the mead-hall. The class went on and they opened their books and dived into the text itself, but it was the stories and songs and legends they wanted. The words and mysteries and how inside the words they spoke every day they carried the memory of this lost world. How it was said that Hitler's troops fought so hard at the end of World War II because deep in their icy German hearts they remembered Ragnarok, and the end of the world. The gods at war with frost giants, men at war with the gods, even the women as Valkyries riding in on shrieking clouds to pick out the heroic dead. And after class that first day, Seth paused at the door and showed his teeth when he smiled. "Neat trick," he said before ducking under the door into the churn of bodies in the hallway.

He was the key to the class, the one they feared. Hold his attention and the rest would follow. Clara had the feeling she had been tested in some crucial way, and she had passed. The moment gave her a strange confidence, and the students responded to this confidence, even if it was all bluff and bravado.

Fifth period became her favorite time of the day. She made the room dark for them by drawing the heavy felt curtains along one wall of windows and then lighting a couple of candles along the lip of the chalkboard. They loved riddles and mysteries, so she put up a riddle each day on the chalkboard from the Anglo-Saxon *Book of Exeter* for them to puzzle over. They drew maps of England, studied the Danish sagas that had inspired *Beowulf,* histories featuring men with names like Ivar the Boneless and Ragnar Shaggy-pants, who was executed by being lowered into a pit of vipers. It was all a little corny maybe, but she had found a way to make this ancient story come alive. They needed her, a PhD washout who hadn't been able to finish her dissertation, a pregnant woman with all sorts of fears and hang-ups of her own, but someone who knew the world and could talk to them about it on their own level. She learned how desperate many of them were to get out of this town, how eager for news of life in the outside world, for what awaited them — a few of them — at college.

Even so, she made plenty of mistakes, pried when she shouldn't have. During a classroom discussion about Grendel descending from Cain, about original sin and monsters, Kelan Gunderson had raised his hand. His black hair was trimmed in a neat crew cut around his square face, and he wore a letterman's jacket in the school colors, scarlet and gold. Kelan, Seth, and Leah had been an inseparable trio in the hallways.

"Mrs. Warren," Kelan asked, "do you believe in the devil?"

Caught off guard, Clara laughed nervously at first, thinking of Dana Carvey's Church Lady impressions on *Saturday Night Live*. But Kelan wasn't smiling, and the rest of the class seemed to await an honest answer. Did she? Was it necessary to believe in the devil if you believed in God? Clara had always considered the devil just an ancient bogeyman, as mythic as Grendel, an excuse for the darker aspects of humanity, but she couldn't say that here, not as the pastor's wife. She was not used to being in a position of authority.

"You heard what happened over in Amroy?" Kelan went on when she hesitated. "Some Satanists killed a farmer's pig for one of their rituals. Cut off its head; gutted the body." This announcement sparked a host of side discussions throughout the class, rumors of rituals back in the woods or on isolated farms that involved molested children, animal dismemberment, secret graves.

"Did any of you see this with your own eyes?" Clara said, trying to get control of the conversation once more.

"My dad's the sheriff," Kelan continued. "He could tell you stories about what goes on in this town." The other students in the room quieted. She felt a collective leaning toward Kelan. Seth they feared for his size and violence, but Kelan held sway with personality. Being the son of the sheriff made every story he told matter that much more. Worse, Clara felt somehow that they needed to believe that these things were happening nearby out in the woods. Such stories offered the delicious shiver that comes from walking in a nightmare and returning safe to your ordinary world.

"Look," said Clara, "if you read the accounts of serial killers, it's not the devil they report giving them marching orders. It's not the devil's voice they claim to hear up in their heads."

It's God who they say told them to kill, she was about to say. But Kelan cut her off. "Do you believe in him, Mrs. Warren? You didn't answer my question."

She wasn't going to lie. These kids had grown up with lies. Adults telling lies to children to keep them afraid or to keep them safe. If Clara held sway here in this room, it was as a truth teller. She hadn't lied, and she wasn't going to start. "What do you think?" she said, turning the question back on him.

"The devil is a roaring lion in this world," he said, his gray eyes shining, and his words flit about the hushed room like bats.

Clara had not meant to think of Kelan now. In truth there was something smug and condescending about the boy that got under her skin. She was trying to remember Seth, the last time she saw him. Clara had been concentrating so she could finish grading a batch of five-paragraph essays from the sophomores on the definition of a hero. She needed to finish them and then get home and start dinner for Logan. It was late in the day, and most of her fellow teachers had gone home, an unnatural quiet spreading in the halls. Clara had the window open to let in a breeze and cleanse the room from the day's gathered odors — chalk and mildewing dictionaries and teenage-boy odors.

Clara had looked up and he was there, dressed in dark jeans, a denim jacket with patches of his favorite metal bands sewn on. His long hair, washed and feathered, glistened. "Seth? I didn't even hear you come in."

"Can I ask you something?" His hands were in his jacket's pockets as he came toward her. "Why'd you come here?"

"We needed a job."

Seth frowned. He was studying her hand, the missing fingers. Most of the students couldn't stop staring, but Seth only seemed curious. "You told us your mother died in a car accident."

She nodded. She hadn't told the full story, just enough to satisfy their curiosity. The unexpected blizzard. The woman with the baby in the backseat. The only bits of the story she knew, really.

"My mom died when I was a baby, too. She only held me once."

"I'm sorry." And this was something she had not expected, either: the way the students came to her after class to talk about such things.

"She had lupus. She had been really sick a long time." He swallowed. "You remind me of her, pictures I've seen."

"I do?" Clara wasn't sure what to say. She thought of the notes and was relieved on one hand that he might think of her in such a way. Maybe that was the connection between them, both missing mothers, both

111

longing to hear a mother's voice. Feral, like her.

"I've got lupus, too," he said. "I found out a few years ago."

She didn't know what it was, just that it could cause great pain. Hadn't it killed Flannery O'Connor?

"That creative response you asked for . . . there's something I don't get about these people."

"Go on," she said, grateful for the change of subject.

"All the gods die in Ragnarok, right? It's like the end of everything. So what's the point?"

"The point? You mean of living?"

"Living even when you know it's all going to go to shit, no matter what you do."

She decided to ignore the profanity. Seth's class was blunt spoken, and early on as a substitute she had developed tin ears. "I guess the point is to make sure your death matters. To die heroically so you can enter Valhalla. To do something of worth."

Seth's Adam's apple danced in his throat. He stepped forward and took something from his jacket pocket, an object wrapped in tissue paper, and placed it on her desk.

"What's this?"

He glanced toward the hallway and then

at her. "Mrs. Warren, you need to be careful."

"What do you mean?"

"Just watch yourself," he said.

Clara stood.

Seth was walking away, his gaze to the floor. Clara unwrapped the tissue paper to reveal two hand-painted miniatures, the kind used for Dungeons & Dragons. The first miniature had the legs of a human, but the shoulders turned muscular and hairy and were topped with a leering wolf's head. A werewolf. The second figure had auburn hair, like Clara, and wore a long sweeping gown, her mouth open as though speaking a song or spell. A priestess. Each figure was exquisitely detailed and painted in bold colors. The priestess clutched a staff in her left hand. Clara felt sure if she studied it under a magnifying glass she would see two fingers missing, cleaved by an X-acto knife. She wrapped the miniatures in the tissue paper and put them away in her drawer. It was only later that she remembered Yggdrasil and the story of the two children, Lif and Lifthrasir, who survive the end of the world by hiding in a tree. Of Balder coming back from the dead, and the sons of gods who witness the green world made again.

It didn't matter anymore; he was dead,

and Clara had failed him or worse maybe even given him some kind of false valor to do something horrendous. His blood was on her hands. And now there was someone out there who agreed, who had put the drawing under her doorjamb like an accusation. Hadn't she been teaching children about doom?

The boy's father had been here and gone. Seth cut the word "wergild" in his desk, and as he had done so, had he known his father would come to her with it? A blood debt. Had he meant that this wouldn't end with his death, that it might trigger something worse? She remembered him, what was good in him, and she was more confused than ever.

Clara looked in the direction the wind had snatched the drawing, off into the cemetery and the field beyond. The sun was setting, but there might still be a chance to find it. In her thin maternity blouse and skirt, she stepped out onto the grass and started climbing the hill. She didn't know where she was going, except that she had the feeling that whoever had left this for her had come this way, a faint scent of cordite on the breeze. In this stage of her pregnancy, Clara had never smelled so keenly what the world had to offer.

Below her the town lay still. She realized she was repeating Seth's journey from a few days ago, heading for the country, for shelter, a hiding place. She was sweating in the muggy air from the walk, her feet aching from the hard ground. She'd walked far enough to reach a deep slough filled with tall, waving grasses. On the other side of the slough stood the waiting corn, the field where Seth killed himself. It had to be it. The cornfield ringed round by woods.

Before she knew what she was doing, she'd taken a few steps into the slough. The thick grasses were high as her waist and alive in the wind, stalks bending with each gust. The seed heads of the grass ticked and frayed in the wind. The corn beckoned to her, but she didn't have the courage to enter. As her eyes scanned it, she saw something that took her breath away.

A figure in a long coat stepped out of the field at that very moment. The boy. Dark hair. The same haggard coat hanging down near his shoes. The vision she had seen that afternoon he came to her door and rang the bell. Seth Fallon.

Her heart pushed up in her throat, and her breathing shallowed. He just walked out of the corn, from the place where he had ended himself, his eyes finding her right away. She stepped back, away from the slough of waving grasses, her blood gone cold.

Impossible. *You are dead. You put a shotgun into your mouth and pulled the trigger. They found your body.* Maybe a hundred yards separated her, but the figure clearly wore Seth's coat, his face a dark smear. He wasn't watching Clara, however. He stood surveying the town, the same spread of valley she had taken in moments before.

Impossible. The morning of the shooting she climbed the stairs after hearing the gun. *I saw you cross the graveyard and vanish. I heard screaming down the street. And all I did was press my back to the wall and sink to the floor, knowing without seeing what had happened. How could I have known? Why won't you leave me alone even now?*

Inside her the child twisted and tumbled. A throbbing at the end of her fingers. She was soaked with icy sweat.

Then the figure turned around and vanished into the corn. Clara hurried home, past the cemetery, shivering all over. She was not supposed to have seen what she just saw. *You've come back for me, my student. You've come back and you're not going to let me sleep, are you? You are restless because you should be in your grave.* There was too

much she didn't know. Why? What could
the dead ask of her?

SWADDLING

Nolan's Funeral Home was on the other side of town, not far from the nursing home and the big concrete walls that protected the downtown from the river during spring floods. Grizz passed through the town itself, his vision focused on the road ahead, ignoring those few who came out of the post office or corner store to witness his rust-pitted Ford rumbling past and wonder over his errand.

The funeral home itself was an ornate, plum-colored plantation-style house with white pillars on the veranda. He shut off his truck, walked right up onto the porch, and stepped into the foyer without bothering to ring the bell. A young man in a three-piece suit and vest was seated behind a polished desk going over some papers alone. He had orange short-cropped hair, a spray of freckles across his face. "Can I help you?" he asked.

He was not someone Grizz knew, likely an apprentice Nolan was training, someone from another town. "Where is he?" he asked.

"Who?"

"I'm looking for my son's body."

A door opened behind the young man, and Nolan himself stepped out. He wore the same dark suit as his assistant, a kerchief tucked in his pocket. Nolan was a short man, his white hair pomaded with Brylcreem, his eyes huge and owlish behind thick black glasses. He nodded at Grizz as though he'd been expecting him and waved his hand at the young man to return to the papers at his desk. "Come this way, Grizz," he said, holding open the door.

When the door shut they were in a narrow hallway together. Paintings of English gardens, the kind with topiary and fountains, hung on the walls, none of them looking like any place around here. A hallway of mirrors and illusions complete with velvety carpet that swallowed the sound of footsteps. Nolan turned as soon as they were in the cavernous hall. "Let's go to my office. We can talk there."

"I want to see Seth."

Nolan paused, his eyes blinking behind his glasses. "I don't think that's a good idea."

"Where is he?"

Nolan remained impassive. "Come to my office. We'll talk about things, make arrangements."

"I was already told what kind of service they have planned for him and where they're going to bury him afterward."

"I heard," Nolan admitted. "But I don't sit on the church council, so that sort of thing is not up to me. My job is to prepare people to say good-bye." He drew in a quick breath and rushed on before Grizz could respond. "There are several affordable packages that might interest you. I am mindful of your circumstances."

Grizz let out an exasperated breath. It would serve this asshole right if he wrung his neck right here in the hallway. He hated his suit, the fake flowery prints on the walls, the richness of the carpet beneath his feet. It was all a lie for the grieving, and now Nolan wanted him to sit in his office while he spun out a dizzying row of numbers, bid him sign some dotted line? But Nolan could still help him. He was not the enemy. "What if I was to bury him on my own land?"

"You need a permit from the county. You'd have to get a portion of your land declared a private cemetery. It's frowned upon by the current commissioner."

"Frowned upon?"

"Now, if you just follow me, we can talk. It's not so bad. Do you really think God cares what section of the cemetery we bury bodies in?"

Grizz narrowed his eyes. "Show me the door that leads to your basement."

Nolan took off his glasses and wiped them with his kerchief. "End of the hallway. Last door on your right."

Grizz went down the hall. When he opened the door, he smelled the dampness and an odor like leaking gas. His iron-toed boots clacked on the concrete steps leading down. He didn't even notice Nolan following until the man flicked on a fluorescent set of overhead lights, the tubing buzzing. The door clanged shut behind the men as they went down. Seth's body waited at the bottom of the stairs in a chilly room. He'd been zipped in a black bag that sat on top of a gleaming metal table, a gurney with wheels underneath, everything polished and clean. Gutters cut into the concrete floor below the gurney led to a large drain.

When Grizz stopped, Nolan set a hand on his shoulder. "Don't do this."

Grizz clenched his fists and stood with planted feet, bracing himself. "I need to be sure."

"It's him. Believe me. But there isn't much left of his head. I'm telling you that now. It'll have to be a closed-coffin service." He rubbed his eyes with his hands. "I'm trying to be honest, here. Look, if it makes you feel any better to know this, when they did the autopsy on Will Gunderson they found his body riddled with cancer. It was all over his chest and stomach. If anything your son saved him long months of agony. They both died quick."

"Leave us be."

Nolan did as he asked but stopped on the way out. "This shouldn't be your last memory of your son. There are better ways to say good-bye. Remember him instead when he was a child." He went up the stairs without looking back.

Grizz shut his eyes and put his hand on the bag. The last time he had been in a room like this was in the hospital after Jo died. The only thing that saved him in the following days was being able to bring home Seth and care for him as a baby.

Seth had never been happy unless Grizz held him or rocked him, and nights passed with him up late walking the creaky floorboards of the old farmhouse. Seth cried in colicky hiccups and spat up most of the formula he managed to get down the baby's gullet. When he heard the baby crying he would head into the nursery room and find the child waiting for him. The two had a truce. By rolling a bottle nipple in sugar he could get Seth to take his formula. Eventually, Grizz ended up bundling the sleepless baby into the car seat and taking him for a ride in the truck.

Already the roads of the town had been so imprinted on his brain he could drive them in his sleep, and sometimes on the long road back, stretches passed with his mind so vacant he believed he had been sleeping. Seth quieted as soon as he was in the cab. Father and son owned the empty streets, the sleeping town, all of it belonging to them at that late hour. To stay awake, Grizz kept up a narration of things he saw on the road: raccoons pillaging a trash can, a hunter's moon, Orion descending. The rumbling truck took them down roads glazed with black ice, Grizz white-knuckling the steering wheel, terrified of the deep ditches opening on either side of the road, down past farmhouses, into the ancient river valley where at last the baby descended into his uneasy rest.

At home he carefully lifted Seth out of the car seat and carried him upstairs to his crib. Before wrapping the baby in his swaddling, he held him, swaying like a branch in a light wind, and prayed, "Lord, this child is little more than a sparrow's weight in my hands. Watch over him. Do not take him from me. What strength I have I will into this child. Down to marrow, let this boy be whole and safe and strong."

Grizz let himself weep for what he had lost until his breath was ragged in his lungs. He couldn't bear to open the bag. Nolan was right. He couldn't do it, and he hated himself for his cowardice. It wasn't Seth here, just the shell of his wrecked body. If there such a thing as a soul, a spirit, the boy's was not here. There was only this to believe in now. Grizz, who only believed in what he could touch with his hands, needed to believe in something else. He had failed his son in life, but he would not in death.

"I'll come back for you," Grizz said. "I won't let them hurt you anymore."

WOLFGIRL

Deeper, further back into her past, there was a wind in the trees outdoors, a wastrel wind. She was six years old, an only child, living with her father in an apartment above the Four Corners, a small grocery store he owned and operated in the suburban town of Savage, Minnesota. That winter, December 1968, it was so cold at night she could hear the elm trees out in the windbreak splitting open, a shriek as their broken branches fell. They dropped with a tremendous thump that shook both the windows and the snow from the roof. Huge icicles draped from eaves, like the claws of some dragon resting on the roof, blown in by the storm. She imagined him up there, scales of his pale lizard belly scraping the tiles. Snow fell and stuck to barren trees and brought more branches to the ground. The night was full of falling snow and falling stars and the wind rising and falling from beyond.

It was the kind of night that made the girl and her father think of the mother, a night when he knew his daughter would bother him long after bedtime, waking him from a deep slumber to ask if she could sleep in his room, because she couldn't stand to be alone. Not when there was a wind outside, a wind with claws.

He came into her room, a thin man, already graying in his early thirties, his eyes deep-set in their sockets like those paintings she had seen of Keats as a consumptive. He smelled of scotch and Marlboros. He had been a Latin teacher once, a man fluent in a dead language, before the state phased it out of the curriculum. "Tell me a story," she would beg. "Please."

He sat beside her on the bed. Sometimes he held her hand in his, touched the ends of her ghost fingers as if the story hid there. This was all he could bear to tell her. "Once upon a time," he began.

A baby girl was born, entering the world covered in a fine wolfish pelt that darkened her cheeks, shoulders, and back. When they lay the baby on her mother's belly, the woman recoiled. The girl's eyes were narrowed to canine slits, and even her cries sounded like subdued yelps. No one in the room, not even an elderly nurse who had seen thousands of births in her lifetime, spoke at first. Then the doctor handed the father gleaming surgical scissors and told him to cut the bloody cord. *"Mein Gott,"* the mother said when she found her breath.

"Go ahead," the doctor encouraged behind his face mask, showing the father the bloodied clip where he'd pinched off the placenta. "Cut right here."

The baby's father nodded. He muttered some reassurance to his wife. Hearing her father's voice, the baby stretched forth one tiny hand. Such ancient hands they seemed to him, all pruned and wrinkled. Old soul. It was as if his wife had given birth to a little furry old person now reaching to take hold of him. The baby squalled this whole time, raspy-sounding hiccups like it was drowning in its own fluids. The father reached out with his other hand, and the baby grabbed his pinkie and held on. This touch startled them both and hushed the baby. The father's eyes filled, and he could not speak. Then a new calmness entered him, and he did what was necessary and cut the cord and let the nurse bundle the child away.

He reached for her in the shocking moment of her birth and would go on reaching until he breathed his last. The baby weighed only four pounds.

A little monster, that's what her mother thought she had birthed. She was being punished; her sin had stained even her womb. She tried to breast-feed the thing and failed. Pale, exhausted, she would go on spilling bloody clumps between her legs long after the doctors sewed her up. It was as if the birthing had torn something out of her, something terrible and secret that she would never have again. And the baby reminded her of nothing more than a runt kitten, something too small and wounded to survive. Slate gray eyes and mewling. "Take it away," she told the nurse. "I need my rest."

If the child had been born with a caul instead, the mother might have known what it meant and not been so unnerved. She would have dried and preserved the caul and then pinned it to a wall above the bed to keep the child from changing into a werewolf when the moon fattened. But this glistening gray fur that covered the entire body, as fine as corn silk, disgusted her. The mother was frightened of wolves, and here one had come from her own belly.

She didn't know all fetuses were furred for a time in the womb, and that babies born more than a month premature, like this one, sometimes still bore a vestigial reminder of humankind's bestial origins. By the time the young doctor came to explain to the mother why her baby appeared so freakish, it was too late. He tried naming the condition, telling her it was called lanugo and that it would last a few weeks before the fur was absorbed into the body. "Your baby is small but fierce," he assured her. "She is going to live."

Much later that night, as the woman's husband slept in an armchair beside her, the nurse wheeled the child and her cradle into the room and left again. When the mother awoke, it was waiting for her, and she knew what she had to do. Quietly, wearing only her hospital gown, she snuck her husband's keys from the lamp stand and took the baby and walked barefoot into the snowy parking lot and was not seen again.

"She was crazy, wasn't she?"

"She gave birth to the child, but she was no mother."

"How come?"

At such moments his pretense fell away, and the girl knew he was picturing her mother as he had first known her and not this fairy-tale vision he had made up for her.

"She was from a faraway place, and she had seen terrible things. She was unwell. Sometimes, women will get really sad after a baby is born, even though it should be the happiest moment in their lives. Sometimes this sadness eats them up and they do something bad."

"Tell me the rest. About the wolves and the baby in the snow."

"That's enough for tonight."

Set it down. That was what her father wanted. The lanugo had long been a memory she carried inside her, but Seth's death and her own impending motherhood awakened it again. Would such sadness also enter her, make her do something awful? Was she even fit to be a mother? Some nights she swore she still sensed the lanugo, a second, bristling existence under all that smooth skin. Fur and wildness. When the moon swelled, she imagined shucking off this outer layer and padding on all fours through the woods. *A wulvas heo.* There she smelled snow in the sharp cold wind, heard rabbits shudder deep in their warrens at the sound of her coming. This was how she had come to think of herself. Look inside the fierce brown eyes her mother gave her, and you would see she was still a wolfgirl all these years later.

SHARDS

Logan was already gone by the time she came downstairs the next morning, but he had left Clara a to-do list, and number one on the list was the dishes, which she hadn't washed in a few days. He had underlined this task so she would understand how important it was, a plea for a return to normalcy. Logan detested messes, and the entire kitchen had a sour smell, the same smell on her skin. Clara tore the list into pieces that she left for him on the table and then set to making cinnamon rolls, Pillsbury, in the oven.

She ate the rolls on the living room couch and licked frosting from her fingertips. The shades were drawn against the day; outside big trucks lumbered past on the one road leading out of town, rattling the glass in the window casings. All the world on the move now, headed elsewhere. Clara sank into the cushion, a pillow propped behind her to support her back, her mind thick with sugar and dough.

The night before Logan had awakened her past midnight. "This is killing me," he said in a drained voice.

"Logan?" His body curled under the blankets in a fetal position, so she touched his hip. "What are you talking about?"

He grumbled something more, still fast asleep she realized, talking to someone in his dreams. Clara couldn't be sure she'd heard him right.

She reached under the covers, found his wrist, felt the erratic wingbeats of his pulse under his skin. "What's killing you?" she whispered, afraid of what he meant, not wanting to wake him up. She had not slept well the rest of the night and a nap was in order this morning. She shut her eyes and drifted off on the couch.

When she woke, Logan was standing over her, his brow furrowed. He must have found the to-do list she ripped into pieces. "Come eat," he said, "I made soup."

"I didn't even hear you come home. Wow, I was really out of it."

Logan didn't say anything as they sat at the table and mumbled grace and set to the soup, which still steamed. Silence and clinking silverware. How could she be hungry again so soon? While she ate her soup, she searched her mind for the right words, something inane about the weather to break the tension.

"I wish you wouldn't eat like that," Logan said.

She had been enjoying her meal until then, the hot salty broth. "Like what?"

"That slurping noise. You don't have to slurp it like a dog. Watch." He dipped a spoon into the bowl, lifted out some soup, and put it past his pinched lips.

"Jesus Christ on a stick. Is that how you're supposed to eat soup?"

Logan set his spoon down, his face reddening. "Don't mock me, Clara. I just wish you wouldn't smack your lips all the time. I wish you would chew with your mouth shut."

Her eyes grew hot.

"Oh, don't. Not this again."

"Don't what?" As if she could stop it.

"It's been this same weepy self-pity ever since Seth shot himself. You know what, Clara? That kid was a little shit. You wouldn't believe the stories I've heard. He was a terror. This whole town is glad he's dead."

She got up before she said something she regretted and carried the remains of her bowl into the kitchen, not wanting to look at him. She turned on the water. She didn't mean to do it at first, but that china bowl was slick in her hands. The first one dropped with a crack into the hard stainless-steel sink and shattered into a thousand pieces. It was an accident, pure and simple. His mother's bone china with the baby-blue etchings. That Dutch boy with his shit-eating grin and the little blue windmills. The sound of it breaking snapped something inside of her, too. One by one she lifted the dirty dishes stacked on the side and started slamming them into the sink.

Logan shouted for her to stop. She heard a clatter as his chair fell over, and then he loomed in the entryway. Clara's vision narrowed to a single red thread. Sometime during the shattering she had picked up a shard of pottery, and she clenched it in her palm.

Logan was saying something, but she couldn't hear a word. A roaring filled her ears. A sound like a growl from her throat. There weren't any words in her mind anymore, just the sure knowledge that if he laid a hand on her she was going to gut him with the edge of this broken dish.

Logan approached, his palms turned up, his arms spread. More words streaming out of his mouth, like he was calling her from a long ways away. Like she was falling down and down, and he was trying to reach her. Her eyelashes blinking furiously. His form blurring. A burning in her blood.

Only a few feet away Logan paused. He was still talking, saying something over and over. The space between them disappeared. He touched her arm. She didn't stab him. She didn't stab him. He was saying, "Clara, it's okay." He was saying, "Clara you're not in danger. No one is going to hurt you. It's okay, it's okay, it's okay." Then he held her in his arms. A deep shudder passed out of her, a moan. She buried her face in his shoulder and let the shard fall from her hand.

He went away again; he had to. They were expecting him for the weekly service at the nursing home. He didn't want to go; she saw it in his eyes. A wariness. Logan was afraid of what she might do. "I shouldn't have said any of that," he said. He tried to smile. Big black half-moons under his eyes, like someone had been punching him while he slept. The dark thing he had been talking to in his sleep. How had she not noticed his suffering?

She wanted to tell him sorry, too, because she was, but her throat felt raw, like she had swallowed something so hot it scorched away the words. She was conscious of her bare feet on the floor. A barefoot, pregnant madwoman. She glanced to the window, wondering if the sound of breaking dishes had carried out into the neighborhood, if people had heard what was happening in the parsonage, if there were eyes upon them even now. She had come back to herself. She was safe in her kitchen, but something still bristled inside her. "I know you're under a lot of pressure, but you shouldn't talk to me like that. Ever."

"Agreed." He licked his lips. "We're supposed to make each other better people. That's what marriage should be. Like two ropes woven together."

"And Seth Fallon may have been a little shit . . . but I can't help feeling responsible."

"Oh, sweetie." He was tender now, regretful. This was the man she had married. His blue eyes clear and pristine as some far northern lake. "You can't save somebody if they don't want to be saved."

"I know." *That wasn't it, that wasn't it at all.* "You aren't mad at me?"

Dust from broken china was somehow on his clerical shirt, and he brushed it off. "No. Tell you the truth, I hated those dishes. Who eats off china every single day? I don't want to think about my parents every time we sit down to eat."

"I lost it there."

"Yeah." He exhaled heavily. "But I understand. You've been through a lot."

She had, but it didn't excuse it. Violence, in her experience, was rarely premeditated. Clara remembered the first time her former fiancé Gregory had struck her. He was a coworker from the bank where she had been a teller, and it happened after a long day at work. They were sitting cross-legged on the hardwood floor of his apartment, eating slices of take-out pepperoni pizza from a cardboard box set between them. They had not been arguing, nor could Clara even recall what they were talking about. The pizza grease was wet on her lips when Gregory got on his knees, almost like he was going to ask her to move in with him. The hope lit in her. They had been engaged for nearly a year, and Gregory was good to her, an attentive lover, a man only a few years older who was both cultured and successful. They hadn't set a date, and Gregory put it off when she tried bringing it up. Clara remembered dabbing at her mouth with a napkin, tilting her chin, when his fist cracked her in the jaw.

She remembered how her mouth filled with blood, how she lay stunned and gasping for breath for only a moment, and then he was pulling her toward him, begging forgiveness, saying "I don't know what came over me" as he tried to wrap her in a smothering embrace. Frightened, Clara had kicked him, her heel striking him in the ribs, and scrambled away on her knees. She only got a few feet before he grabbed her by the ankle, and when she fell she knocked over the lamp stand and everything on it, the bulb bursting, imploding really, his set of keys jingling when they struck the hardwood floor. He had her by the ankle, his words harder now, and he was pulling her toward his bedroom. Clara grabbed the keys and threaded them through her knuckles, like metal claws. "Don't you understand?" he said. "I don't want to hurt you. I didn't mean to do it." She curled into herself, playing wounded, but when he leaned down near her, Clara punched him with the sharp keys in her fist. The blow ripped skin from his cheek, and he screamed and reeled away. She had run out of the apartment, right through the broken bulb's glass, in her bare feet, and then walked all the way home, constantly looking behind her, sure that he was going to come punish her for fighting back.

The faucet was still running, so Clara

reached among the shards to shut it off, her thoughts jumbled as something struggled to stand up inside her on newborn foal legs. She walked over to Logan and adjusted the tongue of white plastic, which had gone crooked in his black collar. She concentrated to keep her hands from shaking. "There, you can go now," she said, because she couldn't think right with him so close. "I'll clean this up."

He touched her face. He swallowed, tried to find his words.

"Go," she said. "The old fogies are waiting for you."

Clara didn't clean up the dishes right away, despite what she had promised Logan. Downstairs the kittens cried out to her. They had heard the uproar and must have been upset. On the stove she heated up milk in a saucepan. This she poured into a collection of medicine droppers for the kittens before trudging down to the basement.

Even in the heat of early autumn the basement remained a cold, whispery place. Stairs painted red, a lipstick smear. Whitewash splashed on the walls to keep down mold, green copper pipes dripping, and the darkness at the bottom yawning like a mouth. There was no rail, so she braced herself against the wall every time she went down, one hand holding the medicine droppers, the other her belly.

The kittens waited, ravenous. They needed their mother. Clara understood. The kittens' mother, the cat she'd named Sorena, spent most of her time outdoors hunting gophers in the cemetery or sunning herself below the neighbor's bird feeder. She did not waste time on feeding her babies. She knew winter was coming, and her babies were too small. They would have been dead if Clara hadn't prepared a box for them, made a nest from torn newspapers, and moved it behind the old oil furnace where sunlight trickled in through a greasy window. Clara knew next to nothing about raising baby animals but was determined to keep them alive. And all that effort, what was it for? Logan was going to take them to some farm, where they'd surely die, though several days had passed, and he had not loaded them up to take them to the Nelsons.

This was the same window where she'd looked out and seen Seth's shoes, the ragged hem of his coat. That day she had felt a hand on her shoulder when she saw him. Icy breath on her neck. A voice inside her head. *Don't answer the door. Stay with me.* The baby inside her going still. A quiet, commanding voice. What Clara had always imagined her mother sounding like.

She picked up the kittens and held them against her, drizzling milk into their pink gums. "I'm sorry," she told each one as she lifted it out. "But you can't stay here anymore." The kittens fought to reach her, and she had to lift them by the hackles to keep from getting clawed, though they were small enough to fit within the palm of her hand. The whole milk from the grocery didn't seem to be providing enough nutrition. She needed to find the Nelson family in the church directory. You weren't supposed to take kittens from the mother until they were at least six weeks old, and Clara was sure Sorena would run away. And yet so far something had kept the cat here. As she fed the kittens she hummed a tuneless nursery rhyme to drown out their mewling.

Then the doorbell rang, silencing her song. The shock of the sound seemed to carry through the wires of the old parsonage because the bulb above her died with a fizzing pop.

She stood uncertainly as darkness washed over her. The blood throbbed in the ends of her missing fingers. That old ache come back again.

The dark was not complete. Sour gray

light leaked in from the window. The bell rang again. She still hadn't moved, waiting for her eyes to adjust. All she had to do was walk over to the window, but she was afraid of what she might see: those dirty shoes, the fraying edge of a coat. The figure she had seen at the edge of the corn. The bell rang and rang.

Silence. She felt her senses shutting down, narrowing, the way they had with Logan in the kitchen. This was the moment her body had been preparing her for. Down in the basement she had no weapon, no place to hide. Adrenaline pumped uselessly under her skin.

There was *something* down here with her. She sensed it standing right behind her. It had come inside. A tremor traveled from her bare feet to the top of her skull, and then she was shivering all over. *Don't turn around. Don't move. This is how you survive.*

Help me, Clara. Please.

The hair prickled on her neck.

That was it, a voice, her name, a cry, before the doorbell stopped and the sense went away.

She waited a minute, catching her breath. The kittens started mewling again, unsatisfied with the little milk she had carried down for them. Then the lightbulb fizzed to life. She turned around, half blinded, but all she made out was a shadow retreating into the watery darkness where she intended to set up a darkroom for her photography. The sound of her name echoed in her ears. She had known that voice, a boy's voice, scared. Seth.

The doorbell rang again, breaking her chain of thought. She wasn't sure how long she had been standing there. Then from above came the sound of the doorknob turning, the squeak of hinges. My God. Someone had come right inside the house; she heard footsteps in the kitchen.

"Clara?" A voice rattling in the empty room above. An old woman's voice.

She didn't realize she'd been holding her breath until she let it out in a rush. Instead of fear the feeling that coursed through her this time was bright, hot anger. It was just an ordinary parishioner upstairs. If they couldn't find Logan at the church, the first thing parishioners did was call or look in here. Because the parsonage belonged to the church, some walked right inside.

"Hello?" the voice called out once more. "Anyone home?" More footsteps, and then she must have spotted the dishes on the floor. "Goodness . . ."

When her breath came back, she shouted

up the stairs. "You can't just come in here. I don't know who you think you are, but you can't just barge into a person's home."

"Sorry," said the voice. "I'll just be leaving then."

"You wait right there," Clara called out. She needed to put an end to this nonsense, make sure these people understood how she needed space and privacy. There were *boundaries* that must be respected. That was the word Logan always used. Clara walked upstairs to find her neighbor, Nora Winters, in her kitchen, standing by the stove. Nora was a gnome-sized woman with a round face that scrunched up into a mass of wrinkles when she laughed; she had blue hair, a dye job gone wrong. She was breathing heavily just from carrying a heavy silver container across the lawn that separated the two houses.

"Hello, Clara," she said. "I brought you something."

Clara drew in her breath. She was mortified to be found in her kitchen in the late afternoon still wearing her robe, not to mention the broken china in the sink. If Nora breathed a word of this to anyone it would spread all over town. "You can't just come in here," Clara repeated, but the heat had gone out of her voice.

"I'm sorry, dear," she said. "I was just going to leave it on the counter with a note. It's hotdish. Tater Tot hotdish. My specialty. I keep one stored in the freezers for funerals and such."

Clara felt tired, so very tired. "No thanks." The thought of soggy Tots soaking in gravy and beef left her queasy.

"But you have to eat for two," Nora rushed on, her lips pursing. "You're far too skinny. Roundness is the natural shape the Lord intended for things. The earth is round and the harvest moon over the corn."

Clara had heard this lecture from her before. "I'm hardly skinny," she said. "I'm fit to burst." Fit to burst? Why was she talking this way? Why hadn't she given the old bag the boot? Nora was one of those women who once lived on a family farm. A cheery, rotund woman who caused everything to bloom around her. It was as though, being round herself, she caused everything to plump and share that shape. And though her husband, she assured Clara on one occasion, had died of a massive heart attack due to clogged arteries, he went to his grave fat and satisfied.

"Why, let that prairie wind take hold of you and you'll be tossed about like a weed," she said.

Clara surprised herself by laughing and then caught sight of the mess in the sink again. Nora's gaze followed hers. "It's my fault. I have a terrible temper and was tired of looking at all those dishes."

"Well, let me help you clean it up," Nora said. "When I was pregnant sometimes the most rotten moods came over me."

Clara looked at Nora, her blue hair, her face ruddy from the short walk, that cheerful voice.

"It's true," Nora said, reading the doubt in Clara's eyes. "I once took a bat to my husband's pickup after he went to the bar and left me alone with the kids on a Saturday night. Got both headlights before he stopped me." Against her wishes, Clara felt herself smiling again as she imagined this turnip of a woman attacking her husband's truck. "So you just let me clean this up. It's one thing these old bones is good for."

"No. I have to . . ."

Before she knew it, Nora had crossed the distance and put her hand on Clara's. Her voice lowered. "Why don't you go upstairs and run yourself a nice, hot bath? You leave this to me." She squeezed Clara's hand, gently insistent. "And don't you worry about talk spreading uptown. I can keep a secret."

Clara's throat thickened, and she didn't want to cry in front of her so she nodded and did as Nora asked. She was almost out of sight before Nora spoke again, an afterthought. "Why did Steve Krieger come by to visit?"

"Who?"

"Steve, the sheriff."

The doorbell she had heard earlier when she was in the basement with the kittens.

"Don't know," she said quickly. "I didn't get to the door in time. Maybe he was looking for Logan. Will Gunderson's funeral is a couple of days from now."

"Oh. He's a vigilant one, our law enforcement officer. Neither he nor Will Gunderson are the type of people you would ever want to cross." She shook her head. "Not that you need to worry about that."

The bath proved every bit as restorative as Nora had promised. Clara put on her terrycloth robe, a towel wrapping her hair, and went to the window. Nora was already heading home. She thought of how kind the woman had been to her on first coming here, how eager she was for the baby, telling Clara how she'd raised eight children into the fullness of adulthood and could salve, rub Vicks Vapo, or chicken soup her way

147

through the most dire illness. But oh! There was one lost one, a boy she could not save from childhood leukemia. She thought about him every living day.

Nora went directly to her garden and knelt on rickety knees in the grass. In the center of the vegetables, now husked brown and raked over, there stood a short statue of the Virgin Mary left there by her husband, Charlie. Nora and Charlie shared one of those marriages, Catholic and Lutheran, which caused so much woe on either side of their families. Nora had told Clara all about it, her voice so loud during the church social hour that people at other tables turned to listen. " 'It's all the same to me,' Charlie used to say. 'To get to New Ulm you can take Highway Twenty-Nine or you can take the Fourteen. They both end up in the same damn place.' "

It had been Nora's husband, Charlie, who insisted the statue be placed in the middle of the green growing things. Nora told her she had resisted at first, but the statue grew on her. In the statue's arms she took some comfort. Here was a woman given a sacred task, bearing God's child into a world that would mock him and impale him on a tree. She did not break when that man was spat upon and crucified. Her love had been absolute. The resurrected Christ came back to women first.

In the days that passed, Grizz held firm on not allowing a funeral. He filed the paperwork asking for the right to bury his son on his own land, then waited on word from the county and tried to keep his mind off it with chores. There was always more work on a farm than any one body could do alone, especially in the fall. Two hundred acres of corn and soybeans to be harvested, fifty-three head of cattle to feed and water, new siding for the barn, twenty acres of bottomland meadow hay and alfalfa to bale and stack in the mow, and machinery to be oiled and groomed for the coming harvest and winter.

He could fill himself up with such numbers and work. It was how he had lived with the boy after Jo died, so much work it stripped away the words he might have spoken across the dinner table, words that might have called Seth out of the darkness he carried inside him.

Any thought of that commissioner set his teeth on edge, even as he sought to lose himself in his labor. The hay in the lower meadow needed cutting, so the day following Grizz's visit to the funeral home he hitched the mower to the International and set out to do the work. Even with the tractor in full thrum and the blades of the cutter scything out long rows of grass, he felt unsettled. Occasionally on the mountain he caught a winking of light, of sun on glass or gleaming metal. As though he was being signaled by a mirror. The hair raised on his nape. There was someone out there watching him; he felt sure of it.

Something else troubled him as well. These last few years Seth's coyotes always came to greet him shortly after he started haying, loping down from their mountain warren to frolic in the fields. He feared the moment as much he longed to see them, for they were only alive because of what Seth had done years earlier, and he had lain awake these last few nights with the windows open to listen for their singing, but the night remained silent.

The coyotes came for the mice the tractor scared up from the grass. When the mice fled, the coyotes leaped after them, pouncing with curved spines to pin the rodents under their paws, then gobbling them up in a single gulp. When Seth was alive, Grizz had recoiled at the sight of them, the way anyone raised on a farm reacts to a predator invading his space, fox or egg-thieving skunk. Seth's little wolves were big, rangy creatures, but their lean snouts and long, comical ears belied something more dangerous. These were efficient killers, and they left little to waste. In the spring when the cows calved in the pasture, the coyotes were always there, gorging on the placenta and afterbirth, their muzzles bloody in the early light. He had told Seth that if they harmed even one of those calves he would shoot them all, but they hadn't, not yet. Seth had held them at bay.

These last few years, the sight of them coming down from the mountain had cheered the boy during the hot work of haying. Grizz would hear his boy's laughter, a rare sound, when Seth sat behind him on the rack. Sometimes he would call, and the coyotes would answer, especially with evening coming on. The coyotes' absence became one more troubling reminder of the boy's absence.

Sometimes a hiccup of dust sprung from the grass in front of the tractor or just behind it as he swiveled the little front wheel and turned into another row of grass. A yellow cloud of chaff smoked behind the cutter and dirtied the clear blue sky. When Grizz changed direction, he turned into the dust cloud, and his eyes and nostrils stung. He kicked into second gear, risking a jam, and pulled the brim of his cap lower. Again the grass erupted to his left, throwing up dirt. Over the grinding of the gears, he heard a distant crack.

Grizz knew then what he was seeing and hearing. Gunshots. He pulled the kill switch to cut the power, and when the tractor sputtered to a halt and the resulting dust cloud whipped past him, he climbed into the saddle seat and stood there with his hat in his hands, swaying unsteadily on the spring seat. *Here,* he meant for whoever was out there. *Go ahead and put me out of my misery.* His breath came short. With his sinuses furred by itchy hay, he wasn't seeing right. Maybe there was nothing out there at all. Shielding his eyes, he scanned the mountain above for a spot where he'd seen that winking light.

He didn't have to wait long. A moment after standing he saw a movement in the grass, higher up than where he first looked, as three forms rushed down, bounding as they came through the brush. Seth's coyotes on the hunt, circling whatever was hidden there. This is what had kept them from coming down. A stranger on the property. A second later, maybe hearing what was coming his way, a figure stood up on the ridge, then bolted. Idiot, Grizz thought. What sort of fool runs from dogs, much less wild animals? Doing so just excited their predatory instincts.

It's no easy feat to run down a steeply pitched hill. The figure fell with the suddenness of a meteor, a thunderous crackling of leaves and branches, gathering momentum as he tumbled. Blackbirds erupted from the bur oaks in a noisy cloud, and his heart turned a somersault inside his chest just to see it. The boy — that much he could make out — spilled down the ridge with a clumsy grace. He had formed himself into a ball, knees tucked into his chest, his arms protecting his fragile skull.

At two hundred yards or more this was not exactly a mountain, but no small hill either. It rose up at a steep sixty-degree angle cut by straight drops and speckled with boulders and orange-tinted cedar trees and massive bur oaks. Somehow the boy missed the steeper drops and the boulders and the iron-hard oak trees. He fell like a child from Dakota legend, a boy out of the sky. Grizz was mindful of the September sun touching his hair, the circling of the coyotes on the hill above, the blackbirds wheeling in protest overhead. I can die now, he thought. I have seen everything, a boy chased by little wolves, falling from the sky.

The boy found one of the smaller ledges and launched into the air, screeching like an eagle when he became airborne. He kicked out of his tuck, shirt billowing, his arms flapping uselessly. Then gravity yanked him to the tall cedar tree below him, and he smashed through bough and branch, yelling all the way down until he struck the mossy earth.

One of the coyotes barked while standing on a rock above the fallen figure, shaking Grizz from his daze. Blackbirds wheeled and settled in a far cottonwood, and forest and meadow eased into silence. The coyotes melted back into the woods, as if afraid of what they had done. Then, because the boy might be hurt bad, Grizz climbed down from the tractor and walked over to where he fell.

He was surprised to find him partly conscious, blinking up into the light. His face and head appeared unmarked, but his shirt and sweatpants had been gashed open. The boy's legs were bent beneath him, and a wheezed gasping bubbled from his lips. Blood speckled the grass around him. "Don't move," he told him, "you might be hurt bad."

The boy's eyes appeared glazed. Grizz was afraid he was going into shock. He knelt in the grass beside him, not minding the blood. He could see now the boy was Lee, the younger child of Sheriff Gunderson. He knew from rumors in town they said the boy was "touched," and the less charitable called him "retard." Lee had long black hair and small eyes set in a pudgy face. Grizz fought a brief anger rising in him. If he had been shooting at him, he had lost the gun during his flight. The whole thing was senseless. Had Lee thought to spill Grizz's blood to even the score? He bit his tongue and concentrated on the child before him. This could have been Seth, hurt after some foolish lark. This should have been Seth, not some child come to work a reckoning.

Lee loosed a hoarse, birdlike cry as Grizz yanked his legs beneath him and probed for broken bones. He didn't intend to be gentle. The boy's eyes were glossy as wet stones. Not knowing what else to do, Grizz spoke at random, fearing the boy's shock would become fatal. He couldn't handle any more blood on his hands. "The damnedest thing I ever saw," he began, "and I've seen many a thing in my lifetime. The way you came down that ridge was a thing of beauty."

Lee groaned again as Grizz poked at his ribs. Along the boy's arm he felt something quick and wet and warm. He took out his pocketknife and cut open the shirtsleeve. His arm was sliced open. He saw tendons, red and glistening. Words left him for a time.

He cut off the rest of his shirt and then ripped it into ribbons. Still Lee had not spoken, but his breathing seemed to steady. Grizz noted a twitch in the right leg and figured the boy had been lucky not to crack his spine or spill the contents of his skull like an egg against a skillet. He wrapped the wound tightly and then pressed down to staunch the flow of blood.

He found his breath again. "I won't be able to describe it, I think, the way you fell. You likely won't remember it. Only me and these coyotes and blackbirds saw you come down that ridge, and by Jesus and Joseph, you are one lucky bastard." Lee groaned as if in agreement with Grizz's rambling. It was all the encouragement he needed. "I recognize you from when you were little and you and Kelan used to come around here." Grizz sucked on his teeth, surprised that the memory of Seth's friends could renew such a sharp ache inside him. His eyes welled, and the boy's features blurred below him. This could have been Seth, he thought. This should have been how it happened, a close scrape, a rescue. He shook the vision away; it did him little good now.

"What were you doing up there, besides trying to kill me?" Lee's glazed eyes found his. Grizz was there to see his consciousness rising to the surface, like some fish swimming toward the light. He was there in the grass wet with dew and blood, and when Lee said, "Seth's wolves. They were after me," in a clipped, frightened tone, he felt a laugh escape his chest, a clean, beautiful feeling.

THE GROVE

Clara answered the phone only to find Ernest Sheuffler, the superintendent, greeting her in his slow baritone. This was their second conversation since she had resigned. "Have you been thinking over my offer?" he asked.

She pictured him on the other end of the line, a fat man who dressed in caramel-colored suits, the seams straining around his shoulders. "I'm sorry, Mr. Sheuffler. My answer's the same as when you called a few days ago."

"How have you been doing?"

"Oh, fine," she said. "Fine, fine, fine."

He was silent, leaving the tinny echo of her voice ringing in her ears. "I believe you have a talent for teaching, Mrs. Warren," he said after a moment. "The students miss you. One came to see me, and we talked about you."

Clara waited. Mr. Sheuffler was proving

to be a frustrating person. Moving way out into the country was supposed to provide Clara the time and focus she needed to finish her dissertation. Teaching had been a mistake.

"You remember Leah Meyers?" he asked.

"Sure." Seth's girlfriend.

"A smart girl. I trust her judgment. She told me you're one of the best teachers she's ever had." Why would Leah go and see the superintendent? She wouldn't, not unless summoned. "It's not a good idea," Clara told him. "I'm due in December. Those kids . . . what they need is some continuity. Hell, what they need is someone who knows what they're doing."

His chair squeaked as he sat back. "Could I come see you in person?"

"Look, I can't think about this right now. I've got too much going on. Busy, busy."

"Okay. A few more days then."

"What? You're not listening."

"I'll call back Wednesday. Good day, Mrs. Warren." He hung up before she could say more.

Logan and Clara ate off paper plates that night, and after dinner he left for another visit, one he'd set up a few weeks ago, before things went wrong. "You work too hard," she warned him on his way out the door. "I worry about you." Really, what she wanted was for him to stay here. They deserved a night together. No responsibilities. Just the two of them up late talking like when they were engaged.

"This is only temporary," he said on his way out, "things'll get better."

She looked away. He was pouring himself into this place. The weight he'd lost made his blue eyes even more piercing and prominent above the hollows of his cheeks. He was pouring himself out as she tried to hold what fell in her hands.

"When the funeral is over and done with, we'll go to Fell Creek, to the supper club there. They make the most delicious popovers."

He kissed her, not on the mouth. The center of her forehead. His lips dry, cracking. She didn't know how to hold him here. What a young wife should say or do.

A moment later, his Nova rumbled in the driveway, and then he was gone.

In the first year of his ministry Logan was on a mission to visit each and every one of his parishioners. Many of the elderly citizens in the congregation had finished their schooling in the eighth grade during the Depression and World War II. The homes and hobbies of these people revealed an unexpected diversity: a bachelor farmer who was a championship chess player; a one-hundred-three-year-old lady who spent her days, summer or winter, tatting snowflakes she gave away each Sunday at church; a veteran who had been there for the liberation of Auschwitz.

He visited homes where newspapers were stacked to the ceiling, occasional homes of filth that clouded his hair and clothing with an ashtray smell of desperation. To all of them he carried simple questions: *What is it you like about your church? What makes you proud to be a part of your congregation?*

In a month's time Logan had visited more than thirty households, and as one they were confounded by his questions. *Pastor,* one of the bachelor farmers had explained, *it's just that we're used to talking about what's wrong.*

Clara stood in the kitchen, looking out into the night that had swallowed up her husband, the gas stove heating a grumbling kettle behind her. She was about to check on it when she noticed something running at the edge of the yard, forms close to the ground. She shut off the lights and let her eyes adjust to the night outside. The coyotes were back again. The largest of them was a gray with a frosty-silver back. A yard lamp behind the church caught the tawny glistening of his fur. The coyotes moved in formation, following behind the gray.

They surrounded an old dog's pen in a neighbor's backyard across the way from Nora. There they yipped and chattered at the dog, who lay inside his kennel with his muzzle on his forepaws, an old man being tormented by teenagers. Then the dog rose slowly to his haunches and loosed a deep booming bark followed by ferocious growling, his fur bristling. The coyotes continued to circle his pen, yipping and dancing. The old dog woofed again, and the coyotes, tiring of their game, trotted off into the night, chuckling like punks.

Clara had never seen anything so strange and beautiful and ritualistic. The kettle spat and jumped on the stove behind her. Just when she was about to turn around, another flicker of movement caught her eye. Sorena, the mother cat. Sorena must have smelled the coyotes out there because she was running full speed, streaking across the yard. Or maybe the coyotes had flushed her from her hiding place, because the gray came on behind her, a flash of silver under the yard lamp. The kettle whistled and then screamed.

The cat shot up a crab-apple tree while the gray and the other coyotes circled the base. Even behind the window Clara could hear Sorena hissing at them below. The gray alpha leaned his weight against the trunk. He was big, the size of a German shepherd, and the crab-apple tree shook and tossed small fruit onto the grass. Sorena lurched, just barely keeping her balance. It wasn't going to take much to bring her down.

Clara was out the door before she even knew what she was doing. She hadn't bothered to gather a weapon, so she raised her arms up to make herself look taller than she really was. "Scat!" she hollered at them. "Get out of here."

The sound of her voice stopped them. The gray left off shaking the tree and peered at Clara with his golden eyes. The other two ambled behind him, their tongues lolling. They did not run. Clara windmilled her arms and shouted at them again. "Ha! Get! Flee!"

The alpha growled in a low voice. His tail bristled as he approached her.

Clara didn't know what to do now. *Run!* A hundred synapses in her brain clicking at once. *Get back inside the house!* Clara stayed where she was. The three approached, sniffing and circling, just as they had with the old dog at the neighbor's house.

She let her arms drop to the side. The gray had piercing yellow eyes that froze her in place. She had been hearing them every night, come from the woods into town. They were all around her, a musky pungency. She should have been afraid, she should have run, but she remembered her father's stories. Clara remembered who she was under her human skin.

She reached out her left hand as the gray came forward. When his nose pressed against her palm, the skin felt coarse and wet. Clara's heart thumped wildly behind its cage of ribs, and she felt the baby stirring inside her. The coyotes looked skinny and ragged, especially the two smaller russet-colored ones. Females? *Steorfan,* she thought, the same word she had for Seth. The coyote's gold-brown eyes watching her. They were starving, she thought. Urchins, like her. "What is it you are looking for?"

The gray's ears peeled back, and he whined softly.

"For Seth, isn't it? You belonged to him?" She was sure of it now. The coyotes had only come from the woods after Seth's death. Somehow the two were connected.

Then a car honked down the block, a blaring sustained honk, and the large gray leaped back. All three tucked tail and fled for the woods, the cat forgotten up in her tree, but not before the gray turned once more and barked, as if asking Clara to follow.

There was a woman lost in a grove, leaves and twigs crackling under bare feet. She wore nothing but a pearly gray gown, and she walked under a sky like slate, even the woods leached of color. She moved toward a sound, what was it? Something was crying. Her baby. Her baby was hurt and calling for her. She hurried through the grove, parting low-hanging branches and stepping over fallen logs. Her pace increased as the child's cries became more urgent, and then she was running. Thorny bushes tore her gown and skin. When she looked behind her she saw that she'd left a track of bloody footprints through the fallen leaves. And still the child kept crying from an unseen place deep in the woods, a call she couldn't resist. The trees closed in, branches writhing.

At last, after it seemed she'd been trudging through the woods for a very long time, she broke through a dense thicket of bramble and found the baby lying on a matting of leaves in the meadow. The shape before her was born out of her but did not belong to her. The baby's cries turned to a wolfish lament. She saw now that it had pale, glistening fur and the face of a child, a pink nose and two glowing eyes that regarded her with bottomless hunger. It loosed another howl and then from the woods around her more shapes trotted into the meadow, wolves come from the place of thorn to lick the blood from her palms.

The church and parsonage were on the town's outskirts, as if built as a protection against the woods spreading beyond. Woods that were still considered a savage place even now. When she was done writing, Clara lay in bed, sleepless, the windows open, her belly immense. The passage she'd set down seemed less one of her father's stories and more a dream of her mother abandoning her. She thought about the child in the woods and then about the legends she'd been teaching her students before the shooting. Beowulf ripped off the monster's arm, and there was rejoicing in Heorot. Somewhere in the swamps his mother wept and bided her time. Something was coming, the coyotes had meant to tell her. *You are not safe, not here.*

Clara shut her eyes, imagining running free with them across the countryside, across miles and miles. Shedding her human skin. The fur and wildness underneath. She was as sleek as silence, a she-wolf whose hearing took in what was happening from far away. She heard the skeletons of abandoned barns caving in the wind, the brittle creak of empty grain bins, the lisping of the corn leaves in a dry time before the harvest. She heard the voices Logan carried home with him, the talk inside the houses after sundown. The folk were afraid. They were afraid and didn't know how to live in a world that was changing all around them. There were coyotes out in the dark running free, come from the woods, from a mountain where the giant lived unseen.

A teenager had murdered the town's hero, then shot himself. There was no mystery to solve, nothing more to fear. Why should it bother her? Something flickered at the edge of her vision, like heat lightning. She had told Sheriff Steve what she had seen, and that was enough, but what had she seen? She had seen his shoes, dirty Converse, the fraying hem of his coat. She heard the gun, saw him cross the graveyard, heading for the waiting corn where his body was later found. Her mind ran over and over the same ground, the images in branded lightning flashes when she shut her eyes. *I'm not ready to bury you like the rest of them. I'm not ready to begin the long forgetting.*

And why had the sheriff come back here? Despite what she told Nora, Clara knew he had come here for her and not her husband. She shouldn't have any reason to be frightened of him, even if he really was the kind of man you didn't want to cross, as Nora had said. Clara had kept the notes, but was that so wrong? Why that presence down in the basement, that overriding sense of fear?

Some of the riddles she had told her students from *The Book of Exeter* had no answer or the answer had been lost to time.

> I give myself far-wandering longing towards
>   my Wolf.
> When it is wet weather and I sat weeping,
> Then the brisk warrior embraced me with
>   his arms;
> That was bliss to me, but it was also pain.
> Wolf, my wolf, my longings toward thee
> Have brought me sickness, thy seldom
>   coming
> The mourning mood, not want of meat
> Hearest thou? Eadwaccer, the whelp of us
>   both,
> Carries a wolf to the wood.

The author had been someone named Cynewulf, a monk scholars speculated lived in Northumbria in the ninth century. Did he invent some of the riddles or, like the Brothers Grimm, gather them from the Kinderfolk? In another riddle he mused:

> I saw a strange sight: a wolf held tight by a
> lamb —
> The lamb lay down and seized the belly of
> the wolf.
> While I stood and stared, I saw a great
> glory:
> Two wolves standing and troubling a third;
> They had four feet; they saw with seven
> eyes!

The two riddles wove together, not answering but asking more questions. A love child that was a wolf carried into the woods? A lamb that destroys a monster?

The next morning, Clara picked up the phone. She needed a couple of weeks, time enough to collect her thoughts, to get the house ready for the baby. Time enough that she could still back out if necessary. If the man she was about to call wasn't in his office anymore, then it wasn't meant to be. *Please be there,* she thought. She dialed the number he had left her. "Hello, yes. Could

I please speak with Mr. Sheuffler? Tell him Clara Warren is calling about his offer."

LITTLE WOLVES

Seth cried out, "Dad, look! A coyote!"

His son had rapped on the passenger side window and pointed. It was a late afternoon in March when the sun's rays warmed the frozen earth just enough that a silvery mist spiraled from the marshes. Grizz had followed his hand and there it was. At first he thought it was a small dog, but then he noticed the lean snout and long, foxlike ears.

Grizz slammed on the brakes, jerking Seth forward in his seat so hard he nearly hit the windshield before his belt snapped him back. The truck slid along the gravel road before grinding to a halt. A second later he was out the door, plucking up a .22 rifle he kept behind the seat. Dust from the road rained down around him. The coyote heard all this and yawned, displaying rows of little razor teeth. It looked indolent and dreamy with the mist rising all around it.

He took his time, balancing the rifle on

the truck bed. If the coyote had not cast one backward glance as it trotted away, it might have escaped into the tallgrass. But the rifle made a small barking cough, and the animal went down. He reloaded while the boy stepped out of the passenger side and followed him into the meadow.

The coyote was a handsome creature with shimmering bronzed fur and round dark eyes and breathed as though in its mind it was still running. It lay on its side in the tallgrass, and the air around them smelled of musk and blood and its terror. The coyote's breathing shallowed. "Aren't you going to finish it off?" Seth asked. He held himself and shivered even though it was a strangely warm spring day.

"It'll be dead soon enough."

"Why'd you have to shoot it? I was only showing you where it was."

"Because," he said. At first the words didn't come right. Why? Because, that was the way of things. No farmer going back to the beginning of time could allow such animals to threaten his living. So he told Seth about summer nights when the ranch house windows were open to allow in a breeze. How his mother couldn't sleep for the sound they made. It stirred her up, that eerie howling. He told him about the calves being born in spring and how the coyotes were always there in the morning licking the birthing fluids from the blood-streaked ground, ghost shapes that were gone again before he could raise a gun. While he told him, he could see it in his mind's eye, a primal scene: cattle tonguing the afterbirth from their calves while coyotes slunk nearby, waiting to drink the rich placental blood from the grass. "Parasites," he said. "Little ravenous wolves. At least now there is one less of them."

Seth's face had gone pale. His features weren't set yet, the bones shifting in his face as if what he would become was still being written. Seth knelt in the grass next to the coyote. It was a female, the heavy dugs showing on her stomach. "Why do you think she didn't run?" he said, and when Grizz had no answer he asked her softly, "Why didn't you run?"

He reached out one hand to stroke her fur.

"Don't touch it," Grizz warned, but she was too wounded to do more than growl with what menace remained in her, her black gums peeling back to reveal long incisors pink with froth. One filmy eye fixed him, and then she went still.

Grizz put his hand on Seth's shoulder and

started to say something when a noise caught his attention. A sound on the hill above where there should have been only silence. Seth jumped up and went ahead of him. She had died not far from a granite boulder ringed by a thicket of sumac. Seth pushed through the branches and reached in. From the dark hole where the coyote had made her den mewling cries echoed. Her kit, probably born just a few weeks before.

"Stop," he commanded Seth. "Don't you go any nearer."

Seth's back went rigid, but he didn't turn around at the sound of his voice.

"You go on back down to the truck and wait for me there."

He gave just the faintest shake of his head.

"You don't want to see this kind of work, but it has to be done. It's the only thing we can do."

When Seth did turn around his eyes were hard and glittering. "No," he said. "I won't let you." He clenched his fist, the wind rustling his baggy jacket. In the distance a red-winged blackbird sang out in warning, hearing them on the hill above. From this vantage point Grizz could see the farm and the stretch of black fields. They would need to take out the spreader now that the manure was no longer frozen, clean out a winter's worth of mess from the barns and fertilize the fields. A long day's work, but the boy would get to pilot the Bobcat in and out of the barn, and he loved driving it. Grizz was anxious to get down and get started.

"If I don't do this, Seth, they're going to starve, a long, slow death." Such a stubborn child. When they had kept pigs, Seth hated when the runts were born. They had to kill them right off so they didn't keep the sow's milk from those capable of surviving. They stretched them on a board and cracked their little skulls with a ball-peen hammer. When Seth was little, it used to make him cry. He would steal those runts and take them up into the loft and hide them in a hole he'd hollowed in the hay. Then he would take out a turkey baster and fill it with milk from the kitchen and carry it to the barn. Grizz knew what he was doing the whole time and didn't stop him. The runts all died despite his best efforts. He left the boy alone to learn that some things aren't meant for this world. By the time he was ten Seth was hardened, and when he started growing prizewinning sows for the FFA he learned to wield the ball-peen hammer himself. And Grizz thought the whole time he had been teaching him about mercy.

"No. Not if we take them home."

Grizz lay his gun down in the grass. "These aren't like puppies from a dog, Seth. They're wild things, and they belong out here in the wild. We start violating the natural order, and bad things will happen." He squared his shoulders and leveled his gaze. "Now get back down to the truck and let me do what I have to do."

"No." Seth's jaw jutted out, and he drew himself up, and Grizz saw how big he was becoming. Still, he could shove him aside, and it would all be over in a few seconds. His iron-toed boots would crush a few baby coyote skulls, and then it would be done.

"What do you think people in town will say when they hear we're raising coyotes?"

"I don't care. I'll only keep them until they get big enough to live on their own."

"The one thing that keeps us safe from such creatures is that they fear us. You take away that fear, and you're going to hurt both them and us."

Behind them, the whimpering of the pups continued. The boy's eyes watered, but he kept his footing, and when Grizz laid a hand on his shoulder, he flinched. That one action, a simple flinch, took away his breath. His son thought he was going to hit him.

177

He never hit Seth, hadn't whipped him in years.

"Okay," he said. "Okay."

"We can take them home?"

"But they have to sleep in the old brood house. We can't have them in the barn or anywhere near the cows. You're going to have to make sure they're cleaned every day."

"We'll get one of the heating lamps," Seth said. "I'll stretch a cord from the barn. And we can keep them in a box with some blankets. And we can feed them with the calving bottles."

"Not a word at school, understand? I don't want people in town hearing what we've done."

Seth drew his hand across his mouth, zipping it shut.

One by one the three pups were lifted, blind and trembling, from the den and deposited in the warmth of Seth's coat. They rode home together with that pungent scent filling up the cab and the sound of them crying so loud Grizz could hardly hear himself think. The boy talked to them in a cooing voice, wincing when a claw hooked his chest under the shirt. "Little wolves, is that what you called them, Dad?"

"It's what some call coyotes, sure."

"My little wolves," he said. "I'm going to take care of you."

All through the spring and summer, Seth fed them faithfully with a bottle they used for the calves and baby's formula from Jurgen's Corner, replacing the nipples that the coyotes gnawed to rubbery shreds. When they were big enough to eat from his hand, he let them go, true to his word. They'd come back every night since. The boy was not supposed to feed them anymore, but Grizz knew he took them scraps and dry dog food, and that was how they came to be so large, the size of wolves instead of bony coyotes.

After stopping the boy's bleeding, Grizz carried the Gunderson child up from the meadow into the yard where his truck waited.

"I can walk," Lee protested, but Grizz shushed him. The boy weighed about the same as a newborn calf, like those that slipped under the fence every now and then, got lost in the grove, and had to be carried back to the pasture. Grizz ignored the aching muscle in his own abdomen, worrying that if he set Lee down and made him walk the boy's wounds would reopen.

Once he got him into the cab, Grizz drove

him to the hospital, remembering the day he and Seth had found the coyotes. It was a good memory, one of a few he had, and thinking on it passed the silent miles that took them over the prairie.

When they pulled up at the Fell Creek Area Hospital, Grizz paused. The parking lot lay empty. "I don't think I'll stick around once you get inside. I don't know what folks will say if they see us together."

Lee was shaking, holding the wounded arm that Grizz had bound with knotted pieces of his shirt.

"When is your pop's funeral?"

"In a couple days."

He hated to ask it, but didn't know when he would get another chance. "Did you know about Seth? Did he say anything to your brother?"

Lee hesitated, his nostrils flaring. Grizz thought he might start crying and worried he wouldn't know what to do if the child did, but Lee only wiped his nose on his sleeve and looked out the window.

"You think you're done trying to kill me?"

He turned sharply. "I don't know," he said. "I guess so."

Grizz knew he wasn't afraid to die. He would have been glad to be shut of his problems. "It's too bad your aim wasn't better."

"I could have hit you if I wanted."

"Sure." He didn't ask about why. He thought he knew. His own son had looked at a man down a barrel and pulled the trigger. This boy thought to do the same. He couldn't account for the feeling floating in his chest, a floating bubble of thought. To die. It would be a good thing. Only by dying could he come closer to what he had lost. Yet he could feel the steering wheel under his hands, the breath in his lungs. A child beside him. He had made promises to Seth. If he died, who would tell Seth's story? Who would see to it that his son was buried properly? His work wasn't done yet. "What are you going to tell people about how you got hurt?"

Lee still trembled. He was expecting for Grizz to turn him in to the law, but he wasn't afraid either. He was hurt bad, maybe not in his right mind. His right mind. Who was these days? The cab reeked with the iron smell of his blood.

"If you don't mention the coyotes, I won't tell about the gun." Grizz held out his hand.

"Okay," he said. His eyes rolled back in his head like he might faint.

"Just tell people that you were out running and some wild dogs were chasing you and you fell down the ridge. Tell them you stumbled out to the road and someone found you and drove you here." It was a dumb story, but how closely would people question Lee? Especially considering what his family had been through. The words his own child had carved into the desk rose up unbidden in his mind. *Wergild.* A blood debt. Grizz heard the words leave his mouth before he even knew what he was saying. "You have a job?"

Lee shook his head.

"You want a job?"

Another nod. "You think you could work for me, help a little around the farm?"

The boy's hand was on the door handle. Their families were two of the oldest in the valley, had been there since the beginning through Indian uprisings and droughts. There was ugliness in the shared story, both recent and long buried. Lee looked at him, and he saw something spark in his eyes. He didn't appear to be as dumb as people made him out. "I don't think that's such a good idea."

"Just think it over."

He grunted as he moved to climb out of the cab.

"You need help inside?"

"No. I'm fine."

The door wheezed as it swung shut. "Lee?" he called, reaching across to catch it before it closed all the way.

"What?"

He considered a moment. "If you come see me again, next time you make sure you come by the driveway."

Lee shuffled along the sidewalk until the sliding glass doors of the emergency room opened. He paused at the threshold, but before he stepped inside he raised his good arm and waved to Grizz.

DUCHESS

Clara had not been back to church since the shootings, but the next morning she meant to meet Nora for a Bible study with her Naomi Circle at a house across town. Going to something as simple as a Bible study was a good way to make the church a part of her life again with the sheriff's funeral tomorrow. When she married Logan, she had made promises.

Clara put on a pair of maternity shorts with a big stretchable waistband, an outfit she completed with a spaghetti-strap blouse and sandals. With her protruding stomach and pale stork-thin legs, she knew she cut an ungainly figure, but the unnatural heat wouldn't let up, even in these first days of October. By late morning the asphalt blistered. Under the sun's glaring eye lawns baked yellow, parched trees let down the last of their leaves, and a film of dust settled like ashes over the streets and houses. Wind-still, even the air had a seared odor, a faint sulfur reek from dying bullheads on the shores of the narrowing river, and as the townspeople went about their daily errands they sought shelter from the heat in what scant shade buildings and trees had to offer.

The walk gave her time to think about the readings, which included every passage about heaven or hell mentioned in Old Testament and New. It had surprised her how little the Bible had to say about what happens after we die. When she asked Logan, he had only shrugged. "The Bible is the record of a living God seeking out relationships with a living people."

"I don't know. I thought the whole point was getting to heaven. If that's the end of the road, the Bible doesn't describe it very well."

Logan had scratched at his beard. "What if it did? What if heaven was described right down to the last cubit? A known place, mapped and explored to the furthest reaches."

"You and your mysteries," she said, wrinkling her nose, sensing where he was headed. "That's your answer for everything."

"God gave us an imagination. It may be one of the most beautiful functions of our brain. He left the space open for us to fill."

Clara wasn't sure what she would say about the afterlife. Her father would grow angry when she tried talking about it with him. *People die,* he had told her, *and that's all there is. No world but this one we can see and touch. No hell but the one we make in our own brains.*

But what about Mama; isn't she in heaven?

No. She's just gone. All you got is me. All we got is each other.

But I want her to be in heaven. I want to see her one day.

And he would get angry, the vein pulsing in his brow. *No such thing. No world but this one here.* Tapping his chest, hard, like a hollow drum, then taking up her damaged hand. *This is what she did to you, your mother. That's all you need to know.*

But —

Enough!

Rosa's home proved to be a low-slung ranch house, the walkway lined with weedy, wavering daisies. Clara was twenty minutes late, drenched with sweat, and praying that Rosa, the host of the Bible study, had airconditioning inside her house.

Rosa didn't. The woman was a widow in a ruffled navy dress that looked hand sewn, pads puffing up the shoulders, and she

186

ushered her into the foyer. She was staring at Clara's bare legs, the sandals on her feet.

All the women were staring at her legs once she went into the dining room where Nora waited along with few others, sitting around a lace-covered table and sipping iced tea from tall glasses. As a group they blended into one at first when Rosa introduced them. Hilda. Doreen. Helen. Gretel. They all wore polyester pantsuits in soft autumn shades, except for Rosa. Clara was the youngest one there by at least three decades.

Clara wiped the sweat of her palms on her shorts and shook hands with each of them. Was she supposed to shake hands or was that considered unladylike? The women had light bird bones under their porous skin, a brittle fragility, and she shook hands gingerly until she got to Gretel. Gretel's iron-gray hair was done up in a tight bun, and she had a grip like a meatpacker. She looked in Clara's eyes and said what some of the others must have been thinking, "You wore shorts out in public."

"Of course she did," cut in Nora. "It's ninety degrees outside." She tried to laugh lightly, and Doreen joined her with a nervous bray. "I'd wear shorts if I had legs like hers." Gretel's frown deepened her wrinkles.

"She's the pastor's wife."

"Gretel was a schoolteacher," said Hilda, "for some thirty-seven years."

"That's . . . impressive," Clara said. Thirty-seven years, she thought. Those poor fucking kids.

"Would you like fresh crushed mint in your tea?" asked Rosa.

"Yes, please."

"Sit down," bid Helen. "We were just talking about our own visions of heaven."

Hilda pulled out a chair next to her and patted the place. "And you should know we're having cake afterward," she said. "German chocolate."

"I hope they have cake in heaven," Clara said after sitting along with the rest. She glanced at the sluggish ceiling fan spinning above the table, which only seemed to stir the hot air in the room. "And air-conditioning." She paused, still nervous with so many eyes on her. She was always afraid they would sniff her out, a doubter among them, the one not raised Lutheran. "Did you know that Hilda or Brunhilda means 'ready for battle' in Low German?" she said to fill the silence. "Brunhilda rode with the Valkyries."

Doreen laughed her horsey laugh, spraying a mint sprig onto the tablecloth. The rest looked puzzled.

"I did not know that," said Alfrieda.

"It's a good, pagan name," continued Clara. "All around us these pagan reminders live on in words and names and customs."

Now that all the women were sitting down, Helen leaned forward. "We've heard that you're a scholar."

A scholar. Clara smiled at the sound of it. "I'm a doctoral student; I just need to finish."

Six gray heads all nodded, satisfied. Nobody asked what her studies were about, but Clara decided to fill them in anyway. Didn't it connect to the afterlife? "For my dissertation I am examining the edicts surrounding the massacre on St. Brice's Day in 1002. King Aethelred the Unready. . . ." Here she paused, clearing her throat. "How's that for a name? Anyhow, this king declared that all the Danes living in England were to be slaughtered. A group of Danes tried to shelter within a church. But the English locked them inside and burned the church to the ground."

"They all died?" Helen's hand covered her mouth, as though the event Clara described had happened in the next town over only a few years ago.

"Cooked to a crisp." Clara felt giddy from the heat. Across the table, Doreen's eyes were glazed, her jaw slack.

"Why on earth would you want to study something like that?" This was from Gretel.

"There's this verse in the Bible about judgment at the end of days, about using fire to separate the cockle from the wheat. Aethelred used it to justify his actions. I've been translating his writings, looking closely at the words, and also studying the Danish impact on customs and language."

Silence. Mercifully, Rosa returned with her iced tea. Clara gulped some down and added, "I hope they have iced tea in heaven."

"Foolishness," grumbled Gretel. "Why must heaven be a place of creature comforts? Streets of gold and all that." She shook her head. "Those are human visions, and I don't know why we settle for clichés."

"You're sounding like Reverend Schoenwald," said Rosa.

Clara knew that the Reverend Gunther Schoenwald had been pastor here for thirty years. For three decades the same portly red-bearded man presided over every Lutheran baptism, every wedding, and every death. This was another reason that Logan hadn't wanted to come here. *They have an unhealthy way of dealing with death,* he said. After so many years under the same leadership, the church could develop rigor mortis, hardening in its traditions. Pastor Schoenwald had been the one who insisted on burying the suicides in a separate section. Saints and suicides and newborns all had their own territory, the tombstones for the unbaptized babies like tiny broken teeth scattered in the grass.

"Why not?" said Helen. "Surely he's up there with the saints."

"Is Seth up there?" Clara said, surprising herself. She hadn't meant to speak her question aloud. She had just come to listen, but she hadn't been able to shut up since coming inside. "Wasn't he baptized in our church?"

"What do you think?" said Gretel. "A murderer and a suicide? What sort of God would let such evil into his holy presence?"

"The same one who lets evil into our world."

Gretel's jaw snapped shut with an audible clacking, like a metal hinge. "You don't know that family, do you? You don't know the slightest thing."

Clara's voice was small. "I knew *him,* " she said.

"Did you? After living here for one month?

I don't believe any of us knows what others think. Only God can look inside a person's heart. Do you know what I am thinking right now, dear?"

"Stop this," Nora tried to interrupt. "I don't like where this conversation is going."

"Something wicked," said Clara, raising her chin and meeting the woman's gaze.

Gretel's smile twitched the corners of her mouth; she was enjoying this exchange, Clara realized, probably not used to people talking back to her. "There's a difference between thinking and doing," she said.

"Not much," said Clara.

"Yes," insisted Gretel. "Sometimes the difference between thinking and doing is a matter of life or death."

After this exchange the rest of the conversation blurred for Clara, and she was quiet, her thoughts elsewhere. The German chocolate cake proved to be dry, spackled with a hard coconut frosting. The women gathered up the plates and headed into the kitchen. Doreen and Helen had left already, but Clara lingered, still hoping to redeem herself from her earlier foolishness. She wanted to walk home with Nora. She stayed because she needed a friend, but when she had offered to help with the dishes, Rosa had gently said, "Not in your condition."

"Condition," muttered Clara. She hated that word, as though the baby was some type of fungus growing under her armpits. Precious Moments figurines sat on the surfaces of sideboards and buffets lining the walls, each occupying its own lace-fringed doily. The figurines had fat angelic faces and teardrop eyes. Clara found them faintly creepy.

Gretel pushed in a woman in a wheelchair from one of the back rooms and left her there, rejoining the other women in the kitchen without any explanation. The woman was so ancient most of her white hair had fallen out, except in clumps on either side of her head. She slumped in the wheelchair, lightly snoring, a yarn afghan thrown over knees despite the heat. When Clara stepped back, she jostled the Precious Moments figurines on one of the buffet tables, startling the woman awake. She raised her head, sniffing like a hound, her eyes milky blue. "Hello, Duchess," she said, when her eyes found Clara.

"It's Clara, actually," she said once she got her breath. "I'm the pastor's wife."

"I know who you are." The woman's mouth was a dark pink cave; her caretaker must have neglected to put in her dentures.

"It's cold in here," she continued, shivering. "That's what hell is like, winter without end. Fire eats you up quick, but the cold is a slow kind of burning."

They had just gotten done talking about eternal life as this woman must have known. Clara heard the others in the kitchen chatting in low voices as they washed and dried Rosa's good silverware and china. "Why did you call me Duchess?"

"It's who you are."

"Oh," Clara said. "How nice to be a duchess."

"Don't put on airs. We took you in as one of our own. Our little displaced person. But you were bad, you and the other one."

The hair stood up on Clara's arms. The woman's whitish-blue eyes had fixed her with a hostile glare. "What did I do?"

"You know what you did." She waved a speckled hand over her afghan. "Always serving tea and then turning the cup over to read the leaves. Telling us when to plant, if our husbands had been faithful. You walked with spirits; you lay down in sin."

Clara froze. If hell was winter without end, it was all she saw in the woman's eyes, emptiness and violence. But the woman's voice ebbed with every word. Even her head sagged slightly, as if the story she told were draining her.

"Well, I won't do it anymore."

"That's what you promised." Her head was like a sunflower, too heavy for the stalk. It sagged toward the blanket. "You promised. But you were a liar. You had to be punished."

"How?"

When a moment passed without the woman speaking, Clara leaned in close. The old woman smelled of talcum powder and decay, as if pieces of her were already rotting from the inside.

Nora appeared behind her. "I see you've met Bynthia."

Clara stood and looked into Nora's periwinkle eyes. "I need to get home," she said, "will you walk with me?"

Once they were outdoors in the heat of Indian summer, the old woman's words seemed insubstantial. Nora hobbled beside her on her bad hip, gossiping. "Sorry about Gretel. Some days, I feel like I have to wash my mouth out with cider vinegar just to hold my own in a conversation with that woman."

The Catholic church's bells rang the hour across the town.

"Bynthia called me Duchess."

Nora halted.

"You know that name, don't you?"

"Stop at my house and we'll talk more there."

They walked the remaining block in silence before going up the steps to Nora's porch. Inside the house, Clara smelled soil and the perfume of flowers. Vines from a pothos plant twisted along the arched entryway and climbed over an inset bookcase. An umbrella tree blocked out the light coming in the living room window, and spider ferns dangled from the ceiling. Even the carpet and sofa were a matching pistachio color, the curtains darkly evergreen. Nora told her to make herself at home while she went to fix them each some ice water. A few minutes later she returned, the ice water sloshing because of her ungainly gait as she passed a cold glass to Clara.

Clara set her glass on a coaster. "You were going to tell me about the Duchess."

Nora sat heavily, grunting as she did so. "First of all, Bynthia is ninety-five years old and she's lived on the wrong side of the crazy river for the last decade or so. She's Gretel's mother. They're relations of Sheriff Steve Krieger."

"Then why does that name bother you so much? Why did I remind her of this woman?"

Nora glanced at Clara's hand. "It's your left hand, dear. How many women have such a . . . wound. Some of the old-timers look at you and remember. There's been talk, but we couldn't be sure. Who are you, Clara? Who are your people?"

"My people?" Clara settled into the couch's soft cushions. "I don't really know. I was raised alone by my father. He refused to talk about his family or my mother. He would only say that she died in a car accident in the wintertime. He would tell me stories, but they were fairy tales, really. There was always a mountain in them, sometimes wolves and winter storms. That's all I know, not even my mother's name. After he died, I couldn't find my own birth certificate among his records. I don't know how he registered me for school without it, how he got me my social security number. It's as if I don't exist, except through his stories."

Nora was quiet for a long time. "Why did you come here?"

"My husband was called. The call committee hired him."

"Yes, I heard. I also heard from Simon Wiley that he was sure your husband was going to turn us down. We were all surprised when he accepted. So I figure you talked him into it."

"I did. I've been looking for records of my mother for a long time."

"You might just have found her," Nora said.

A hard knot in the center of her chest tightened her breathing. This was it, the news she had longed for. The air grew light up in her head, and she had to take a drink of water to compose herself. "All my life, I've lived with this gap inside me. This empty place. I need to know about her."

Nora sipped from her glass, then set it down. "Sylvia came here a little after the war, married a schoolteacher in town. She was an immigrant, but we couldn't be sure where she was from. She came here under the Displaced Persons Act. She was petite like you, but darker, raven haired. Shortly after the wedding, she leased out a building downtown. Lord knows where she got the money, considering her husband's salary. Draped the windows with posters of Paris and London. The Duchess's Beauty Emporium opened a few weeks later."

"Did you ever go there?"

"Oh, all the young girls did. Sylvia was good with hair. You could bring a picture from a magazine, and she could weave up any bob or beehive you asked for. But that wasn't the real draw."

"Bynthia told me about the tea leaves."

"Yes. She would tell fortunes after serving you tea. She had this thick, dreamy accent. It was all very European, mysterious. She predicted I would meet Charlie at the dance hall over in Henderson, predicted him right down to the color of his eyes."

"Bynthia made it sound like the town punished her."

"Punished?" Nora's expression darkened, her lips thinning. "Nobody punished her."

"I saw that woman's eyes. Pure malevolence. Surely, she was guilty of something worse than reading some leaves."

"Sylvia was a free thinker, if you know what I mean. One of the high school boys came to see her. She was helping him with a correspondence course, near as I remember. They worked together late at night, and I guess you could say they grew close."

Clara twisted her hands nervously on her lap. She was trying to take all of this in, not sure what to believe. First, there was the toothless old woman, who had looked like she materialized straight from an episode of late-night cable television, *Fright Show* or something. Now this, her mother's story. Duchess. A woman Clara's father had hated so much he erased her from his life.

"We don't talk about this. Nobody has talked about this in many years. Then you show up. What I'm saying about Sylvia and the boy is that they were caught together. Naked in the back storeroom of the shop. Remember we're talking about the early 1960s. Hell, if that happened even today there would be trouble. Still, it might have all blown over, but Sylvia pressed for a divorce from the teacher. She said she was in love with the boy."

"Wait. What happened to her?"

"You mean your mother?"

"If that's who she was."

"Your father's name was Stanley?"

"Yes."

"He spoke Latin?"

Clara nodded. "He ran a corner grocery store up in Savage for most of the years I was growing up, but we had whole shelves in our apartment stacked with books in Latin. I must have been the only sixth grader in the county who'd read Ovid's *Metamorphoses* in the original language."

Nora looked wistful, absently running her hands through her hair. "Sylvia had a nervous breakdown, from what we heard. She had to be institutionalized. Your father moved to the Cities to get away from all this. Start fresh. This Sylvia Meyers was your mother. I'm sure of it. She had the same eyes, dreamy and farseeing. Like she was looking on into a world of spirit none of us could see. Your father and mother were gone as far we knew. Shamed. We thought that was the last of it."

"She came back, though."

"For her lover, in December, a few days before Christmas. I think they were trying to run away. They left in a hurry, in the midst of a storm. But the car must have slid off the road into a slough. It turned over at the bottom of the canyon, crushing the roof. Sylvia made it out of the car. She tried to walk back to town, but she never made it here."

"She had a baby with her."

"It was Sheriff Steve who found the baby. He took the baby, but he had to leave Sylvia behind. He couldn't carry both her and the baby through the deep snow."

Clara's head was spinning. She sank deeper into the couch, shut her eyes. It was the vision of the woman she had seen, lost in the woods, surrounded by wolves. But there were no wolves in this story. "Why did she take the baby? Why not just leave me if she wanted to run away with this guy?"

"Why do people do anything? Maybe she wanted to hurt your father."

"I don't understand why he wouldn't say anything."

"What father could bear to tell his daughter such a story? How could he forgive his wife?"

"I'm going to have to say something, aren't I? Tell them who I am."

"No. It doesn't make any difference. You are Clara Warren, the pastor's wife. You are a schoolteacher. A damn fine one from what I hear. You are an expectant mother. That's all anyone needs to know. Leave the ugliness in the past."

Clara sighed. "There must be some kind of article from a newspaper, something to substantiate all this?"

"No. The first newspaper office burned down years ago. Why would seeing something in writing make it more or less true? The only article ever printed didn't even mention a baby, just the accident and the death of the woman. Sheriff Steve made sure of it. No one knows, really, but a few people like me."

"And Bynthia."

"I knew Stanley. If he didn't tell you, he had reasons for it. He told you enough to bring you here, didn't he?"

"What did they do with her body?"

"She's out there, has been this whole time.

Sylvia Meyers was buried in the suicide section."

"The suicide section?"

"Pastor Schoenwald didn't want her with the saints. She's right out there at the furthest edge near the woods. Kids still tell stories about her, about the woman in the woods. It's said that some nights if you are back there in the trees you'll hear her calling and calling for her baby."

Nora put her hand over Clara's and squeezed. "Now her baby has come home."

Grizz took the International out in the fields with a haybine and rack running behind it. He was late for this final cutting and in a foul mood, realizing he would likely have to buy hay from the next county over to feed his cattle through winter after the poor harvest. Haying this way took two men, normally, one to catch the bales spitting out the bine and stack them on the hayrack, the other to drive the tractor and scoop up the loose hay into the thresher, running along the even rows. Without Seth, Grizz had to stop every thirty yards or so and hand carry the tumbled bales to the rack and climb up to stack them himself — long, slow, hot work.

It took him two hours to get the first rack filled, so when he came up from the fields and saw a strange truck in his driveway, a rust-eaten Silverado, he cursed under his breath. What stepped out of the truck was not the young, boyish pastor Grizz had been expecting but an old spidery man with long arms. He was clad in a wool suit and carried a slender black briefcase.

Even after Grizz shut off the tractor it continued to hum and tick. The worst of his work awaited him. He'd have to unload the rack and shoot the bales up the conveyor belt into the hayloft, where the temperature likely broiled near one hundred degrees. It was too hot for this late in fall, the heat and drought relentless. He rinsed his face at the pump, in icy water drawn deep from the well.

"Looks like hard work," the man said as he came toward Grizz.

"It's nothing I can't handle," he said, water dripping from his beard.

The visitor introduced himself as a preacher from over in Amroy named Cyrus Easton, and when he opened his Bible and began to read to Grizz about the end of times, Grizz stopped him by setting his hand on his shoulder and squeezing hard. "You don't even know where you are or who I am, do you? I'm Seth Fallon, and this is just outside Lone Mountain. Almost a week ago my son killed a man and then went into the corn and ate his gun. So, I'm not meaning to be rude, but you're the last person on earth I want to talk to right now."

The end of the world. The apocalypse. Grizz smiled, completely unhinged. What a sick sense of humor God must have to send a man like this to him on such a day.

Cyrus pulled away from him and reached into his briefcase, extracting a brochure he left in the grass rather than hand him directly. "I heard about it on the radio," he said, softer. "I'm sorry. Maybe I'll come back another time." He snapped his briefcase shut and peered up at the other man expectantly. "Might be I could tell you about heaven and how it's possible for you and your son to be among the chosen."

"You come back here and I'll snap your neck with my bare hands."

"Well, okay, then," Cyrus said, gesturing at the brochure and walking to his truck. "You can look that over." Then he seemed to think of something important because he paused midway. " 'Here I tell you a mystery,' " he said, lifting his voice as though he were addressing not only Grizz but the cows in the pasture and the rest of creation. " 'We shall not all sleep, but we shall all be changed.' "

Here I tell you a mystery. Grizz had been waiting for news from the county, biding his time. He was not a man to bide time. After the little preacher man left, Grizz abandoned the rack of hay bales. Let the rain ruin them, let them rot. There were questions about Seth he had been pushing aside.

An hour later he parked his truck under the trees at the old landing. In a normal year the shade near the river hummed with bloodsuckers, but the summer of drought had palsied the oaks and stripped the cottonwoods bare. He left his truck and made for where he thought the place might be, freshly fallen leaves crackling under his boots and releasing a dusty smell, like burned cinnamon, into the grove. The river beyond was little more than a stream, so shallow he could walk across it and hardly wet his ankles.

A little ways out, a channel catfish with a body as long as his arm rotted on the bare sand. All that remained were the barbed whiskers, hinged sucker jaws, a cage of bones. A prehistoric creature of mud and deep currents, it had probably been marooned here as the river dwindled to a shallow pond and then to nothing. The sun had bleached the scales gray, and a few crows worked at the head, picking at the flesh, before they saw Grizz and flapped their wings lazily in the heat, moving to the other side of the river.

Sweat crept down his spine. In the middle of the river a long golden sandbar gleamed under the sun. He thought of his son out here with that girl just a few months before. There would have been enough water then that Seth and Leah would have had to swim to reach the sandbar.

He let himself imagine it as it must have happened. A fire crackling from the shore in a sandy pit, a beer can sweating in his boy's hand, the river a band of caramel under the moon, Leah dipping a red-painted nail into the water and asking, *You want to go swimming?*

Can't. Didn't bring any suit.

It was innocent, the girl had told Grizz. But had it been? He imagined her undoing the buttons of her cutoffs and letting them slide to the sand, showing long legs like a gazelle's. And then quickly, while Seth gaped openmouthed, the shirt peeled off and fluttered behind her, before she dived in in her bra and panties, popping to the surface a ways from shore, her blonde hair dark and wet against her pale shoulders. *You coming in or not?* And when he had followed, stripping shyly with his back turned to her, and dived in after and found her in the river, had she tasted of the beer and

208

the river itself, the salty mineral heat of her true self, sweet breath and the carbon of stars?

A kiss, a long kiss, Seth fighting for footing as the lazy current pulled at them, Seth trying not to think of the channel cats the size of barracuda swimming near him, all the things sliding past him in that secret river. A long kiss before the girl pulled away and went for the sandbar, laughing.

They had not been alone, Leah had implied. Someone had stood on this shore as he did now, back in the trees, watching the two teenagers in the shining river. And if it had been Will, why hadn't he arrested them for trespassing, two half-naked minors under the influence? Will Gunderson had not been the kind to look away while others broke the law. Unless Will himself had secrets out here. Unless this was not the first group of teenagers he had spied on.

Grizz breathed through his mouth, steadying himself. He had a hard time letting go of that vision of his son in the river with the girl. For a short time in the early part of summer he had stopped fearing for his son's future, and let his guard down.

A beaten path led to a small cabin in the clearing. This was the place Grizz had been heading for all along. The cabin leaned on

its river-rock foundation, something mud-
ded together in a bygone century. This was
the place Leah had told him about, where
Will brought vagrants and strangers to scare
them. A sign warning that this was county
property was nailed near the door, but some
kid had spray-painted FUCK YOU, PIG in red
letters over it.

A rusty lock sealed the door shut, but one
kick of Grizz's boots splintered the spongy
wood around it and sprung it open. When
he stepped inside, the first thing that hit
him was the abrasive smell filling up the
room. A table was pushed up against one
wall and on it sat a Coleman camping stove,
a kettle, and a tin of instant coffee next to
some chipped mugs. Above this table tools
hung by nails in the planking, pliers and
brands and sheers. Big iron-jawed traps for
beavers and muskrat also spread around the
room. Grizz saw a bottle of Stop-Rot, a
woman's hairbrush, toothbrushes, a hot-
glue gun, and a rusting hacksaw all arranged
on an old potbellied stove. Along the wall
rested the source of the stink, gallon buckets
where dead things bobbed in what he
guessed was formaldehyde.

"Oh, Christ," he said when he realized
what else was here. Deformed stuffed
animals were posed around the room on

benches and chairs made from logs. He had glanced over them at first, thinking them ordinary taxidermy creations, animals Will had trapped and stuffed. But he had sewn the corpses back together in unusual ways. A muskrat's body joined with the head and wings of a pheasant rooster to make what looked like a baby griffin. A doe's preserved head sprouted a single polished bone like a unicorn's horn. The body of an old boar, gray and bristly, had been stood up on its hind hooves and then joined to a mannequin's head draped with a shaggy wig. Half pig and half child, the creature's front hooves raked the air as though fending off some attacker.

His mind tried to match the creations to the man he'd known, his dark good looks and military buzz cut he'd kept after leaving the service. Will had been a man who watched and saw everything.

A lone chair stood against one wall.

Grizz sat in it and felt it creak under his weight. His fingers traced the wood and found the place where it was scarred by rope burns. His son had been here. He had been roped into this chair.

He shut his eyes, tried to see it. Will lifting the pliers from the wall, running them along the blue flame in the stove. The black, ashy smell of it. Will bringing it close to Seth, pulling up the boy's shirt to expose the soft, pale flesh. The burning. Burning him in secret places. Following it with a fist to the ribs, a slap. Seth wetting himself in fear and shame. Will hurting him just enough so that Seth could walk away once more.

Had Grizz seen marks on the body? He hadn't looked. He had lacked the courage. It came to him that Sheriff Steve Krieger had known about this place from the beginning. He had been the one who trained Will Gunderson about law and order. As in-laws the two had trapped and hunted these woods together.

No one wanted to see this, Grizz knew. In town they already had the story they wanted, one about a Vietnam veteran, a hero, and a violent teenage delinquent. Grizz breathed in the acrid smell of the room, his eyes stinging. Across from him the pig child stretched open his mouth in a solitary scream.

Grizz stood and let the chair clatter behind him. Somewhere out on the road a car passed, spitting up gravel. He was aware once more of the outer world, those crows cawing as they fought over the last of the fish down at the river. Farther off in town the bells were ringing. The bells of Trinity

Lutheran. Grizz knew in that moment he was hearing the end of Will's funeral service.

RITES

Logan faced the congregation in his alb, a white robe meant to remind them of their baptism, as he began to tell them about Sheriff Will Gunderson. Clara listened to his homily now and measured his words against the man she had known, if only in passing.

Gossips had told her that during divorce proceedings his wife, Laura, alleged physical abuse. Within a few days Clara had been warned what might happen if she drove even a few miles over the speed limit or failed to come to a full stop at any intersection. The ex-wife sat in the very front pew, flanked on either side by her sons. Directly behind the family sat Steve, Laura's father, and the rest of the sprawling Krieger clan, including Gretel and Bynthia in a side aisle in her wheelchair.

Clara's only encounter with Sheriff Will Gunderson had happened in the town

214

grocery store. Will had been a thin man, black haired, his arms long and ropy. When she entered the store, he had been leaning against a counter, his hand lightly touching a cashier's, a teenage girl laughing too loudly at something he said. His smile vanished the moment the bell dinged to announce Clara's entrance. She had felt his gaze on her, tracking her as she moved to the next aisle and left them alone. No, she had only seen him in passing, but Will had seemed a man at ease in his skin, a man of appetites. The entire town packed the sanctuary. Normally, the front of the church was a no-man's-land that only Clara occupied, but today she was wedged in tight a few rows behind the grieving family, surrounded by people she had never met. Like others in the crowd, she fanned herself with her bulletin. It was too damn hot to be dressed like this, and she felt sympathy for Logan in all his priestly layers, his face shining in the heat. Though the windows were open in the hopes of a cooling breeze, the air remained stagnant.

Midway through Logan's homily, a wind picked up out of the east, and the sanctuary filled with a putrefying odor. Logan, his face scanning the crowd, froze. The unnatural smell swelled in the room, a searing cloud that burned inside Clara's nose. Stricken, Logan suffered a coughing fit, and the smooth and orderly service began to break down.

The nightmare. Clara remembered his dream of seeing the devil out in the crowd, an ordinary man in a suit. She looked around her, and he could have been any of the men here. Logan's face purpled, as if the smell had stolen the breath from his lungs. People began to shift in their pews, muttering among themselves, and a good minute passed before the church secretary emerged from a side door bearing a cup of ice water. Logan shook as he guzzled it, spilling some on his alb and vestments. The terrible odor seemed to gather strength.

A man spoke from the balcony, and Clara craned her neck along with many others. The balcony, occupied by the hard-liners, the ones who could remember when the service was still conducted in German, was entirely gray haired. The man spoke again. "It's all right, Pastor," he called down, "just a little fresh country air."

Logan handed the glass back to the secretary. He smiled faintly and wiped his brow while nervous laughter rolled through the room. The smell had seemed to rise from the fields where the boy had killed himself, but it hadn't. It had come from the hog barns east of town. The Gunderson farm, which the boys were going to inherit, the biggest in the valley with six barns and vast holding pits for all that manure. It was ordinary hog shit they were smelling, nothing supernatural. The laughter didn't last long; they all knew why they were here and were anxious to escape the cloying heat. Clara roasted along with them, her dark dress stretching around her big stomach, imagining the baby inside her baking like a lumpy potpie.

"With the death of Sheriff Gunderson we lost a hero, a father, a protector. We cannot forget his sacrifice. With his passing, we want to know that we are safe. We want safety for our children. We want to be sure God will protect us in our hour of need."

His eyes scanned the room as he found his words. "And yet, God does not call us to lead safe lives. If anything our faith makes us more vulnerable to the world, which belongs to the devil." His words made Clara nervous. She felt the rest of the congregation straining toward him. He was not going to gloss over what had happened. He named the sheriff's death a murder. He named the boy a suicide. Clara knew the congregation around her also listened intently because people had stopped fanning themselves with their bulletins. A stillness settled.

"This is not our home, not here, this hard place, this heat. There is a house with many rooms. It was bought and paid for on the cross, and not by anything we have done. It is a place beyond all earthly strife, where we will be free of our troubles and in the presence of the Prince of Peace. Our Father is calling us, if we have ears to hear. He tells us to forgive those who have wronged us, if we ourselves want his forgiveness. He reminds us to love our neighbors, even when that is the hardest thing to do. Even when our neighbor is a child like Seth, who has done a great evil, for it is only in forgiveness that we will be made whole again. A God who sends his own Son into the world is one who knows our pain. A God who marks the fall of every sparrow, knows the number of hairs on our heads." Logan touched his own thinning scalp, smiled with twinkling eyes. Then his voice grew quieter, softening. The smell in the room had dissipated but not the heat.

"He is calling to you now. Listen. Come, Holy Spirit, come. We need you here. In Christ's name we ask forgiveness for our sins, so that we'll be made whole. As we are forgiven, so do we also forgive. We remember Seth Allis Fallon, who was baptized here at this church. As we are forgiven, so do we find the strength to forgive him. We ask that you watch over the family of Will Gunderson, who was your faithful servant in this life. We turn our eyes inward, and there we find you. We ask you for your healing presence. We will not live in fear but instead in your perfect love." Logan paused. "Please bow your heads with me for a moment in prayer."

After the service, Clara normally stood with Logan to greet people as they walked out, shaking hands, but the widow had taken their spot, chatting with people heading down into the basement to fuel up on sandwiches, bologna on buttered white bread, with a heaping of potato salad to the side, a comforting meal before heading out to the cemetery for the burial.

The widow wore a black dress short enough to show some leg. She didn't have on any stockings, and her toenails were a splash of red. Her hair was honey blonde, permed in a frowsy yellow cloud around her face. She looked like a woman who wasn't ready yet for old age. Widowhood had granted her a passing fame. A circle of well-wishers surrounded her, but they parted to make way for others. The widow greeted Logan, thanked him for his kind words, and then turned immediately to say, "Why, you must be Clara." Her smile was warm, gracious. "I'm Laura Gunderson, the sheriff's wife."

Clara searched herself for words of comfort to offer but came up empty.

Undeterred by her tied tongue, Laura went on. "Well, I'm officially his ex-wife, but as I was just telling these ladies here, we got back together only recently."

The other women she referred to had melted away, gone downstairs for the luncheon. Cold sandwiches and colder air in the basement. Laura's two sons stood nearby, Kelan in a blazer two sizes too large for him. His father's? He looked uncomfortable in all his layers, desperate to be anywhere but here. The younger one kept his arms wrapped around himself, his eyes red from crying, his misery tangible. "You must have had some guardian angel on your shoulder," Laura continued. "That's what everyone is saying." This statement, vapid in some mouths, was disturbing from a woman whose husband evidently didn't have any such angel.

"Something like that," Clara said, thinking of the hand on her shoulder that day. She glanced at Kelan, saw the boy studying her. The older boy dry-eyed, maybe not knowing what to make of a world that no longer had his father in it. He smiled slyly when their eyes met. *Do you believe in the devil?* she remembered him asking. How would she answer that question now? If the devil had passed among them he had worn the shape of a boy, a long coat, dirty tennis shoes. Clara rubbed the ends of her fingers on her left hand, nervous in this family's presence. The widow's cheeriness. The sullen older child.

Laura surprised her then by putting her hands on Clara's belly. Clara's dress was cotton, thin and stretched, and she felt the shock of those hands right through the fabric. "You're going to have a boy," she announced.

"Umm . . . we don't really know yet." Clara felt unsteady on her feet.

"A boy," she insisted, finally taking her hands away.

Clara wanted to be away from her. The rest of the congregation milled uncertainly behind them, trapped in the hot room. You were only supposed to shake hands and speak a few words and then keep the line moving. She had the feeling that Laura was enjoying being the center of attention, making everyone wait so she could talk to her.

Laura leaned in. "I'm pregnant, too," she confided in a low whisper. She shook her head. "Will had been visiting me every night before he died. We were planning on getting married all over again."

"Congratulations," Clara mumbled. She felt Logan's impatience next to her, because they needed to keep going. People bunched up behind them, clotting in the heat.

"Laura," he said, interrupting the conversation. "We're very sorry for your loss. I want to assure you that you and your boys are in our prayers."

"Yes," said Laura. "That's very kind of you." With a regal nod, she let them pass.

Ashen sunlight washed through the curtains the next morning, and the air in the room smelled crisply of burning leaves. Autumn had arrived at last, all at once, a cold front blasting down out of Canada. As if God were clearing the air now that the sheriff was under the ground. It felt like a good morning to laze under the sheets. Clara fluffed her pillow and settled back while Logan dressed.

"Good Lutherans don't believe in ghosts," he was saying, fresh from the shower, clad only in tighty-whities and black socks, his chest and legs pink with steam.

"But what about the Holy Ghost," Clara said. "It doesn't seem fair if God gets to have a ghost, but none of the rest of us does."

She had finally told him about her sense of Seth's ghost troubling her, the drawing of the wolf someone placed at the door, the figure at the edge of the corn.

Logan plucked his ironed khakis from a wire and stepped into them. "Whoever said that God was fair?"

"Not me. Glad I don't have that job."

"I don't have that job, either." He straightened. White-blond hair circled up from his stomach and feathered his pale chest. His muscles were taut and tense, the blue veins prominent. Her beautiful, boyish husband smiled briefly at her sarcasm, but his eyes were serious. "I would be careful about encouraging whatever it was you think you sensed. This ghost or spirit."

"What's that supposed to mean?"

He took down an indigo-colored clerical shirt and shrugged it on. "In Ephesians it says we struggle not against flesh and blood but against powers and principalities, the powers of this dark world. Against evil."

She clapped a hand to her forehead. "So

now I'm possessed?" Hysteria, she thought. In Greek the word meant "from the womb," since supposedly only women could get hysterical. It was useless to try talking to Logan about these things. *There are more things on heaven and earth, Horatio, / Than are dreamt of in your philosophy.* She had let him have his devil, but he wouldn't allow her a simple ghost.

Sighing, Logan sat at the foot of the bed and pulled on his socks. "You never knew your mother. I think you long for her."

What did that have to do with Seth's ghost? And yet she had told Logan once before about running away, about that sense of her mother calling to her. "You remember what we talked of when we first talked about coming here?" she said. He rubbed her feet through the comforter, listening while she told him what she'd learned about her mother from Bynthia and Nora. Who her mother really was.

Logan was quiet for a long time. "Do you think it's true?"

"Nora seemed sure of it."

"I worry about you." His hand smoothed the blanket over her legs, stopping just above her knee, squeezing. His voice gently insistent. "What if you don't like the answers you find?"

She caught his hand, squeezed back. "We're all mixed up in this, aren't we?"

He sighed in answer. "Maybe there are some things we aren't meant to know. And you think you're hearing things again now in a moment of great stress. Seeing things."

"I know what I saw."

"It's just this. If there really is something not of the living talking to you, then you should be careful. I believe this spirit means you harm."

Clara let go of his hand and turned over on her side, away from him. *Poltergeist:* from the Low German, meaning "rumbling spirit." She didn't know what was worse, that Logan believed her or that he had made what she saw into something frightening.

On his way out, Logan paused at the door. "Let the dead be dead, Clara. Let the dead rest."

"And what if I can't?"

Later that afternoon, she decided to paint the bedroom down the hall using the only passable shade of yellow she had found at Toby's Hardware downtown. She needed to take her mind off her unfinished dissertation waiting in the desk drawer. The wolf stories her father had told her wandered through her imagination while what was

225

supposed to be her true work, her lonely research, gathered dust. And now there was a job offer. In less than a week Clara would be a teacher again.

The paint can promised to evoke memories of a summer afternoon, but once applied looked like partially digested mustard. She had taped plastic sheeting to the hardwood floor and laid down newspaper, but the paint came off the brushes in thin, watery streams that spattered and speckled everything — the oak paneling, the floor, her arms and face and clothes.

Logan returned later that day, his tread heavy. For a thin man her husband carried himself with gravitas.

"Ta-da," Clara said, spreading her arms, when he came in.

He raised an eyebrow. "Who killed Tweety Bird?"

"This, my darling, is Lemony Surprise." She wanted a happy color with the baby due in December. An antidote for the long, dark winter of the child's birth.

"It's a surprise, all right. Looks like someone threw up creamed corn everywhere."

She drew in a deep breath, which should have calmed her except for the chemical fumes of the paint. She hoped there was no lead in this cheap stuff, nothing that might harm the baby. The fumes burned inside her nose. "I'm almost done. The ceiling took forever. There must be a million nooks and crannies in these textured ceilings. God, when these walls were still that awful gray color it was like being in a cave." With a stroke of her brush she covered the final gray spot and stood again, her hands on her hips. Logan hadn't said anything, so she turned to him. "Did you finish your sermon?"

"It's as finished as it's going to get," he muttered. "It's the end of Pentecost, and I'm preaching from the Book of Acts instead of the lectionary. I don't know what possessed me — the Book of Acts is not exactly easy to preach on."

Red was the color of Pentecost, she remembered. For a moment she pictured doing this room up in red, saw herself standing inside it like standing within the bloody chamber of a great heart. "It's because you don't like the Holy Ghost. The Holy Ghost is all over the Book of Acts."

"Holy Spirit," Logan corrected. "And I like him well enough. It's a blasphemy to say otherwise."

Or *her,* she thought. Clara knew the word for spirit translated from the Greek as "wind" or "breath," and she liked those translations best of all, something fierce and invisible moving in the trees, her hair. A caress in spring, a slap in winter. And the two of them living in a country of wind out on the prairie.

Logan crossed the room and pulled the curtains shut. "Doesn't look so bad in the half dark."

"Like swimming in a big custard pie." The thought made Clara's stomach grumble.

He turned to her, smiling. "And look at you," he said.

"I know I'm a mess." Paint freckled her arms and face.

"A glorious mess, yes. Beautiful. With your hair up in that kerchief you're like some homey vision from the past."

"Are you saying I should dress like this more often?"

He wrapped her in his arms, the shelf of her big stomach an awkward barrier between them. "Thank you," he said.

"For what?"

"For this." He spread his hands to encompass the room. "And for putting up with me when I behave like an ass."

"I'm sorry for my own part." There were those notes, which she still hadn't thrown away, but she knew in that moment that she would never speak of them. There were all the ways she felt she had failed him as a wife. The pregnancy. The kittens. The boy she had not been able to save. Bringing them here to this place.

Her eyes were damp again, but this time he kissed her tears away. "I need you," he said, and he led her back to the bedroom. He undid her kerchief and Clara shook out her hair. He kissed her mouth, her throat, the hollow above her breastbone before unbuttoning her shirt. He even let his hands linger on her stomach, but the baby was quiet inside her, asleep. Clara helped him undress, and then they climbed under the sheets together, Logan pressing against her from behind, his teeth against her shoulder blades, his hands reaching around to cup her breasts.

Outside, Clara heard the trash cans tip over. A neighbor's dog barking and then silence. Logan's lips along her shoulder, his face in her hair, his teeth nipping at the softness of her neck. Then he shuddered; they both did. It had been so long, so very long, and never like this, from behind, with such urgency. He kissed the lobe of her ear and moaned once, softly, a sound that was almost like an apology.

The next morning Clara dropped the notes into a Folgers coffee can sitting on the garage floor, lit a match, and let them burn. "Yes, I know it's not a practical disposal method," she said to Loki, the smallest of the kittens, who circled her ankles, purring, "but the Danes would have approved."

The kittens now occupied a box in the garage, their litter box near the door. After their mother had disappeared one morning, gone or eaten by the coyotes, Clara talked Logan into letting the kittens live out here. He did not like having to park his Nova outside, but it was better to have the kittens here rather than in the house, and he agreed that the Nelsons could wait until next year when the kittens were big enough to survive on their own before they gave them away. As long as Clara promised she would give them up when the time came. She had managed to keep these kittens alive, had bargained them a home.

She sat on the cold concrete floor, and they came to her — Loki, Freya, and Gandalf the Gray — and let her gather them in her lap. Last of all, she dropped in Seth's final gift, the werewolf and priestess minia-

tures in their tissue wrapping, and watched
as flames took them.

BOYS AND GUNS

It took Grizz an hour of searching through
the brushy hillside before he found the gun,
the barrel speared into the dirt. The dusty
coating couldn't hide the weapon's beauty,
a burnished walnut stock trimmed with
silver etching, the scope powerful enough to
draw down stars from the night sky. A Colt
Sauer 30-06. If Lee had hit him, he would
have put a good-sized hole in his chest. The
boy must have stolen it from his father's
gun collection. A single round was still
housed in the chamber, and Grizz levered it
shut once more with a satisfying click. Even
in the heat, the rifle was a cold deadweight
in his grasp.

The farm boys in this stretch of country
grew up with guns. Hunting was one of the
rituals that gave fall meaning, a release from
the hard work of the harvest. Farm boys
here grew up shooting sparrows from the
telephone wire with pellet guns, learning a

steady aim from targeting squirrels at the bird feeder, or practicing on rabbits that invaded their mothers' gardens. They grew up with guns and became teenagers who shot at street signs from moving cars or shot loads of buckshot straight up into the sky and then scurried for cover before the deadly lead rained down. They grew up, and as they grew bigger the guns grew with them. A .410 could take down a coon or even a small deer at close range; a 20 gauge could pluck a fleeing pheasant or goose from the blue. Shot or slug, steel or lead, they could cite velocities and tell stories of the improbable kill or the one that got away. They ate what they killed, mostly, but sometimes they killed out of boredom, a long-legged gray heron that wandered into range on a fall day, the red-tailed hawk circling ducks in a pond, kills they later mourned but could not undo. Every boy, every one, Seth constantly reminded him. Every boy but his. Other than the .22 rifle that Grizz kept behind the seat in his truck, little more than a varmint gun, they didn't own guns on the Fallon farm. They did not hunt, did not trap, did not kill, except for stray foxes or predators. And when Seth asked him, begged him, for a gun of his own, he had held off as long as he could, until last Christmas when he bought his son the twelve gauge, hoping that the promise of hunting the next fall would keep the boy in school and out of trouble.

A few weeks before hunting season his mother, Gail, had chased his father across the front lawn, slashing at him with a big kitchen knife until he sheltered amid a canebrake of raspberries. Grizz saw this happen from his spot on the porch, where he was whittling a new walking stick with his pocketknife. Gail went in after his father, cursing, and the raspberry bushes lashed and fell as they struggled. Grizz heard shouts and whimpers of pain, but a few minutes later they emerged from the canebrake, both scratched and bleeding, his mother disarmed. They went inside, his mother still shouting something about him "catching worse if she heard he'd been around that woman again." A few minutes later his younger brother Wylie came out and joined Grizz on the porch.

"They at it again?"

Wylie nodded, his eyes huge. Even from out on the porch they heard curses and breaking furniture.

"Let's go for a walk," Grizz said. Sometimes, he felt like he was the one raising

Wylie, that he was more a father than an older brother.

As they went down to the lower meadow, Wylie started to tell him about the pageant this coming year, and Grizz let him chatter, grateful for the distraction. "The real Hiawatha is nothing like the one in the play."

"Yeah?" The tall meadow grasses heaved and tossed like a green sea in the wind. There would be enough wind to keep off the mosquitoes, a fine fall evening. If their parents were still at it when they went home, "making up" noisily in the bedroom, Grizz would walk with his little brother into town and buy them a burger and shake at the pool hall.

"The real Hiawatha was a Mahican, not Ojibwa. He was a warrior, a cannibal. He would have eaten a poet like Henry Wadsworth Longfellow for breakfast."

"I bet it would have given him indigestion."

"What would?"

"Eating a poet with a name like that." Grizz burped to prove his point.

Wylie laughed. The play wasn't until spring, but the kids from the middle school auditioned for it in fall. It was the biggest event of the year. Everyone in town gathered on picnic blankets on the grassy hill above the amphitheater at the start of summer. People drove all the way out here from the Cities to see it. There would be beer for the adults, popcorn and Cokes for the kids. Longfellow's famous *Song of Hiawatha* broadcast in an abbreviated monologue from grainy speakers while actors pantomimed the drama on the stage below. This year, Wylie had been selected for the lead part and couldn't stop talking about it. At the finale, Hiawatha lit a flaming arrow that he shot in a beautiful arc into the black waters below before diving off a steep rock into the waiting pool. His little brother, the hunter in white doeskin. He was going to redeem the family name. They would no longer be the son of a poacher and drunkard, the children of a broken woman, whom people whispered about in the streets. Wylie, his lucky, good-natured little brother, was going to be a hero.

A few days later the boys went deer hunting with their father. The only time they did not need to fear Dermot Fallon was during hunting season. The ritual of blood and violence calmed him. For days afterward he didn't need to drink. He didn't lay a hand on any of them.

It was still dark outside when they stepped

toward the mountain. Their father had warned them about staying away from the road. Deer-hunting season didn't technically start until the next weekend, but their father was not above poaching when it suited him. "What's on this land belongs to me," he often told them.

They positioned themselves at the edge of the woods, the father choosing one tree and the sons choosing another on the opposite sides of the meadow. These were old outposts; lumber handholds nailed into a tree trunk led up to a shelf of plywood amid the lower branches. The brothers climbed up and waited for the deer to come down to the meadow and feed at first light. Grizz loved it, the crisp October air, the flashlight carving a wispy trail through the dark. He loved the stillness and the cold and the creepy primeval screech of night birds making one last sweep through the woods.

Together in their tree house, the boys watched and waited. When first light came and went and nothing stirred, they whispered back and forth. Grizz taught Wylie what he knew about the world, which wasn't much. *Hang your coveralls in the barn the night before a hunt so the deer can't smell you coming. You got to walk like this, on the balls of your feet, so the branches don't crackle. Injuns don't drink no water when they hunt; water makes a body weak. Crush a leaf in your fist and let it go so you know which way the wind blows. Don't kiss any girls French style because it makes you go cross-eyed. Not even pretty Jean Fletcher; I seen how you look at her in church. Sure you say that now. What? The French style is when people get down on all fours like a dog. Sh! Quit your jibbering. Didn't you hear that? A crow only caws twice like that when there's something near.*

They waited all day and didn't see much more than a few squirrels scampering in the woods. A couple of times their father came over, and they walked the stretch of woodland nearest the river to see if they could chase anything up. The last time, as evening fell, their father passed his flask around. Grizz refused, but Wylie tried a few sips, wincing when the whiskey hit his throat. Their father roared. "Look at him," he said. "Shit. The boy's getting a taste for it."

Both Grizz and his father were big men, broad shouldered. Only sixteen years old then, Grizz already had hair on his chest. Wylie, three years younger, was small and wiry, a dark-haired serious boy.

When Grizz said nothing, his father slapped him in the mouth. "Answer me when I talk to you."

Grizz swallowed his blood and rubbed his chin. His father usually didn't hit them like this when they were out on the hunt. The slap, the ringing sting of it, caught him off guard.

"You aren't going to cry, are you? Big blubbering baby. I heard about you in town. They're all talking about you and that little girl. She's just a child in pigtails for Chrissakes."

"She's in high school, same as me. Shut up about her."

His father slapped him again, harder. Grizz tasted his own blood, and he spat it out.

"They better just be stories, boy. She's not for you."

"This sure tastes good, Pop." Wylie spoke up, playing the fool. "Better than Coca-Cola."

"Damn straight. You're more a man than your pussy older brother."

Wylie pretended not to hear. "I feel it right down to my toes."

He laughed, took back his flask. "Save some for me."

The three walked home following a slough. The heat of the day buzzed in Grizz's skull, and he was sweating inside his coveralls, drowsy from waking up before dawn. Grizz and Wylie came along one side, their father on the other, a small canyon of fetid water and cattails between them. Grizz dreaded what was going to happen when they got home. No animal blood spilled out here meant blood would be spilled in the house. Gail, the boys' distant mother, had wires in her jaw to support the bones that had been broken. Her nose still sat slightly crooked on her face. Grizz wouldn't touch liquor, not at that point in his life, seeing what it did to his father, but the old man was already corrupting Wylie, turning his spirit dark.

Grizz walked slowly, his brother weaving from the whiskey, when the biggest buck the Fallons had ever seen rose up from the water where it had been hiding, belly deep in the mud. Years later, standing on this mountain with a dead man's gun in his grasp, Grizz could still see it.

His father reacted instantly, the butt of his twelve gauge finding a groove in his shoulder, his finger squeezing the trigger. It didn't matter that the boys stood on the opposite side. It didn't matter that if he missed he would have killed one of them. All this he realized later. What he remembered came in fragments: Wylie going down in the grass,

240

Grizz raising his own shotgun, sweat stinging his eyes, the form of the deer blurring,
the shadow of his father on the other side.
He pulled the trigger over and over, jacking
out spent shells into the grass around him,
the gun slamming against his shoulder.

When he was done shooting, he saw the
buck as it bounded away, each leap covering twenty feet, a beautiful stag with a massive rack of antlers, the trophy deer their
father longed for, with enough meat to
smoke and make into sausage to feed them
in lean winter months. The buck stopped at
the edge of the woods and looked back at
Grizz as if to share the joy and surprise of
still finding fire in his veins.

Smoke spiraled from his gun. Wylie stood
again, wiping his mouth on his sleeve. He'd
been bent over vomiting up the whiskey.
"Did you hit it?"

Grizz shook his head, his mouth dry. The
opposite bank, where their father had stood,
was empty. "Wylie," he said. "You wait
here."

"Where's Pop?"

Grizz slid down into the murky water of
the slough, the shotgun held above his head.
Wylie called for their father, but there was
no answer. The muddy water sucked at
Grizz's boots, and it took all his strength

just to cross the slough and climb the slick canary grass on the other bank.

Dermot Fallon was not difficult to find. He was still alive, his body shuddering, the grass flattened all around him. The slug had burrowed into his belly, and he was trying to push his guts back inside. A matting of red, the cattails splattered. A smell like brimstone, something sweet and charred, drifted in the air. He moaned and pounded the ground with his fists. Then Wylie rushed past Grizz and knelt beside their father. The boys' father tried to sit up, but the pain brought him low. He looked up at Grizz, he looked up at him in his blood, and said, "I didn't think you had it in you."

"Run get help!" Grizz told his little brother.

Wylie climbed to his feet. "I'm sorry, Daddy. Oh, Jesus." He stopped to retch again in the cattails.

"Hurry," Grizz said to him.

When his brother was gone, Grizz made sure to kick away his father's gun, where he couldn't reach it. It didn't matter by then. The man's breathing had grown labored, his eyes rolling back in his head.

"It hurts," he said. "Hurts worse than I thought it would." His voice softening. He waited for his father to curse him, waited a

242

long time before there were sirens in the distance. Volunteer paramedics. Sundown. The sky violet, then deepening into indigo. Geese going overhead, racing the falling night. A long time more before the paramedics walked out here from the road. The grass turning brittle with cold. There was an aurora that night, the sky ablaze with energy, green and red lights reaching down like burning fingers, as if the universe were tilting to show some molten secret.

At the house that night, the sheriff interviewed both boys in the kitchen. Grizz told the same story over and over. A deer rising up between them. The slug. It must have ricocheted. An accident. It had been an accident, right? He hadn't meant to do it. A deer, a beautiful buck. Both his brother and mother weeping. He hadn't known until then. Hadn't realized they loved his father. They loved him even though he was a monster. And Grizz? What did it make you, if you were the one who killed the monster? What he felt in that moment was a profound sense of calm, of relief. He was glad his father was dead and could not hurt any of them again. Yet it had not mattered. Within ten years both Wylie and Gail were dead. The sheriff taking notes, glancing from older son to mother. That terrible scar along her jaw.

"You don't seem too upset," he said to Grizz.

"It won't help him to cry now."

The sheriff nodded, closing up his notes. He was so young then, with daughters Grizz's own age. His wife had left him a few years back, run off to California with another man. He knew the boys' father, knew this whole family. "What's done is done," he said. Sheriff Steve had suspected Grizz all along and despised him for it.

Grizz thought for a long time what to do with the gun Lee had left on his property. When he came down from the mountain, he carried it with him.

BOOK TWO

LOUP GAROU

One day when Clara was walking down the cereal aisle of the grocery store with her father, a woman had paused to appraise Clara. "What a beautiful little girl," she said to her father. "She must favor her mother."

He had smiled, thin lipped, and put his hand on the top of Clara's head. "No. She doesn't look a thing like that woman." Something in his tone made the stranger draw back.

Clara wasn't any more than seven when this happened, but she knew an opportunity when it came her way. While the woman was still in earshot, she asked her father, "What did my mother look like?" But his hand only tightened atop her head, tugging at the roots of her hair, and he hurried her down the aisle without speaking.

In the next aisle her father leaned down at eye level and said in a low voice, "Don't ever shame me like that again." When he took his hand away from her head, strands of her brown hair were stuck to his palm. To this day, remembering made Clara's scalp ache.

She ran away the first time that afternoon. While her father napped on the couch in front of an episode of *Bonanza,* she loaded up a canvas tote bag with a loaf of Wonder bread, a jar of strawberry jam, and a copy of her favorite book, *Madeline and the Gypsies.* She didn't make it far from the apartment where they lived in Savage, because it started raining as soon as she stepped out of the door.

Clara took shelter under an old weeping willow and listened to the *plink-plink-plink* of the rain striking the river. The long green branches of the willow swept the grass like a woman's tresses, the hair of some Medusa whipping in the wind. With her back against the trunk she had a vision of her mother for the first time, a woman stepping through the beaded curtain of the branches to stand before her in a summery dress the color of emeralds, her chestnut hair flowing past her shoulders. Her eyes were green, green like the tree, the grass, the rainlight. Her smile was so sweet and sad it made Clara's breath catch in her throat. She seemed to beckon Clara toward the river's slippery bank, where water licked at the shore.

Then in the distance Clara heard the screen door slap shut and her father calling and calling her name, and she turned in his direction, and when she looked back again the woman was gone, the branches waving where she had stepped through, and she felt so downlow and lonesome in that instant that she pulled up her knees to her chest and wept and that was how her father came to find her. He wasn't mad. "This is a pleasant spot," he said, and he sat with her awhile on the damp lawn, passing her his handkerchief.

Clara did not tell him about her mother's ghost, because she knew he would dismiss it. Instead she snuggled close to him. "Tell me about the wolf boy," she said, "the one Copper rescued from the prairie fire."

"Do you mean the *loup garou* he later became?"

"The werewolf," she translated with a delicious shiver. Now that she had grown older, the stories had darkened. This story he told during the daylight hours only. "Yes, that one."

"But as you know, to tell his story, I must speak of another one. Of the trapper and his daughter."

■ ■ ■ ■

This happened in the springtime, a starvation season on the prairies when the winter stores were exhausted and the ground too cold for planting. In this time there was a girl who lived with her father in a valley shadowed by a lone mountain. Every year the girl's father left her to go trapping north of the Purgatory River, and every year he was gone longer and returned with fewer and fewer furs to trade at the post.

One year he had been gone for only a few days when late at night she heard someone banging at the door. "Come quickly, girl," he cried out in a querulous voice. In the dark she fumbled with the latch. When the door opened he rushed inside, slammed it shut, and bolted it tight. He leaned the half-stock prairie rifle he always carried with him against a log cabin wall and then further blockaded the door with a log chair.

"Papa?" the girl said in confusion, still half asleep. He had not been due back from his trapping expedition for another three days. "What's happening?"

Even in the darkness of the room she could see a horror story written on his face. Claw marks gashed open either cheek, one eye puffed pink and swollen, and strings of dried blood matted his beard.

"Shush, girl," he said, holding a finger to his lips when she gasped at the sight of him. "It's coming."

Before she could ask what, an eerie wailing erupted from the woods. The girl went to the window, blinking as her eyes adjusted to the darkness. In the moonlight she saw a shadowy streak out near the oak savanna. Her father snatched up his rifle and checked the priming. Deep in the woods an animal reared up on two legs. The girl beheld shaggy hair around its face, a lean, muscled torso, and long, curling claws. It stood unsteadily as a bear might stand, sniffing the air. Two large eyes caught and held her in a lambent gaze. Even from this distance she saw something flash in those eyes, a glint of recognition.

"Get away from the window," her father said. He eased up the glass from the casement and balanced his rifle on the ledge so that it poked out into the night. The creature wailed once more before the trapper answered with his gun. A cloud of smoke filled the cabin, and when it cleared the moonlit glade where the thing had stood lay empty. The trapper bit off a fresh cap and poured it in the half stock, cursing as he tapped it down with a priming bolt.

251

She was glad he had not hit it. Those eyes had been luminous in the shadows, summoning.

At a puncheon table she used lucifer matches to light a lantern. Her father sat on a stump so she could tend his wounds, dabbing them with a cloth and then wringing out blood into a bucket. He took long pulls from a bottle of rye whiskey. "How deep are the wounds?"

The worst ran down the center of his cheek, an ugly ribbon of skin through which she glimpsed bone. "I'll need my needle for just the one, but the rest should heal on their own." While she worked, drawing tight the thread, she asked him to tell what happened, hoping to distract him.

He began by telling her how the animals he had caught in his traps were unlike anything he'd seen. By the time he checked his traplines all that remained was the fur. Something was eating the muskrats in the traps, devouring the meat and blood, and leaving behind only tufted pelts.

For three days and nights he ran his traplines and collected what pelts were salvageable, until one morning he came upon something else: a prairie wolf, a shaggy bitch, alive and struggling in the teeth of the trap. He figured this was it, the source of all his troubles. He'd heard of cunning wolves doing this before. He drew his knife and put her out of her misery, and when he did he heard something behind him. An unearthly shrieking.

The girl shuddered. She had heard the pain in that howl.

"I didn't even see it, just felt it. It was all over me, biting and clawing. I fought back, lashing out with my fists. Somehow I hurt it enough to chase it away. God help me, but I ran after that. I left behind the remaining traps, the few pelts worth saving, and took my gun and ran. For two nights I've been traveling here, stopping to light fires at night, hearing that thing out there, circling the edge of the flames."

He slept for a short while on his rope bed, his breathing labored, his bottle of rye whiskey empty. In the light of the lantern she surveyed his wounds, knowing the deepest one would scar. Abruptly, his snoring stopped, his eyes popped open, and he woke screaming. She went to him and touched the back of her hand to his forehead, which burned as if with fever or infection. "Oh, Papa."

"No human or animal moves like that. There is a powerful dark magic in that thing. It was a *loup garou*."

"I know," she said, thinking on what she had seen. "I believe you."

"I can feel the taint spreading inside me. The next moon, I'll begin to change, and then you won't be safe around me anymore."

"You wouldn't ever hurt me."

"I'm going to have to go away."

She touched his shoulder. "Please. Let's go see the preacher. He'll know what to do."

He groaned. "I'm so tired. I'm going to rest for just this night. In the morning, I'll go. You'll be safe, because the *loup garou* will follow me. I'm going to go where I will be far from any people, out on the prairies."

"The Indians are out there," she said, thinking of the Dakota warriors who had been their worst fear until this night.

He shut his eyes again. "There is only one way to fight the *loup garou.* You have to draw its blood. Draw blood from it, and it will change into its human form and tell you the secret it holds."

"Papa, what will I do if you are gone?" But his breathing had deepened. She went to her side of the cabin, descending into restless sleep. She did not hear him leave in the night, but in the morning his bed lay empty. That he had left his rifle here frightened her, as though her father was surrendering, offering himself as a sacrifice.

The girl did what she always did to pass the day. She gathered eggs from their laying hens, collected maple syrup in buckets from the trees in their grove. She was thirteen years old, and not strong enough to plow, but she knew these woods, the places where the wild grapes and berries grew.

A week passed until one night she heard something outside padding around the cabin. The boards of the porch creaked. When she called out "Papa" it went silent again. A hand scratched at the door. It whined softly, searching for a way in. Moonlight flooded in through the window. She pictured those claws, the gouges on her father's face. It pressed against the door, but the latch held fast. She lay awake, listening to it. "Papa?" she said again, but whatever was out there was not him.

"What happened next?" Clara asked. "That's not the ending."

Her father coughed into his handkerchief. "This wet grass has soaked straight through my backside. Let's get inside before we catch chill."

These stories were less frequent now that Clara had grown older, and she feared the day they would stop entirely. Like the man in the story, her father was going farther away from her, or she from him. Clara let him lead her by the hand back to the apartment they kept above his store.

She had realized she could see her mother, this woman whose memory her father denied her, but only when he wasn't near, so she kept running away. She didn't consciously mean to hurt him. Each time she ran away, the weather changed, as if her father had the power to call down storms. And each time he came to find her, no matter what it cost him physically. He didn't ask questions nor did he scold her. For a long time after he died Clara had the sense of him out there, still searching for her, trying to keep her safe. The dead carve out a space inside us, taking up residence like a man stepping under a willow tree in the rain to sit beside the ghost of our former selves. In this manner each of us is haunted, and who would have it any other way?

Before she knew it, school started on Monday, and Clara was back in the thick of things. The sophomores of first and second period came to class toting ten pound bags of Gold Medal flour wrapped in panty hose along with their usual notebooks and supplies. "How do you like my new baby, Mrs. Warren?" the first girl through the door asked Clara, swinging the thing in her arms. Foam-filled panty hose bulged out in the shape of pudgy arms and legs around the flour sack. She had sewn round blue buttons into the lopsided head for the eyes and mouth. This smiling head lolled on the neck when she balanced it on her hip.

"Baby?" Clara said, confused. It looked like a doll dreamed up by Dante. She struggled to recall the blonde's name. Her chirpy voice, at 8:15 in the morning, hurt Clara's ears.

"It's baby week in home ec," said another, a brunette who always had chewing gum packed into her chipmunk cheeks. She trailed behind the girl, lugging her own flour-sack baby. "We have to carry these around for a week, to learn what it's like to have a baby. That way we won't get knocked up."

Clara smoothed down her blouse over her stomach. "Does the sack of flour wake you up six times a night?"

"Not exactly," she said, sagging into her desk. What was her name? Tara? Tina? That was it: Tina. "We have to call Miss Drimble sometime between two and three in the morning and leave a message on her machine. Every night. Then we have to call back and tell her the baby is sleeping fifteen minutes later."

"Isn't that like the dumbest thing ever?" the first girl chimed in from her own desk.

Clara nodded. Like totally, but who was she to judge another teacher's methods? The flour-sack babies were all the sophomores could talk about. They had to introduce Clara to them as they came in the door. Each baby had a name, a Crayola birth certificate, and a little book where the student recorded the times they supposedly changed diapers and administered feedings. Clara was walking the rows when she came across Lee Gunderson, the sheriff's younger son. She'd forgotten he was in this class. Unlike his older brother, he kept to himself. He had long hair, his eyes slightly slanted. The taint the boy must feel was the same as any soldier or policeman feels after surviving bloodshed, family trauma. Clara knew that psychologists called this sense of always feeling branded the mark of Cain.

There was something mechanical to his smile. Clara paused at his desk. His baby had uneven eyes, a smile like a gash along the lower jaw. "Hi, Lee. What's your baby's name?"

"Billy," he said without looking at her. It took her a moment to realize that Billy was short for William, his father's name.

Clara patted his shoulder. "That's a good name," she said.

He nodded again. His clothing, she noticed as she continued down the rows, smelled faintly of mildew and smoke.

Though the bags made a mess, a faint white powder coating the floor from the careless boys, the ones who tossed their flour-sack babies back and forth in a juggling game — daring Clara to report them to Miss Drimble — by the time the first two classes left she was glad of the distraction. The smell made her hungry. On her aching feet, with a baby adrift in her stomach, sloshing around as she moved to put up the daily vocab words on the chalkboard, she smelled the fine, invisible powder and daydreamed of sugar cookies and buttermilk rolls hot from the oven, of sweet houses made from gingerbread set deep in the woods to snare the unwary.

The students seemed happy to have her back. Some complained about the strictness of the substitute, Miss Hartle, but they bent to their work after making a few lame jokes. Clara had entered the fray of their lives once more, just another odd addition like the sacks of flour they were forced to lug around. They were happy to see her again, but it seemed clear that, for the first two periods at least, they would have been fine without her.

■ ■ ■

After school she was erasing the board following seventh period when Leah came in. She hadn't even heard her enter the room, just the squeak of the desk as she sat. Clara clapped her hands to remove the chalk dust. She smiled, but Leah's smile in return was faint. They had already hugged earlier, during fifth-period English lit. "What is it?" Clara asked.

Leah nodded at the door, and Clara reluctantly shut it. She knew she was not supposed to be in an enclosed room with a student. Leah's hair was unwashed and stringy, and she wore a boy's baggy sweatshirt with an Iron Maiden print on the front. "I'm so glad you're back, Mrs. Warren. I wish you could stay."

Clara smiled. In truth it had felt good to be up on her feet in front of the room, leading discussions, telling stories, parsing words. She still carried a small, energized glow from the day. She had realized how wrapped inside herself she had been these last few weeks, tangled up in her own problems. She belonged here in the classroom. Perhaps she even belonged in this town. "Oh, you'll see me again. Once this baby gets born."

Outside in the parking lot they heard cars starting and loud boasting about the game this coming Friday, the blast of celebratory music to signal freedom from school's daily oppression. Clara had the windows open to let in a cool breeze and cleanse the room from the lingering odors of the flour-sack babies. The big green felt curtains stirred slightly as an icy breeze that tasted of blowing grit passed through them.

Leah chewed at her nails, already ragged. "Do you still think about him?"

"I do."

"He talked about you all the time. He was obsessed with your class. It was all your stories of battle and warriors."

Her feet aching from the long day, Clara sat on the edge of her desk.

"I've been going to Kelan's house after school," Leah went on. "We can do whatever we want down in his basement. His mom doesn't care. Kelan knows stuff. He knows things that you wouldn't believe. Have you ever done a séance, Mrs. Warren?" She trailed her finger along the smooth surface of the desk.

"You should really be talking to a counselor, Leah."

"I am. Useless old prick over in Fell

261

Creek. My dad makes me go." She tapped her nails on the desk.

Leah's eyes looked cagey, darting about the room. "Do you hear the coyotes? Sometimes it sounds like they're right under my window. Like they've followed me home, and they're just waiting for me to go outside. Everyone in town is talking about them."

"They belonged to Seth, didn't they?"

Leah nodded. "They were the only thing he loved, really. He said the world hates them, but they find a way to survive. He wouldn't let any of us go near them, even though Kelan begged him. Seth said they were dangerous." Leah exhaled and then tugged at her baggy sweatshirt. "I must look like shit."

Is this what she had come to tell Clara, that she was damaged now? People could see Clara's damage, the bad hand, the person who could never be whole. She wanted to tell Leah that she was beautiful, that she would find someone to love her one day, and that all of this would seem like one bad dream she'd woken from, but she didn't say any of those things.

Leah's mascara ran in black streams from the corners of her eyes. "I'm so messed up." The sound of footsteps clumping past in the hallway outside made her tense. "I have

262

to go now."

"You come see me anytime, okay?"

Leah hugged her once more, burying her face in Clara's shoulder. "I gotta get out of this fucking town," she said, and then she was gone.

In the quiet of the room, Clara went to the back and sat at Seth's desk, the princely island of space around the desk still in force with him dead. She had to wedge her big stomach to fit in, and the wooden chair groaned under her weight. The desks had iron legs painted copper and wooden lids the students could lift up to store their textbooks and papers within deep cavities. Clara lifted the lid and peered inside. Empty, except for the heavy textbook Seth had dropped to the floor to silence the other students the first day of class.

On a hunch, Clara cracked open the book and flipped to the pages at the front where the Beowulf text was laid out. The students weren't supposed to write in their books, but intricate illustrations decorated Seth's. He'd been scrawling the runic letters she had taught, just like at the bottom of the drawing someone left at her house. *HeWhoSleeps is waking. HeWhoSleeps has heard our call. HeWhoSleeps is coming. HeWho-*

Sleeps will bring death to us all. The final rune smeared, as if he'd drawn it in a hurry.

Clara touched the runes with her hands, felt the grooves the words cut into the paper. He'd pressed down hard with his pen, almost tearing the page. His last week in class, Seth had turned sullen, let his hair hood his eyes. He'd known even then what he was about to do, was talking to the demon inside him. The skin prickled on the back of her neck. Clara stood and shut the window against the chilly wind blowing in.

THE WILDING

He drank until he blacked out most nights, and in the dark, feverish phantasms troubled Grizz's sleep. Every morning his head throbbed, but he liked the hurt. He woke with the shakes, with cotton mouth; he woke in strange places, once out on the lawn with dirt under his nails, smelling of the grave, once in Seth's bed, surrounded by the boy's animal smell, a scent of wet leaves and sweat, where he had looked up to see his son's *Heavy Metal* movie poster, a drawing of a leather-clad blonde riding a winged demon through the clouds, pinned to the ceiling above him.

The Dakota who once roamed this land did not speak the name of the dead. To speak the name of the dead was to call their ghost from the hunting grounds, to ask for possession, but Seth's name swelled in his brain like a wood tick, feeding on blood and regret. His thoughts kept circling back to the day of the shooting, Seth loping to town with the gun against his ribs, the pastor's wife in her basement hideaway, Will Gunderson pulling up in his cruiser, the field of sheltering corn calling to his boy. It was all there, all the story he needed, but the pieces wouldn't fit together right inside him. All he needed to do was believe in his son's cold rage. And then in his mind's eye he saw the trapping cabin with its gutted creatures sewn together in unnatural ways, Seth tied to the chair, his eyes rolling back in his head as Will took pliers to the tender skin under his ribs and pinched it in the metal, twisting until Seth screamed. No. Maybe that was the story he made up to absolve Seth of his evil. Two darknesses canceling each other out.

The muscles in his shoulders and arms ached as if he'd been swinging something heavy the night before. A memory, a tiny blood-dark spot, spread in his brain. He had done it, he knew deep down under the throb of his headache: stolen his son's own body from the funeral home and buried him up on the mountain. Grizz dressed in the clothes he had tossed on his floor the night before, chewed four aspirin from a bottle beside the bathroom sink, and after rinsing his face and combing his hair and beard, he got into his truck and drove to town.

Trinity Lutheran had the classic clapboard siding of a country church. It stood as a remnant of another time, a whitewashed vision of the past that Grizz's family had a role in preserving as much as any of them. His great-grandfather had donated the land the church was built on, and Grizz's name was still on the membership rolls, though he had not darkened the door of this place since Jo's death.

He pulled up out front, parked his truck against the curb, and climbed the steep concrete stairs. The heavy oaken door groaned when he squeezed the handle and yanked it open. From inside a stained-glass window on one side showed Jesus in the Garden of Gethsemene, his face upturned in prayer. Roads curved through the countryside behind Jesus, leading to a hill with three crosses, and Grizz stopped to trace the pathway with his fingers, as he had done when he was a boy. Early evening light leaked through the rosy glass to touch him where he stood.

The anguish on Christ's face made him think of Seth. When he was thirteen Seth went through a stage where he slept with his lights on. At night Grizz heard him grumble as he twisted in his sheets and strove for sleep and it sounded to him as if there was another voice in there, a lower timbre, a voice like footsteps crushing leaves. Seth cried out because his bones were stretching inside him, his muscles lengthening, even the bones in his face shifting. Black hairs sprouted around his mouth and under his arms, and a rash of blackheads and acne spread on his face and back, sores that wept when he scrubbed them. Grizz had forgotten how much being a teenage boy hurt, the strange aches and pains, but when Seth got sick, throwing up after meals, refusing to get out of bed in the morning, Grizz knew this wasn't ordinary growing pains.

In the examining room, the nurse had paid the boy compliments as Seth sat up on the papery sheet without his shirt on, his back and chest blotched with acne. "Such a fine young man," she said, winking in Grizz's direction. "You play football?"

Seth mumbled his response.

"He doesn't like organized sports," Grizz offered for him. "He doesn't like taking instructions."

Seth slumped on the table, his head down, not looking at either of them. He'd quit the team the year before, just stripped off his padding and helmet and walked right off the field without looking back. He'd been fast. The best runner in the school, but the coach said he was a negative influence on the others.

"That's too bad," she said, before leaving the room.

"Why are we here, Dad?"

"We need to know for sure."

"They won't be able to do anything. They couldn't for Mom."

"You don't know that." Grizz ran his hands along the seam of his jeans, looked away. "They've made advances since then." Jo hadn't ever complained. He wasn't even sure how much the lupus hurt her. She took her pills and went to bed early when the flare-ups were worst. Sometimes, when she snapped at him for smelling of the barn, for the way working with cattle seeped into his skin, under his nails, he told himself it was the lupus, the pain of being eaten up from the inside out, speaking.

"They call me freak at school."

"Don't pay them any mind."

Grizz knew this was bad advice. Ignoring bullies only made them grow worse, inventing more devious methods of inflicting pain, verbal or physical, to draw a reaction, but when he looked up he saw Seth was studying him, his eyes curious. "How did Mom

269

live with it? You never talk about her."

Grizz had always had a hard time talking about Jo. He thought about what to say now, not wanting to describe her illness. Sometimes Seth smiled his small secret smile because there was music inside him when he was alone in his thoughts. And Grizz had to turn away, the familiar expression reminding him too sharply of the boy's mother. Seth's hand for drawing, his fancy-flighting, his desperate capacity to love the wrong things: all this he inherited from her.

"She wanted a baby more than anything," he began. They talked awhile longer, the two of them in the examining room, not looking at one another. He told Seth about how his mother liked old folk songs. He told about how she longed to see the ocean, and here he fell into the story without meaning to. They had started on a trip to Florida a few years before Seth was born but broke down right outside Seaforth, only a hundred miles away. "The money for the trip went to pay for a new tranny instead. At the motel that night she filled the tub, added in bath salts. We put on our suits and climbed in." He smiled at the memory. "Sure, she cried a little, but then she shut her eyes. 'Tell me how it is,' she said. Well, I had never been, so I did my best."

A knock came at the door, Dr. Salverson with his news, but they already knew what he had to say.

"Mr. Fallon? Seth?" The pastor's voice calling him by his Christian name startled Grizz. No one called him Seth anymore. The pastor must have heard the door open and come looking. He didn't look much older than an altar boy himself, a thin spiderweb of a beard around his mouth, pale hair and skin. His eyes skimmed over Grizz, noting the mud spattering his jeans, the dirt around his collar, his very nails black with it.

"I've come to ask you something," Grizz said.

"Let's go to my office and talk."

They stopped at a fountain where the pastor took a paper cup from a dispenser and filled it to offer to Grizz. After Grizz refused, they continued down the hallway to the pastor's office, where he gestured toward a seat and retreated behind his desk. "I want to tell you how sorry I am about your son," he said as he sat down in his swivel chair.

Grizz stayed standing but took off his seed cap and kneaded it in his hands. "I'd like you to come out to my property and do a private ceremony. A cleansing or blessing to get rid of bad spirits. Whatever you people call it. I'm asking on behalf of the boy's mother."

Pastor Logan coughed, then sipped some of his water, his frown deepening. "You mean like an exorcism? I don't know. It's not really something Lutherans do. But maybe after the funeral —"

"There isn't going to be any funeral."

"Pardon?"

"Not here. My son won't be buried with your suicides."

Pastor Logan swiveled in his chair, nervous. "You got the permit the county said you were after?"

"No."

"Then he's going to be cremated?"

"They didn't mention that option at the funeral home."

"I've been thinking about it for some time now. It might be a good way around this . . . impasse."

Grizz continued to twist his hat in his hands. "I haven't met anyone who buries people that way." He thought of his uncle Harry who lost his hand in an accident with the corn picker. He retrieved it and kept it up in his icebox all his life, among the rump roasts and frozen peas. When he died, he was buried with it so the Lord could resurrect him properly for Judgment Day.

Logan nodded and went on. "Regarding your son, I am bound by the church's rules and bylaws, like it or not. What I mean is that if Seth was cremated we could put all of this behind us."

Grizz felt his mind clicking, justifying his actions. "You're not following. How would he be resurrected then, if he was only ashes?"

"I follow. But God doesn't play by our rules. It says in the Bible that we will be given new bodies in heaven. New bodies, a new earth."

Grizz hadn't come to argue over such things. Cremation, strangely, hadn't crossed his mind. It was not something done in his experience. You died and you were put in a box and your place in death reflected your place in life. To be ashes, dust. It was what people did in the Cities. Or like the Hindus or Vikings. But it didn't matter, not after what he'd done. "What I am asking is for you to come out to the house and speak a few words."

The pastor began to massage the center of his forehead. "There is something I'm not understanding here."

Even in his tiredness Grizz could see why.

"Headache?"

"It feels like nails were driven there."

"You been drinking the water from that fountain regular-like?"

"Sure."

Grizz said nothing.

"Is there something wrong with this water?"

"Well, for one thing it's so full of minerals you could build a bridge with it. There's rust in it, and even if the fountain is new, the pipes that bring the water in are full of lead."

"And no one has told me until now?"

"Everyone knows. Makes me shit fire biscuits every time I drink it. But it won't kill you. Long as you let that faucet run for a while so the lead can drain out."

He sighed, appearing even paler than before, and blinked at Grizz with his watery eyes. "Look, Mr. Fallon. There's no easy way to talk about this, but we need to speak plainly about your son's death. Your son was baptized here. He was a child of God."

"The only thing that matters to me or anyone else is that he was my child, a Fallon. That name means something in this town."

Logan leaned forward and set his elbows

on the desk. "I know that you feel perse-cuted."

"What do you know about my family? About this town?"

"I know about the accident that killed your father. I know that you did time in Sauk County for statutory rape. And that the girl waited for you until she was eigh-teen, and she married you before the justice of the peace, despite her family's objections. I know this wife died shortly after giving birth to Seth and that you raised him alone. I can only imagine how hard it was for you."

Grizz froze. What had Steve Krieger told this man? Steve had been the one so many years ago to encourage Jo's family to press charges against Grizz after he caught them in the backseat of Grizz's Impala. Grizz had been thinking that the pastor might be an impartial witness as an outsider. Once he came out to his property he planned to tell him about that shack in the woods. But if Steve had already painted him as crazy or criminal it might not be any use. That word "accident." How had he pronounced it?

"They say your great-grandfather was at the hangings in Mankato. They say he was the one who cut the ropes that dropped thirty-eight Indians to their deaths. They say one of those Indians laid a curse on your family and that you bring bad luck to the area."

Grizz smiled grimly. "They say all that, but they don't tell you about the water?"

"Some is stuff I've been reading in the archives in the library. It's been a hard week. I wanted to understand. I know about the statues, why you make them."

Grizz went ahead and sat down. He was quiet for a long time. "Do you know when Seth was only thirteen he bit a boy in his class?"

"I know he was troubled. That he had a history —"

"I'm not talking just teeth marks. He bit a chunk out of the boy's face and swallowed it. The other boy needed surgery. No one bullied Seth ever again. Instead he became the bully. He became the nightmare."

The pastor sat back in his chair. "It doesn't do any good to think about those things now."

"I can't stop. I can't stop thinking about the day he came into town. I still don't understand. Seth was violent. He could be cruel, but something like this — it was beyond even him."

"You may have to live with not knowing." His hands traced his thin beard, and he was quiet for a moment. "You ever hear of sin eaters?"

Grizz shook his head.

"The Welsh had a tradition. When a person was dying they brought in a sin eater, some outcast from the community. They put bread on the one dying and let it soak in the sins. Then the sin eater stepped forward and ate the bread."

"What are you saying?"

"In unhealthy systems, I'm talking families or communities, there will be a scapegoat. I know that's what they've done to you. I'm telling you that I'm on your side, Mr. Fallon. You're not an outcast in my eyes. Whatever they told me, it doesn't matter. Whatever it is you think happened that day, it's over if you want it to be. I only know that we need to put your son to rest."

"You believe in hell?"

"Yes."

"You think my boy is in hell?"

"I don't know. I'm not God."

"But the Bible has to be awful clear on this point. He committed murder then shot himself. If I want to see my boy again, then I need . . ."

When Grizz couldn't finish his sentence, Logan added, "I don't know what was happening in Seth's head when he went out there. It's said that nothing can separate us from the love of God, no power or principality. I believe in your son's baptism. I believe that God loved your son. And I know that God loves you. Do you believe that?"

"No."

"I don't have any such thing as a cleansing service. Not like what you're asking for. But I will come out to your land and pray with you. I will break bread with you."

"It's for his mother. His mother would want it."

"It's for you that I'm coming."

Grizz didn't even make it out of town before he saw cherries in his rear view mirror. Jesus, just what he needed. He pulled off along the edge of a slough. Sheriff Steve let him stew for a good minute before he got out and approached his truck. He paused, studying the cargo Grizz had left in the pickup's bed and then plucked out a crowbar. He used this to tap against the window, which Grizz rolled down reluctantly.

"Mind shutting off the engine?"

"I do. I don't know if she'll restart."

With his other hand, the sheriff reached past Grizz and twisted the keys. The engine coughed and stuttered to a halt. When it was quiet he went on calmly. "I got a call from the funeral home this morning. A break-in. Someone pried open the back door with a tool of some sort or another. They must have done it last night."

Grizz said nothing while Steve tapped his door with the crowbar.

"How do you like that? Only thing missing was a corpse. The body of your son. Can you imagine it? Who would do such a thing?"

Grizz looked off down the road. He didn't owe him a single word.

"It's a strange thing, isn't it? I know from Nolan your discussion with county authorities didn't go so well."

"It's true. I had to get part of my land declared a cemetery. It might take months."

"So, you know why I pulled you over?"

"Not really."

"You don't seem too concerned that the body of your only child has gone missing."

Grizz shrugged.

"I'm going to ask you politely just once. Did you bury him up on the mountain, Seth? It's what I would have done. Why don't you take me and show me the spot where you put him?"

"Why don't you go fuck yourself?"

Again, he moved quickly, or maybe Grizz was so beyond exhaustion he hardly saw straight. He felt the fist rather than saw it, smashing into the side of his face. His mouth filled with blood. When he bent over, streams of it gushed into his lap, a lone tooth in the hot rush of fluid.

Out of the corner of his eye he saw Steve massaging his knuckles. "I could arrest you right now, goddamnit. I found this crowbar in your truck, the tarp you probably used to drag his body through the woods. You tampered with state evidence when you took his body. You committed a felony when you broke into the home. I should, but I won't. You want to know why? Then all this mess stays on people's minds. Then I have to deal with another set of reporters coming in from outside asking questions, hounding our schoolkids and parents. We take care of our own messes here, Grizz, and your family is the biggest mess of all. Has been from the very beginning."

A car passed them on the road, and the sheriff turned away to lift his hat, likely smiling to let them know that there was nothing happening over here. Grizz rubbed his chin, checking to see if the jawbone was broken. His tongue found the empty place where the tooth had been knocked out. He sopped the strings of blood from his chin with his sleeve, thinking, *When the time comes I am*

*going to hit you back, again and again and
again, until I smash every bone in your face.*

When the car was gone, the sheriff leaned
in, resting his elbows on the window. He
went on in his subdued voice, "They're all
dead now, all except you. Kind of makes
you wonder, don't it?"

"What are you talking about?" His words
slurred; he needed to hold on to his rage to
make it home.

"Your dad. Will. Seth. Jo." Jo had been
Steve's second cousin, his godchild. "And
the whole time you were over in Sauk
County, she waited for you. She was so
damned stubborn. Why anyone would come
here to live with you, even knowing what
you are, is a mystery to me. Why she wanted
you."

"Jo was happy."

"Then you had to go and get her pregnant.
You knew what would happen. You could
have taken care of matters. There were ways
even then. Can you imagine if you had? She
would still be alive. Will might still be alive.
This whole ungodly mess would never have
happened."

"No. Jo was sick. Even if it wasn't for the
childbirth, the lupus would have killed her
within a couple of years. Doc said so."

"All dead, all except you," he repeated.

281

He tapped the side of the door with the crowbar again and then tossed it back into the pickup's bed. "Here's how the rest of this is going to shake down. A few weeks from now a group of us will come combine your corn. The money will go to Nolan, to pay his expenses and for his discretion."

"I need that money to pay the bank."

"You should've thought of that before you tried this stunt. Stupid, so fucking stupid."

Grizz had only one bit of leverage. "I know about the hunting cabin," he said. "I know that Will Gunderson took people there. I've seen the inside."

Steve was shaking his head. "You best forget such rumors. It won't do you any good to think about it."

Grizz gripped the steering wheel. "I saw those things he made with my own eyes. You know what I'm talking about, don't you?"

"No, I can't say I do." He swallowed the dry air, spit in the road. "Listen, Grizz, the money will also pay for a stone, right in the section where I said he was going to be buried. Far as the rest of the town will know, your son was buried in a private ceremony. Only you and Nolan and I will know different. You say anything to anybody, try any more stunts like this, and I send cadaver dogs onto your property, and I will find and dig up the body and put it where it belongs according to the law. I will make sure you do jail time for this, and you'll lose the farm for sure. Are we understood? Next time, you'll lose more than a few teeth. This is what mercy feels like. I'm letting you go for the good of this town. You hear me, Seth Fallon Sr.? This is over. The end."

Grizz smiled through his blood. "There isn't any ending," he said as he turned the keys.

Clara and Logan were in the kitchen carving pumpkins when Stormy Gayle announced on the radio that coyotes had attacked a small child in town. She didn't say the boy's name, just that he lived near the edge of town, and he'd been playing in his backyard when his mother heard him scream. By the time she made it out of the house the boy rushed toward her across the lawn. "They were trying to eat me up, Mama! Wolves!"

A mouth-sized chunk of his parka was missing, down spilling out. The child told his mother the coyotes had tried to drag him toward the trees, but they got scared by the roar of a leaf blower over in the next yard.

The town's part-time mayor, a chain-smoking lawyer named Brian Neske, coughed into the microphone. "It's one thing," he told Stormy, "to lose a cat or small dog. But when our children are threatened we must take action. I want to assure listeners that the authorities are doing everything possible. We've called in an expert from the DNR, and traps have been set. If you have a dog or cat, don't let it wander outside, especially not at night. If the coyotes don't get it, we've laced meat with antifreeze and spread it around the woods. And if you have small children, don't leave them unaccompanied in the yard or even walking to school."

"Would they attack a full-grown adult?" Stormy asked.

"It's not likely. These are scavengers. Dangerous ones, but we'll catch them before the week is out. I'm here to announce a bounty. You can already get ten dollars a pelt at the county courthouse, and remember, you don't even need a permit to shoot coyotes. Consider it your civic duty."

"Will you shut that off?" Clara asked Logan. The news story was the last thing she wanted to hear. She had trouble believing those coyotes had attacked a small child. Not the same ones who had encircled her. If she shut her eyes, she could still feel the gray's coarse black nose against the softness of her palm. Now Seth's coyotes were hunted things.

Clara sat Indian-style on a floor spread with newspapers, sawing open the skull of a pumpkin with a serrated knife. Once it was properly lobotomized, she lifted off the lid, rolled up her shirtsleeves, and scooped inside. Soon her hands reeked sweetly of the orange guts, but she didn't mind the mess.

"What's that supposed to be?" Logan asked after he turned off the radio. He'd carved his pumpkin to look cross-eyed, finishing with a gap-toothed smile. His pumpkin-bumpkin, he called it.

"What do you think?" Clara's had moon-sliver irises. Long incisors dangled from the cavern of the mouth.

"Looks a little ghoulish for a fall festival at a church."

"I'll take that as a compliment." Clara plopped handfuls of orange goop on the newspapers, carefully sorting seeds into a colander. She planned to dry the seeds overnight on wax paper, salt, and bake them crisp in olive oil tomorrow night. "But if you must know this is Grendel's mother."

"Ah, I should have guessed. Isn't she the last monster old what's-his-name has to fight?"

"She's the second. There's always another monster in epics. Until you die. It's the third, a dragon, that slays Beowulf, leaving Wiglaf to moon over his body as an age of darkness spreads over the land."

"Gloomy business, being a hero." Logan thumped his gourd on the ground and wobbled it in the direction of Clara's. "Prepare for battle, foul-smelling hell wench. It is I, Beowulf, wooer of maidens, mighty mead drinker, all around ass kicker. You will be smoten."

Clara smiled. It was good to be here in the warm kitchen with him. This was the Logan who had made her laugh when they first started dating. "How will you smite me if you have no sword?"

"Oh," he said. "I have a sword."

She was about to say something really naughty, but just as she was making the last cut, a slit under the eyes to represent a scar, the knife slipped and swiped across her left palm. Clara didn't feel anything. She lifted up her hand, fascinated. Bright blood mingled with cords of orange pulp that dropped wetly to the newspaper. Across from her, Logan said something as he reached for her. The knife clattered to the floor. Clara heard an oceanic sound in her ears, and she stood too quickly, making for the sink, wanting to wash the wound, and slipped on the slimy newspapers. She managed to twist as she fell, but still struck the linoleum hard enough that her breath was punched from her lungs.

Logan knelt beside her as she caught her breath. He wrapped a kitchen towel around her hand, pressing down to apply pressure. "You okay?"

She blinked up at him. "I think so." Her other hand went to her stomach. At least she hadn't landed right on it, but she couldn't feel the baby. She shut her eyes and sent out a prayer. *Are you all right? Mommy's sorry she scared you.* In answer, a wave of nausea made her rest her head on the cool floor.

She felt a stinging sensation in her hand as Logan dabbed at the wound. "Doesn't look too deep," he said. "I think we can bandage this, but you knocked yourself a good one when you fell."

Clumsy girl. Look at what you've done.

"We should get you to the hospital, get you checked out."

"You think so?" A new terrible thought branched inside her. What if there was no baby? What if the baby was lost? Here now, all Logan's attention focused on her hand. What would happen to the fragile peace they had built once the baby arrived? And yet she was grateful when Logan insisted

288

they go to the hospital to get her checked out.

The drive to Fell Creek took them into a starless dark split only by their headlights. The highway rose up out of the river valley, out onto flat, open prairies, passing isolated farmhouses, each huddled next to its own yard lamp and shelterbelt of trees. Clara shut her eyes and imagined what would happen if they just kept going past the hospital, past Mankato, all the way up to their old life in the Twin Cities. They didn't talk, but Logan drove with one hand on the wheel, the other lightly touching her arm.

After the on-call doctor probed the wound with iodine and mummified it in fresh gauze, he bid Clara undress and put on a papery gown so he could check her for vaginal bleeding. The doctor was middle aged, a thick barrel mustache around his mouth, the ends like tusks. "Why don't you wait in the other room?" he asked Logan in a firm voice. It didn't sound like a suggestion.

"I'm staying." The doctor frowned, the ends of his mustache drooping, and had Clara climb up on the examining table, put her legs in the air. He snapped on his on rubber gloves and hovered over her, pressing at her belly and side, then hard against the inside of her thighs as he inched up the gown. When his fingers slipped inside her without warning, Clara gasped audibly.

"That hurt?" he said.

She nodded, more shocked than anything.

He drew out his hand and studied the glove. "You're not bleeding at least."

No, just violated, she thought. Clara's gynecologist, Dr. Frank, was a tall beanpole of a man who reminded her of Ichabod Crane, but his hands and voice were gentle, and she trusted him in a way she didn't trust this man.

With his stethoscope, he pressed up near her breasts before moving it to her stomach. "Sounds just fine in there. Little savage beating on his drum." He turned to Logan. "You wanna hear it?"

Logan came over and put the stethoscope in his ears. His eyes found Clara's while he listened to the baby.

On the drive home, he didn't hold her hand. The pure country darkness of the open prairies spread all around them, swallowing up the Nova. Clara had never imagined a darkness so vast.

"I'm scared, too," Logan said after a long silence between them.

She didn't have to ask about what.

"I never really imagined myself as a father.

This is going to sound strange, but babies scare the shit out of me. Every time I do a baptism in church I'm always worried I'm going to drop one. They're in these long, ruffly gowns, squirming all around. How can anything so small even survive in this world?"

Love, she thought. A mother's love should be the most powerful force on earth. She hoped it would be true of her when the time came and that Logan would find the same inside himself. "Maybe, it's more natural than we think. How many couples out there actually feel prepared for the baby when it comes?"

She looked away. The road bent, and her stomach lurched as they began the steep descent into the valley. Traveler, she thought, "one who travails." The old word promising the birth of both suffering and wisdom. She felt a sudden sense of vertigo as the road dropped. The woods, the shade, the wolves, the mountain she had never seen. She was afraid, too, but also relieved to be away from the open prairies. Whatever happened, this was where they were meant to be.

Logan squeezed her hand. "What I'm try-ing to tell you is that tonight, hearing the baby's heartbeat, I'm glad the baby is fine."

"Our baby," she added.

Clara had moved back in with her father following her brutal fight with her fiancé Gregory. She was between jobs and apartments, between just plain everything. By the time Clara came to live with him, Stanley had also been on dialysis for two years.

A hospice nurse came to visit in the mornings, because his kidneys were failing. When Clara got home from her new job waiting tables at a local diner, she went around correcting the woman's mistakes, shutting the drapes and curtains in rooms throughout the house, the way her father liked it. Her father had been a fearful man, as if he were waiting for someone to come punish him for his past.

As Clara shut the curtains, she imagined her father's slow terror as the nurse insisted on throwing them open, exposing him to the world. He lay on the bed like some creature fallen from primeval trees, his fingernails coiling like a sloth's talons. She would need to cut them, since the nurse refused. Her father trembled when she came in, blinking up into the light when she turned on the lamp beside him. The IV beside his bed dripped steadily into the taped and bruised opening in his arms. "Hello, Daddy," she said.

"Clarie." His voice was a husk of itself.

"They drain you again today?" Tuesdays another nurse also came, trundling in a dialysis machine that siphoned out his blood and ran it through a filter.

"Vampires."

Clara squeezed his hand. "Vampires don't put fresh blood back inside you."

"It's what she called me here, living in the dark."

"That bitch. You want me to call and complain again? She shouldn't be opening your curtains when both of us have told her not to."

"No use."

"Did she clean your bedsores?"

He coughed wetly. The nurse, a woman named Regina, would scrub him raw and bloody, or not at all, leaving his sores to fester. Sometimes Clara had to clean him, a task she dreaded. When she pressed her hand on his forehead, the skin felt clammy. The nurse had told her that he wouldn't live to see the snow melt. He was going to die and take his secrets with him. Clara went into the bathroom and fetched fingernail clippers. Stanley's eyes were shut when she came back in the room, his breathing raspy. She cut ivory half-moons from his left hand, holding the palm gingerly, careful not to draw blood. Each snip of the clippers made his eyelashes flutter, but other than that there was no response. "I want to know about my mother. I want to know if you loved her."

A vein pulsed thinly at his temple, the only sign of his irritation. "I've told you everything you need to know."

"You've spoken in riddles. When you're gone I'm going to go looking for her."

One rheumy eye flicked open. "You must never go back there."

"Why not?"

But the eye had sealed shut again and soon, despite her questions and her clipping, he was asleep. Clara carried the curving nails into the bathroom where she balled them up in a tissue and discarded them in the waste bin. She went back into his room, pulled up the sheets around him, and was turning up the dials on his electric blanket when the doorbell rang. Clara frowned. If this was the nurse Regina, she was going to have words with her.

But waiting for her on the porch was a young man in a dark coat, his face chapped by blowing wind and snow.

"Can I help you?"

"You must be his daughter, Clara."

"I am." Clara hadn't invited him in yet. The house's heat rushed out the door, another thing her penny-pinching father disliked. "Who are you?"

He pulled off leather gloves and held out his hand. "I'm Pastor Logan," he said. His eyes were pale blue, almost turquoise, with lovely lashes. He had whitish-blond hair, high cheekbones. Clara held his perfectly smooth hand in hers, which he must have taken as an invitation to come inside. "I'm sorry to bother you, but I was coming home from church, and I saw your car in the driveway."

Uninvited, he took off his coat and hung it from a peg. Clara shut the door reluctantly. She saw his collar now, the dark clerical shirt. His presence here, his seeming familiarity, bothered her. "I still don't know why you're here."

His brow furrowed. "I'm your father's pastor, from St. Mark's Lutheran a few blocks down. Your dad didn't mention me?"

"I didn't even know my dad went to church."

"Oh, Stanley's been a member for years. He even served on the council before he started dialysis."

In the foyer's tight space she was aware of his aftershave, a hint of cinnamon, and underneath the earthy scent of his skin. "We didn't even go to church growing up."

He absorbed this as if it was old news to him. "How's Stanley doing?"

"The same." There was something airy and elemental about the pastor's Nordic good looks, his gleaming white teeth.

"Would you mind if I gave him communion?" He held up a slender black case.

"I doubt he's even awake. He's just had his dialysis treatment." For some reason she felt angry with this pastor and with her father for not telling her, as if he was leading a secret life. And it was a good secret, unlike the rest of what he kept from her, but it bothered her the same.

"Okay if I look in on him? I've been coming every week."

Clara relented, and when they went into his bedroom, her father's eyes were open, and he even smiled for the young pastor. Clara looked at her father with a sense of mingled wonder and betrayal. After all these fiercely agnostic years, the old man had been taking religion on the side. Was he taking out insurance with the reaper knocking? His eyes blinked in the lamplight, hooded by furry gray brows. He had a lifelong drinker's face, his nose split with red veins. "I'm so glad you got to meet my Clara," he said. "She's living with me, just temporarily. She's a student, you know, a linguist. She's going to be a professor one day."

"Yes, I know." The pastor turned toward her, smiling. "He talks about you all the time. It's good that you're here with him." He set his black case down on the nightstand and cracked it open. Inside, plastic cups shaped like thimbles nestled in red velvet lining. He took out the cups along with a canister of wine and a thin tube packed with crackers. "Would you like to join us?" he asked Clara.

"No," she said, crossing her arms.

The pastor filled the small cups with wine, his hands shaking so that some spilled on the nightstand. She saw that he was preparing her father to cross over, to go somewhere she couldn't follow. It shouldn't have mattered, the stale wafers, the bitter wine, but when the pastor said, "This is my body, broken for you," snapping the wafer in half and placing it on her father's tongue, the old man exhaled lightly, his eyelashes fluttering. And when he said, "This is my blood, spilled for you," and tipped the cup past her father's cracking lips, he shut his eyes and his breathing deepened, as though

297

the wine were spreading inside him, cleansing impurities. Clara looked away, her eyes full.

The young pastor visited twice a week, and Clara found herself timing her day so that she would be home when he arrived. Sometimes, when her father was sleeping, they went into the kitchen and talked.

"The closest I've come to religion is reading Rilke," she told him one afternoon. " 'For beauty is nothing / but the beginning of terror,' " she recited from memory.

" 'Which we still are just able to endure,' " he continued, surprising her, " 'and we are so awed because it serenely disdains / to annihilate us. Every angel is terrifying.' "

Clara cupped her face in her hands, leaned toward him. "You know the *Duino Elegies*?"

"I read them in the original German the year I studied abroad. I adore Rilke." He was quiet for a moment, considering. "Rilke says that we live out our lives in the horizontal." He drew his hand slowly along the surface of the table, "but every now and then, even in an ordinary life, we touch the vertical." He lifted his hands from the table, spread them. "We get some glimpse of heaven. Faith is like that. Most of the time, I don't sense God. I stumble through my days as blind as the next person, but every now and then I touch the vertical."

Somewhere during this recitation, Clara had touched his hand unconsciously after he lowered it to the table, and she held on. They had both blushed when they realized, and even then she hadn't let go.

After they returned from the hospital, Clara lay in bed waiting for the baby to rise as a fish does from the depths. Why was she so sure this child was a boy? *The boys cause the most trouble,* the widows told her. Logan sighed in his sleep beside her, tired out from the drive, but Clara was stirred up. Gusts of wind and rain shook and rattled the house. The north window flexed inward like a membrane, and outside the bare maples scraped one another.

Mother. Clara's first ghost, her childhood imaginary companion. In the wind she heard her mother trying to get home through the snow. The snow was coming, a winter out of time. Clara's eyes grew heavy, lulled by the sound of falling water. She shut them for a moment, but somewhere distantly a door banging open and shut woke her. The wind moaned long and low, and it was so cold in the room she wanted only to nestle under the covers, spooned against her husband. Her left hand hurt, the missing fingers stretching out in the dark, regrowing from the nubs. The pure pain of it popped her eyes open.

She was here in the room, having arrived with the storm. Clara heard her before she saw her, the sound of dripping, a board groaning. She had plugged a night-light into the wall so she wouldn't have to stumble around if she needed to use the bathroom, but the bulb crackled and went out. In the new darkness, Clara sensed her near the bed, a deepening of shadow. Logan turned over in his sleep, muttering incoherently. The floorboards creaked again, a sound like a sigh. Clara pushed up against the headboard, shut her eyes to banish her. The nerves in her hurt hand bristled.

"I'm sorry, Mother. You've been out there the whole time, and now you have a new companion in the suicide corner, don't you? Did he wake you up from your sleep? I heard about you, Mother. I know your story now. Go away."

Clara opened her eyes again, and in the pitch of the room she saw her. The woman's hair rose and fell as though the wind had come inside along with her. Her skin blue as moonlight on snow. Her hospital gown shimmering. She looked cold, covered by a

300

sheen of thin ice melting and pooling in a puddle at her feet.

"He left you, didn't he? Left you out to die in the snow, so he could carry me back. And now you're angry with me. That's it, isn't it? You would have been free and alive if it wasn't for me?"

The woman carried something in her arms, a bundle in the shape of a child. A present for her daughter. The bundle squirmed.

Clara heard a thin screaming. A child lost somewhere and crying for help. Then the blanket her mother held out to her un-wrapped. What spilled out at first looked like a baby but was white as a corpse. The child was no more than a round ball of mag-gots, seething and boiling. These maggots spread up the woman's arms, burrowing into her blue skin or unfurling one by one before dropping to the floor. The crying turned to a shriek, full throated. Her mother was still coming toward her even as the maggots ate her alive, her icy skin peeling away in clumps until she was bone, a skel-eton woman, a skull with livid dark hair. She reached for Clara, disintegrating as she came.

Then the light switched on, and Logan, above her, pressed a finger to her lips.

Her throat ached. She had been scream-ing. She had been the one making that aw-ful sound.

He stroked her forehead. "You're burning up," he said.

He brought her Tylenol.

Clara took the pills and watched as he toweled up a spill of water on the floor — she had knocked over her glass in her sleep.

She and Logan were a young couple with too few belongings to fill a big parsonage echoing with a century's worth of memories. When you walk in a place, she thought, spill blood, surely the echoes of your passing remain long after you were there.

A Good Day's Work

His wife Jo's last summer had been a scorching season like the one that just ended, nights so hot the two of them slept naked, an evening ritual. He would shut off the lamp, disrobe, and cross the room where she waited for him atop the marriage quilt her mother had sewn. As soon as he lay down she straddled him, her skin feverish. When she kissed him their mouths smacked together, and her breath was hot on his neck before she bit down. His shoulders were tattooed with these teeth marks, wounds that never quite healed. She had never been like this and would never be like it again. It didn't matter how bone sore or sun sapped he might be from working in the fields because her hunger for him had no end, and sometimes he thought she wanted to swallow him, sate herself with his mineral and salt, take him inside her and make something new.

When he shuddered into her, he prayed that what was dark in him would not root in her womb and that what was light in her would instead bear fruit. He prayed that the sins of the father would not follow the son, and if some summer nights he hesitated at the foot of the bed, he could not be blamed any more than he could possibly resist her summons. Summer passed in this way, and her belly did not melon-swell, and some mornings he caught her kneading the flatness of her stomach, praying fervently over and over the way farmers pray for rain in the dry season. God heard her, eventually, and gave them Seth.

When Seth was a boy he threw the most terrible tantrums, and all Grizz could do was hold him while he thrashed and frothed at the mouth. In the firm cage of his arms he could rage for hours, it seemed, until the demon went out of him, and he sagged and was his frail self again.

He knew what they were saying about his son in town, but they didn't know him. Had Jo not died of systemic lupus shortly after the boy's birth, how might Seth have turned out? Had he been born in another age, he might have done something great, and his name and Grizz's name would have been remembered for different reasons now.

Something of Jo had lived in the boy, even in the final terrifying moment of his life.

Grizz had lied to get the pastor out here, and the man seemed to know right off. Still, it hadn't stopped him from following Grizz up the ridge to the burial mounds at the base of the mountain where Grizz buried the boy the night before, a rose-colored stone marking the spot.

Under the round, rolling hummocks of grass all around them rested many bodies. Dakota. Fox and Sauk Indians. Before them, the Cheyenne. Before them, a thousand nameless generations. This was an ancient, spooky place, and Grizz didn't usually come here. A man from the university had walked this property and wanted to come back with a group of students and do a dig, but Grizz refused. Such an act seemed a violation.

And now Seth had a place among them. In the dark, he'd unzipped the bag he'd dragged up through the woods and let the body spill into the deep grave he'd dug. Skin touching earth. Not looking, grateful for the cover of darkness, covering his child with warm black dirt. Seth hadn't belonged in this century, and Grizz hoped he might find rest here in the wildest place left in the valley. And if the sheriff did ever try to follow through with his threats and send out the cadaver dogs, they might never find this body among so many others.

A tumbling of leaves rushed up from the woods and spilled past them, and the twilight quickened with swift clouds. "If Seth had lived this is where he would have come. There's a cave behind the spot where's he buried. He would have hid here. There's a limestone spring close by. He would have had food and water. Maybe that's what all the shells were for. The ones in his pockets."

These last few nights Grizz had dreamed of fire. Fire licking up from dead leaves and the underbrush on the forest floor, cracking and spitting as it ate twigs and leaves and branches, growing into the very trees. The oaks and maples blazing from within, as though they had been given inner beings of light. They were transfigured. The fire grew and grew until it made its own wind, a living thing, hungry for flesh, and it moved on toward his farm and the sleeping town, drifting under a pall of ashes. In the dream he saw his son running just ahead of it, his long coat fanning out, saw him stop in the grove, out of breath among the statues, and turn toward the flames.

The pastor took off his glasses. He seemed

angry to have been brought out here under false pretenses. "Let's get this over with, then." He chewed on his lower lip. "And I want to make this clear. I believe your boy intended evil. All that ammunition wasn't just to kill one man. It wasn't for hunting out here. Seth went into town knowing he was going to die, by his hand or others."

Fire in a dry season, in desperate days. Fire consuming them all so that the world could start fresh again. He woke with the taste of ashes on his tongue. He woke thinking of his son.

"I know you loved Seth," Pastor Logan said when Grizz didn't respond.

"I would give my life to have him back."

"You blame yourself for his death?"

He nodded, his eyes stinging. He had not meant to cry. It unsettled him to cry in front of another man, but once the tears started he was powerless to stop them.

"Do you believe that you can be forgiven?"

Grizz settled himself by looking out over the woods, the parched trees stretching all the way to his farm and town beyond it, dusky in the fading light. "Let's not talk about me anymore. I want you to do the funeral rites. That's why we're here."

The pastor took out his Bible, and Grizz came toward him with the lantern. Here were two men on a high hill that passed for a mountain in these parts, one carrying a light, the other a holy book. The risen moon hiding behind shreds of cloud and then re-appearing once more and touching everything with silver. Something silvery moving in the woods below, among the stone statues that lined the driveway. Something unquiet where there should have been only peace. Something near calling out when the moon appeared. One man crying, one afraid. A secret ceremony, as grass closes over a body like a green wound.

By early autumn the sugar maples stood bare out in the yard. The trees had retreated inside themselves in a bad time, letting down dusty leaves and dreaming of the promised season, abundant rain and a fat summer sun. The absence of leaves told him a story about more than drought. The sight made Grizz anxious.

He turned when he heard footsteps crunching in the frosty leaves. A boy in a bright red Windbreaker approached, his head hung low, but Grizz recognized the younger Gunderson. The boy didn't even know he was being watched until he left the woods and entered the yard. Grizz raised a hand as Lee approached, a dough-faced kid in work boots and jeans. "Morning," Lee Gunderson said, his breath ghosting in the cold.

Grizz nodded. It seemed a long time had passed since he had driven him to the hospital. "What can I do for you?"

"I'm here about the job."

Grizz rubbed his eyes. He'd forgotten his spur-of-the-moment offer, hadn't seriously thought a Gunderson would take him up on it. "What time is it?"

Lee glanced up at the sky, then back at Grizz. "It's around nine, judging by the sun." Grizz noted the watchband on the boy's wrist, one of those lumpy deals that also played video games or some nonsense. One of Lee's eyes tracked lazy, following its own orbit. Odd Lee. The sheriff's boy. Right here on his property. "Your mother know you're here?"

Lee toed the dust with his boots.

"Okay, then. But I need some coffee before we get started. You eat any breakfast?"

He mumbled something Grizz didn't catch, his chin tucked into his chest.

"Look at me when you're talking."

"Chocolate cake. Two slices."

"Your mother feed you that?"

"She doesn't get out of bed much these

days. The cake is from the church ladies."
Looking at this boy who had come through
the woods without telling his own family,
Grizz remembered his body and felt hun-
grier than he had in a while. "That isn't a
proper breakfast. Come inside and I'll fry
you some eggs."

A few nights ago Steve and a few other local farmers had come with their combines
to harvest his corn. There must have been
at least a dozen men from surrounding
farms. Grizz had recognized Steve's cousin
Harvey and the two Folshem brothers and
Jim Brogan from down the road, among
others. They brought trucks and gravity bins
for transferring the corn to the silo, and all
those machines had lit up the night. Grizz
had watched them from the house and had
not come out on the porch to thank them
when they were done because he wouldn't
see a dime from the corn they were taking
from his fields. There was a part of him that
said they were doing this for themselves, so
they could go back to their houses and talk
later about how Christian and forgiving they
had been, and their plump wives would nod
and say *That poor man,* and the men would
say *Well,* and perhaps speak of how he had
not come out into the yard to thank them,
not even once. He knew it was unkind to

think this way, because he had not deserved their mercy, and their mercy had only made him feel more desperate and alone.

Now one boy had come onto his land, a boy from an enemy family. While the coffee percolated on the stove, Grizz fired up another burner and cut nubs of butter to coat an iron skillet. He whipped the melting butter into a froth and then cracked eight eggs, folding them together with a spatula. "I would make toast, but the loaf's gone moldy." The rich smell of the eggs mixed with the aroma of the coffee. It had been a long time since Grizz cooked breakfast for anyone but himself, but he enjoyed it. Seth had slept in late most days, a constant battle to get him to wake up and go to school on time.

The Mirro percolator thumped this whole time as water rose and washed over the grounds. When the eggs were done, Grizz shut off the gas stove and carried over a plate for each of them. For a boy who claimed not to be hungry, Lee shoveled in his food.

"How's your brother?"

Lee shrugged. "The same. That girl Leah comes over all the time."

"You mean the girl who just moved here from the Cities." Seth's girl.

"I'm not supposed to follow. They keep to themselves. Mostly, I take care of the pigs. My mom calls me her little man, says it all depends on me on account of me being the responsible one. It's not easy. That's what she's always saying. This isn't easy for me, you know?"

Grizz made a humming sound in his throat. "How often does the girl come over?"

Lee shrugged once more, and Grizz decided not to press him. What had it been like growing up in the household of Will Gunderson? Lee raised his gaze. "I charge three dollars an hour, and I can only come on Saturdays, when my mother is working at the nursing home."

"Those are fair terms."

"What kind of work do you have for me today?"

Grizz took him out to the truck garden, among the viny rows of potato plants overgrown with weeds. He pointed out the difference between the potatoes and the weeds, the velvety lamb's ears and pestilent burdock that grew among the crop. The plants were carefully hilled, and Grizz loosened the ground with a spade and then tugged one up by the base and shook out the loose black dirt from the small clump of potatoes. "These are Yukon Gold," he said, "about half the size they should be."

Lee whistled. "We only got eighty bushels an acre this year in corn. It's bad all over the county."

"I planted sweet corn and peas and carrots, but this is all we have left." Earlier in the summer, Grizz had hand carried buckets of water from the well to save what he could from the relentless sun. Now he rubbed the potatoes to clean off the dirt and tossed them into a gallon bucket.

Without being instructed further, Lee worked the dirt with his shovel, crouched, and tugged out a plant of his own. He held up a potato mealy with holes. "What do I do with the bad ones?"

Grizz took it from his hand and hurled it off into the trees. He left the boy to go do chores. There was a surprise he was preparing in the woods, something he'd been working on to keep his mind occupied, to escape his troubling fire dreams. When he came back an hour later, Lee had finished a row and filled three of the gallon buckets. He was a better worker than his son had been. Together they carried the buckets up to the porch, where Grizz had filled a pitcher with well water and grape powdered

Kool-Aid. The well water was so cold it made his fillings ache.

Lee stood and dusted his jeans when they were done, heading for the back field. "Hold on," said Grizz. "We'll finish the potatoes another day. I got something to show you." He trundled over a wheelbarrow he'd made ready for the purpose and slit open a bag of dried concrete with a spade. Grizz showed Lee how to mix it with gravel and water to get just the right consistency. Chilly well water splashed up and soaked Lee's sleeve, but he didn't complain. Grizz let the boy push the laden wheelbarrow up the driveway and into the woods.

An empty figure of mesh wires waited there, leaning against a tree. Metal posts had been driven through the legs and spine to give it support.

"You're making more of them?" Years had passed since Grizz had added anything to the Frozen Garden, his forest of statues growing mossy with time. "What's this one going to be?"

"That's Minnehaha herself, the hero's bride."

She leaned against a silver oak, her head drooping. Around them on the ground lay more gallon buckets with broken green glass bottles and the cowrie shells Grizz used for skin.

"What happened to her?"

"She dies of sickness in the story. It happens before his last battle, before Hiawatha must face Pau-Puk-Keewis, his ultimate enemy."

Lee touched the empty metal wires. "Why do you make the statues? Everyone in town says it because you're crazy."

"What do you think?"

Lee rubbed the arm he'd wounded coming down the mountain, kneading the muscle as he peered up at Grizz. "I think it's because you're sad. You've been sad for a long time."

Grizz swallowed. "I guess that's a good enough reason. They were for my brother. Maybe an apology for all that I couldn't do for him."

"I didn't know you had a brother."

"This was all before your time. You never got to see the pageant, did you?"

"I was just a baby when they did the last one. Dad said it got to be too much trouble for the town. And every year less people visited to see it."

"It's true." Grizz picked up the spatula and started scooping in the cement before it could dry. Minnehaha was going to be his largest statue yet, well over eight feet tall.

"Why do you miss it?"

"Nostalgia, I guess. It brought people together. It was an old story that people made sure to keep alive and pass on." But even as Grizz spoke he knew it was more than that. The play was a direct line to his family's past, his great-grandfather's role in the hangings, an entire town craving redemption for what they'd done to Indians a hundred years before, dressing up in the costumes of the ones they had killed or driven away. He handed an extra spade to Lee, and they filled the base of the empty skeleton with concrete, Grizz smoothing and shaping the rough edges into a textured skin.

"Now comes the fun part. Before the concrete dries we got to put in cowrie shells and glass. Make her pretty. So when the sun shines people will see her from the road."

"You going to put some clothes on her?"

Grizz had styled realistic clefts in the buttocks and given the giantess a massive bosom. "Nah. It'll scandalize the little old ladies driving by on the road."

Lee stepped back to study the statue taking shape, maybe trying to imagine. "Seth used to tell us about the naked woman they found here in the woods."

Grizz sucked on his teeth at the mention of the woman, unsure how to respond. "Hypothermia. That was why she didn't have any clothes on. If you're freezing to death it feels like you're burning up. When did Seth tell you all this?"

Lee was about to say more when the sound of snapping twigs made them turn. A young man in a russet rain slicker approached, his eyes grim and slitted. Kelan, Lee's older brother. Lee dropped his spade into the wheelbarrow and lowered his head.

"You get on home," his older brother told him.

"He was just helping me," Grizz said, standing. "We have an arrangement."

"Fuck your arrangement. Let's go, Lee."

"I want to stay," Lee said. "It's my choice."

In answer, Kelan came forward and grabbed his little brother by the ear. "I've been looking all over for you. Mom thought you had fallen into one of the hog pits. She was worried sick."

"Let him go," Grizz said.

Lee struggled and kicked, and there were tears in his eyes, but when Kelan released him he bunched his hands into his coat pockets and started walking, not looking behind him.

"You stay away from my brother," Kelan

said, jabbing a finger in Grizz's direction.

Grizz could have caught the finger in midair if he wanted and snapped it like a chicken bone.

The boy was walking away. The strange presence of both brothers on his land troubled him. *You may have to live with not knowing,* the pastor had said, but Grizz couldn't leave it at that.

LOCK-IN

Lee Gunderson surprised Clara and Logan when he showed up for the Luther League's fall festival lock-in. He had walked from his farm outside town and arrived without sleeping bag or change of clothes. He also didn't have the required signed permission slip, so Logan tried to call his mother but was unable to reach her. It seemed cruel to send the boy back home, so they let him stay. The other children left a circle of space around him. Clara was there to keep order along with a couple of other adult volunteers. Logan had told her how he struggled working with young people, and the kids might be especially wild on All Hallow's Eve. "Children and bees can smell fear," he said.

"Try stronger deodorant."

But she was here. She oversaw the apple bobbing and watched the older teens play hide-and-seek in the darkened sanctuary and basement, a few still finding shadowy recesses where they could make out. Only around sixteen youths from the Luther League came, most parents wanting to keep their children close to home this year. There had been talk of canceling all Halloween trick-or-treating because of the coyotes that had been seen roaming the night. No one knew how dangerous they were.

Around midnight, Logan put in a Betamax tape of *The Goonies* for the boys to watch while they fell asleep, and Clara took the girls next door to the parsonage. The girls unrolled sleeping bags on the living room floor and passed the hour telling ghost stories about the woman in the woods. She had long claws they said, her hair a ragged nest, and she wanted a child, any child. If she snatched you she would take you off in the woods with her, and you wouldn't ever be seen again. The ghost stories devolved into gossip about boys and then to giggling, which Clara finally silenced.

The girls slept well, much better, she would discover, than Logan and the boys.

All sounds magnify in the dark, especially the sound of something wounded or afraid, Logan later told Clara. He had given his blankets to the Gunderson child and made a makeshift bed of choir robes in the corner of the room for himself. A few hours before dawn, Logan woke to the sound of whimpering.

He propped himself on his elbows to better hear. Boys mummified in sleeping bags were cast about on the chilly linoleum floor, their lumpy shapes glistening like seals on some unfamiliar shore. The children were all worn out from the games and movies, soundly sleeping, except one.

When the crying rose to a choked sobbing, Logan picked his way among the sleepers. He found him still shuddering, his breathing husky and labored. The boy's face was a blank, contorted mask, and he cringed when Logan loomed over him.

"Hush," Logan said, speaking in a low, soothing tone as he touched his shoulder, smelling the blankets he had loaned him a few hours ago were soaked with urine. "You were having a bad dream."

The boy mumbled something inaudible. A dream language. Logan crouched beside him to give him time to rise from his nightmare. Lee had oily, dark hair and the chubby, shape-shifting features of a teenager whose adult face was not yet formed. Logan could only imagine what he had been dreaming as he slept on a cold floor in a strange room less than a block from where his father had been murdered.

Lee's nostrils flared. "Do you smell it? Do you smell the gunpowder?"

"No." This was a lie. When Lee named the odor, Logan smelled it, too. Peppery and sulfuric, the gunpowder burned inside his nostrils. But it was simply not possible, not here.

"I'm all wet."

"We'll have to call your mom, have her bring fresh clothing."

"No. You won't be able to wake her."

"Won't hurt to try," Logan continued. "You never know. She might be awake and thinking of you right now."

Lee trembled, urine chilling against his skin. "No. Not when she's taken her pills."

The other boys were stirring. They'd wake soon, their senses heightened by hunger, and know this child had wet himself. The girls, sleeping with Clara next door, would be over in a few hours. Time was of the essence.

"Come with me, then," Logan said. "We'll find something for you upstairs." He helped the boy bundle the blankets and carried them to an out-of-the-way corner. Then he led Lee up a rear stairwell in the dark. The neon glow of an exit sign bathed the stairs in red light, and Logan thought of what eerie places even churches seemed at night; something hellish must have touched the boy in his sleep. The gunpowder smell remained on them both.

When they reached the back room, he hit a switch, waited for the fluorescent bulb to flicker on, and then fetched a dark choir robe intended for a petite woman from a mothballed closet. "Here," he said. "You can wear this until morning. Take it to the men's room and rinse yourself in the sink. Use the paper towels for drying."

Lee's stink saturated the tight quarters. He took the robe reluctantly. He was shivering all over, as if lice boiled under his skin.

"You want to tell me about your dream?" Logan asked.

A shake of his head.

"Sometimes you feel better if you name your fear aloud."

"He's hunting me," Lee said, his gaze to the floor. "Seth is after me, too. I saw him. I saw him all covered in blood."

The boy's voice was flat, toneless. Logan said nothing, waiting for him to go on.

"I could feel him in the church. The blood was dripping down his clothes. Then he put his hand over my mouth so I couldn't scream. He leaned down and he was laughing; he was laughing but it sounded like something breaking inside him. I kicked and struggled and tried to wake up, but I just couldn't."

"Lee, do you want to pray with me?"

His head was still lowered. "I'm sorry," he said. "So, so sorry." In that moment it sounded like all the sorrows in the world were wrapped in his voice.

"It's okay. You just go change. Then I want you to meet me downstairs in the kitchen. Milk and cookies are the best cure for nightmares that I know."

His shoulders still quaking, the boy went down the hallway to the bathroom. Logan walked to the kitchen, carefully shutting a swinging door so as not to wake the other boys. He put on a light above the stove and set out two plates with some cheap store-bought cookies, the kind with cream inside. Then he poured two tall glasses of milk. In the room beyond, the other boys slept on, oblivious.

Logan waited and waited. Lee did not come.

Eventually, he walked down the hall and knocked on the bathroom door. When there was no response he opened it to find the empty robe lying on the floor in a black puddle.

Lee was gone. He had walked off into the

icy night in his wet clothes. He had run, run as if being pursued.

Later, as Logan told Clara all this, he shook his head in disbelief. "I can't get over what he said to me. How he apologized. It was about more than the blankets. It sounded like a confession."

The girls' story of the woman in the woods made Clara dream of her mother again, and when she woke she knew what she had to do. After all the teens had gone home and Logan left on errands, she set out the next morning. This whole time Sylvia's grave had been right outside Clara's window. Why had her father buried her here instead of taking her back to the Cities? Why had he never told Clara where she could find her? In the days since Nora had told her, the knowledge she was out here prickled inside her brain, made her hyperattuned to her body and breath.

Now she was out in the yard in the early day. A north wind whisked clouds as thin as tissue paper across a peerless sky milky with early morning light. The grass below her was yellow and water starved, the earth stretching taut in the cold, like the skin on her stretched belly, thick as a drum. While the air tasted of snow, none had fallen yet, but Clara felt it gathering somewhere, building strength as it swept across the Dakota prairies.

Did anyone see her in the town below? She had on Logan's red down jacket because her own was too small. Underneath it, a wool sweater covered a shapeless maternity dress, brown as a potato sack. Clara was having trouble finding decent clothes this far from any shopping centers. Her breath smoked in gauzy streams in the cold. Below her she saw the grid of the sleeping town, a few trucks moving along the main drag, but she felt cut off from them. Why then this strange sense of being watched? This sense that eyes were on her even now?

She walked the rows, seeking out a pattern of organization. The older tombstones bore laments in German. SEELIG SIN DIE TODEN DIE DEN HERRN STERBEN, DEN IHRE WERKE FOLGEN IHNEN NACH. Clara traced the cold marble with her fingers, guessing at some of the words since Anglo-Saxon was close to Low German. *Though he is dead, his work follows after him.* People had left plastic flowers, the bright yellows and reds the only color in this place. She recited the names: Gunther, Helga, Wolfgang, Frieda. Names of the original settlers who carved out "civilization" from these woods, who killed the Indians and tamed the wolves and made the land safe for livestock and crop rotations. Shannon. Halvorsen. Brecken. Scheuler. Names of those who continued to hold sway in Logan's church, whom her husband dared not anger.

She went deeper into the cemetery, the marble tombstones growing less ornate as she came to what she guessed was the suicide corner here at the edge closest to the woods. No more angels. Clara found no grave for Sylvia Meyers. Maybe she was not here? It didn't make sense for her father to bury her here. She had been so wrapped up in her search that she hadn't even noticed where she was until she saw the name below her. It was a simple gravestone of polished purple granite. SETH FALLON: DECEMBER 11, 1970–SEPTEMBER 13, 1987. Logan had told her the story of the boy's strange burial, Seth's body now up on the mountain.

Clara knelt in the grass. She felt a prickling along the ends of her fingers. The leafless woods loomed nearby. All the corn had come out of the field where Seth killed himself, only a few bent stalks leaning crookedly in the tilled black rows.

A crackling in the leaves made her turn. Only two of the three coyotes stood there, panting in the cold, their ribs showing through their skinny hides. The big gray was not with them. One came forward, whining, but danced away again when Clara stood, dusting the grass from her knees, and approached. They retreated into the woods, but stopped to look back at her, beckoning.

A pregnant woman alone in the woods with dangerous animals. Something like them had harried her mother through this very stretch of woods. She had died here, less than a quarter mile from town. She had died with Clara shielded close against her, absorbing the last of her warmth.

Wolves. But there were no coyotes back then, and the last wolf in the county had been killed more than a century ago. The old-timers had told her this. It had only been a few years that coyotes had come back, migrating from South Dakota to fill a place on the food chain.

She was our Duchess. A displaced person. She had to be punished for her sin.

The coyotes loped down an old deer track. Even without leaves the woods were thick and shadowy, the branches of the bur oaks braiding a canopy above her. She pushed on through sumac and bramble, following the sounds of the coyotes ahead. Eventually, they reached a small meadow, where the gray lay on his belly in the grass.

The two smaller ones circled it warily. The alpha lay gasping, and bright blood splattered the ground around him. Clara saw when she knelt beside him that he was caught in a trap, the serrated teeth closed around his front paw. She smelled spoiling hamburger, or whatever meat the trapper had used to lure him in. He'd gotten greedy, careless.

This coyote nosed her hand. Clara stroked his soft fur gently. He growled but did not snatch at her with his jaws. "This is going to hurt," Clara said. "I'm sorry but there is no other way." The gray tried to heave himself off the ground and strained against the trap that held him, snarling and gnashing as his tendons tore and fresh blood sprayed from the wound. The trap, bolted into the ground by a chain, hardly budged.

Clara backed away. The other coyotes yipped as he thrashed and then finally settled in a heap.

She came close once more. "You can't do that," she said in the quietest voice possible. She knelt again beside him. Under her breath she was singing an old spell, an Anglo-Saxon *galdor* to soothe a monster. His lids were shut, and she thought maybe he had lost consciousness, but when she reached for the trap, the yellow eyes snapped open. He growled once more, his black lips exposing his razor canines.

Clara's fingers fumbled with the metal. The great hinge did not want to give way, the iron cold against her naked fingers. When the coyote suddenly lunged forward and clamped down on her arm, she started to scream, but realized he hadn't punctured the cloth with his sharp teeth. He was just holding on. She swallowed, finished her spell, and slipped her hands deeper into the trap to get more leverage. Then she tugged with all her might, straining until the trap opened just enough that the gray could slide his injured paw out.

He pulled away from her, limping on three legs. Clara saw that he had left behind digits from his partly severed paw in the trap. When she let go off the hinge, the trap snapped again, causing the gray to snarl. Delicately, she plucked the long, bloody claws from the grass and put them in her pocket. The smaller coyotes licked the gray's face, sniffed at his wound, and then they bounded off together into the woods.

Clara should have headed home, but down in the valley she could make out the farm where Grizz Fallon lived, smoke coiling from his chimney. If it was true that Seth had tamed these coyotes, his father might know what to do with them, some way to keep them from coming into town where it was only a matter of time before they were killed. Or hurt someone. She followed the same old deer path down through the woods toward the house and then cut across the property, passing a wheelbarrow abandoned next to the stump of a fresh statue, a creation twisting into the tree itself. The statues were leering figures under the November sky, their pearly skins glittering as they watched, through bottle-green eyes of glass, Clara walk among them. A forest of stone monsters, the foes of Hiawatha. She imagined Seth as a boy playing among them, a toy bow flinging arrows at the frozen figures.

The farmhouse below stood on a small rise overlooking the yard. Though the white paint of the boards peeled away, betraying its age, the limestone foundation looked sturdy, except for a warping, wraparound porch.

Skeletons of abandoned farm equipment were tucked back in the grove, an old H tractor up on blocks, a rusting cattle trailer beside an open corn bin that had willow trees growing inside it. The barn had the same matching limestone foundation as the house. Cattle milled uneasily in their pens, wading through deep pools of manure that also caked their hides and hung in dirty green strings from their faces. They pressed close to a wire fence as she approached, and one, shorter than the rest, bellowed, his primal challenge ringing through the empty yard.

The house faced east to take in the mountain and rising sun. The mountain. Clara had caught glimpses of it from the road, but now with fall stripping the leaves from the trees it rose before her, the curved slope like the gray back of some immense sleeping animal. She saw the form of a giant in the shape, the small hills beside it his shoulders, the rounded head of waving grasses. As mountains went, it was smaller than she'd imagined it, no more than three hundred feet by her estimate, but it was like nothing else around it. A sacred place, her father promised, with a healing limestone spring that spilled down to join the river. Some large bird, an eagle or a red-tailed hawk, circled the summit, riding a thermal in a gyre. The kid was buried up there. It was where the coyotes denned, the place of her father's stories. *I've told you all you need to know,* he'd promised her when they last spoke. Here was the mountain, and Clara had found her home, though she could not climb it today, with the smell of snow in the air, with all that was happening in this place. Her earlier sense of worry had not evaporated. She faced the silent house, fingering the coyote's claws in her pocket, for courage or luck.

"Hello," she called out, knowing before she even stepped up to knock on the door that no one was there. The walk had done her good, woke up her sluggish mind. In the cold, she felt her blood beating and the snug presence of the baby inside her. She sat on the porch to catch her breath just as Grizz Fallon walked out of the grove, lugging a bundle of wood, an ax slung over his shoulder.

He had not spotted her yet, and for a moment she thought of ducking around the porch and hurrying home. Instead, she waited as Grizz walked her way. She'd forgotten his size, broader in the shoulders than Seth, his long arms looped around the logs he carried, the knuckles thick and scarred from years of labor. He wore tan coveralls and a quilted flannel shirt, an orange hunting cap pulled low. "Mrs. Warren? What brings you here?"

"It's Clara," she said. "Should I come another time?" She had her arms wrapped around herself. Grizz registered something familiar about her face, the sharpness of her features, those luminous brown eyes. She didn't wear any makeup, didn't need it. He felt he had known her from somewhere long before this.

He rested his ax against the porch and glanced toward the cattle. What had brought her here, walking all this way from town? It seemed the world wasn't ready to leave him alone just yet. "I got chores to do, but I suppose I can spare a few minutes." He carried the wood up the steps, shouldered open the front door, and nodded to the entryway. "It's a little messy. I haven't had many guests."

She followed him in. The radio he'd left on spread murmuring voices through the house, Waylon Jennings. Grizz set his bundle of wood down on the bench, shrugged out of his flannel, and then unlaced his boots before gesturing toward the living room. "You can wait there. I'm going to get a fire going and then I'll heat us some coffee. You drink coffee, right?"

"Sure. I won't be staying long."

He hefted the wood in the living room and set it beside a potbellied stove. Then he levered it open, balled up some newspaper, and stacked the wood around it. He struck a match, let the paper catch, and blew on it to get it going before levering the door shut once more.

"Make yourself at home," Grizz told her while he went to brew coffee. From the corner of his eye, he noticed how she was eyeing the two matching blue recliners dubiously, probably not sure if once she sank into the cushion she could climb out again in her condition. "It's okay," he encouraged. "I don't have fleas."

She lowered herself and waited, rocking in the chair. Grizz went into his kitchen and fired up the gas burner under the percolator. This morning's coffee, a little tarry on reheating, but his hospitality had limits.

"I added in cream and sugar," he told her when he returned with two mugs. "The coffee's a little thick otherwise." He stayed

335

standing, leaning against a bookshelf that held his collection of Zane Grey and Louis L'Amour novels.

Clara took it from his hands, mumbling her thanks. "You probably wonder why I'm here." She took a sip, winced. Her other hand was in her pocket, and when she took it out, two hooked and bloody claws lay curled against the pinkness of her palm.

"Is that what I think it is?"

"It'll live, I'm sure. I rescued it from a trap."

"How'd you manage that?"

Her palm closed around the claws, and she pocketed them again. "I've heard talk that you and your son raised them."

"Seth did. I didn't want anything to do with coyotes. I warned Seth what might happen once they got big. They stayed out of trouble, till now."

She watched his face. "I have a feeling they're looking for him," she said. "They don't understand he's gone."

Grizz was quiet, thinking on how Seth loved the land in different ways than him. The farmwork he detested, anything involving machines. Had Seth inherited the land he would have let the lower forty, down near the river, become CRP land and return to its natural state. "I don't want anything bad to happen to those animals. They're a living reminder of my son."

"What can we do?"

"I don't know," he said.

Her smile was faint, nervous. She still seemed agitated, her hands in that pocket as though the claws were some kind of totem. Not many women would have gone to an animal in a trap or picked up something like that from the ground.

"There's another reason I came, something I have to ask you. Around twenty years ago there was a car accident. A woman went off the road not far from your property. She tried to make it back through the storm. I was told a baby was rescued."

The Duchess. Yes, those eyes. He knew her now.

Clara held up her damaged hand. "I was that baby."

Grizz came over and sat down in the other chair. "Seth knew didn't he? He figured out who you were."

A log broke inside the stove and settled with a crackling thump. If Seth had known, then so had others. "Will you tell me the story? I'd like to hear it. The sheriff saved my life if what they say is true."

Grizz rubbed the side of his chest where a knot had formed, a tightness in his breathing. "Saved you? That's the story they tell?"

She nodded, and he tried to concentrate as she told bits and pieces of the story that had come to her from her father: her mother's madness, the car abandoned in the storm, the snowy woods she tried to cross to safety. "Other people have recognized me. One old woman even called me Duchess, which is what they called my mother. There's a lot my father never told me. I think he was still very angry with my mother."

Grizz drew in a deep breath. "Not a winter passes when I don't think about her. The man in the car with Sylvia, the one who broke his neck? He was my brother, Wylie. I was going to stay on the farm so Wylie could go away to school. He had a knack for languages, always did, but he was in all sorts of trouble. Fights at school. Hot-wired a car and ditched it in the river. Your father taught at the high school, thought all the boy needed was some purpose, direction. Wylie started correspondence classes in German from the university. He needed a tutor, and here was this woman, a refugee from the war."

"My dad arranged it?"

"She was lonely by then." His mind raced, remembering. "Pastor Schoenwald had gotten fixated on the idea that she was some kind of witch, and he spoke against her. People stopped going to her salon. So my brother would visit in the early afternoons, and they drank tea together, practiced in her home language." He paused. " 'She's seen things you can't imagine,' Wylie told me once. I guess you could say they grew close in more ways than one. Both our parents were dead by then, and I think he was lonely, too."

"What happened?"

"When the affair was discovered, her shop was shut down for good. She went away. They both went away. We heard later that she was in some kind of institution. A mental breakdown. Her English wasn't so good. She may not have even understood what was happening until too late. When she got out, she started writing Wylie letters again. I paid the phone bill and saw the long-distance charges to the Cities, nearly twice a week. I made my brother go and see Pastor Schoenwald, made him confess. For a time, the phone calls stopped, and I thought that was the end of it."

"He never saw her before she got pregnant?"

He looked at her, for any sign of his brother in this woman. Wylie, small and dark and wiry. No, it wasn't possible. "I know what you're asking. I believe Stanley was your father. I feel sorry for him, despite everything that happened. He didn't ask for any of it. She came here, you know, driving from the hospital just ahead of a storm. Blizzard predictions all over the radio, and she shows up in a DeSoto. Wylie went with her with only the clothes on his back. I grabbed hold of him, shook him. She was a married woman. But he shoved me aside."

"It was you who called the sheriff." Clara held herself, rocking in the chair.

"No. I didn't know she had a baby with her in the car. I let them go. I didn't expect to ever see them again. It might have been that your dad called him from the Cities, but Sheriff Steve has always had a sense when something's wrong. They told me later that Wylie died at the scene of the car accident. He never made it out. It wasn't until the next day I heard all this, about her getting out of the car, coming on through the woods."

"Were there coyotes back then? Some kind of wild dogs or wolves? It's how I've always imagined it because of my father's stories."

His mind had often gone over the same territory. The woman found without any clothes on. Sheriff Will Gunderson, freshly graduated from the vo-tech, had been out there that night as well. "Wolves?" he said quietly. "If there were any wolves, they came in human form."

Both of them startled when a rotary phone sitting on a small table rang. Grizz had finally bought a new phone a few days ago to replace the one he had destroyed. "Did anyone see you come here?" He couldn't account for his paranoia. The ringing phone was a jarring sound, and at first he just let it go, wanting to finish his story. He had always suspected that something else had happened out there. The DeSoto had been found at the bottom of a ditch with minimal damage, a missing headlight, the windshield caved in. Sheriff Steve had hated Wylie for the headaches he caused. The story, the adulterous couple punished by Mother Nature, was too convenient for him to fully believe.

When the phone's insistent ringing kept on, Grizz finally answered it.

"Mr. Fallon?" said a quaking voice at the other end. He heard the hesitation in the voice and what sounded like another voice in the background, whispering instructions. "We need your help. Please hurry. It's Leah. She's fallen into the hog pit."

"You call the paramedics? The sheriff?"

The other end of the line had gone dead.

"What's going on?" Clara asked when he hung up.

"That was Lee Gunderson. He said Leah fell into one of the holding ponds of their hog farm near as I could tell."

"They can't get her out?"

"It's worse than you could imagine. The chemicals will suffocate you if you get too near. I have to get there, or she'll drown. He must have called here because this is the closest farm."

"I want to come."

"No. There's nothing you can do. I wouldn't want you to see this." Grizz already knew what he was going to find by the time he got there. No way he could make it in time. "Go home and pray. That's the best you can do right now."

The Gunderson ranch house sat up on a ridge climbing out of the valley, sloping woods on one side, rich flat prairie table-lands spreading on the other. They owned two thousand acres and then some, with four hog barns and vast holding pools for all the manure so many animals produced. Grizz downshifted into second gear as he pulled into the steep driveway and sped uphill.

While other farms failed and families moved away, the Gundersons' and Steve Krieger's family operations kept on growing. Bigger combines and bigger equipment worked the ground more efficiently, all of it paid for with bigger loans from the bank, where both men had friends, and all of it subsidized by the government. But it was because of moments like this that Grizz hated the factory farms the worst.

Hundreds of hogs piled into each reeking barn; on some nights he could hear them screaming during feeding times, a high-pitched whine that carried throughout the valley. Worst of all was the smell, a dangerous mixture of ammonium hydroxide concentrated in the manure. Hog shit could kill you. Just last year over in Lyon County a young boy helping his father pump out the pit had walked too close, been overwhelmed by the fumes, and fell inside, asphyxiating before he could be pulled out. Now this girl Leah was in the same predicament. An outsider to the area, she must not have known how dangerous it was to get too close. And why would a girl be wandering so near such a foul-smelling pit? Had it been some kind of stupid teenage dare?

He was going forty miles an hour by the time he reached the crest and pulled into the turnabout, dust and gravel spraying out behind the truck. Then he was out the door, running toward Lee, who stood at the edge of the buildings.

"Where is she?"

Lee didn't speak and spit bubbled at the corners of his lips. He pointed at one of the holding pits.

"How long has she been in there?"

His eyes widened, and he moved his chin, as if trying to draw Grizz's attention to the hog barn nearest.

"Goddamnit. You got to tell me more." A girl might be drowned, and the only witness was this idiot child. The boy was clearly unhinged, the skin slack around his eyes. Was he on drugs, going into shock? Grizz took him by the shoulders and saw how dilated the pupils were, darkly brimming so they filled his eyes. Pot. That was it. They must have been smoking out here, and the girl tried something stupid. He was angry now, and so he shook him. "Now, listen to me, because we have to act fast. You call the paramedics again. Get an ambulance here. You got to do this, okay?"

Lee mumbled something.

"Speak!" Grizz roared the word, his patience gone, but when the boy couldn't get the words out he pushed him aside and went toward the holding pond. Even from a distance he could see the place where the pump's guide wire had broken. She must have been trying to retrieve it with the come-along line, helping out Lee with his chores, both of them stoned to the gills. Everyone else around the place seemed to be gone, even the older brother. Grizz crouched as he came closer. He held his shirt front over his face to block out the smell. He was a bigger man, much bigger than any child, and maybe his body mass would save him.

He crawled on his hands and knees, conscious of the sound of the pigs screaming in the barn. The sound make him think of the story of Legion begging Jesus to let him possess the swine and that herd casting itself from the cliff, a story that fascinated him as a child. Grizz had never liked hogs. If a demon were to select an animal, it would choose swine. Grizz went forward until he caught the come-along wire in his hands. Maybe he could lower it to the girl, fetch her out of the way. He thought he heard something as he got closer, a thin watery voice crying out for help, or the voice came from behind him. He couldn't hear right over the hogs.

She must have still been clinging to the

other end of the wire. The smell of shit burned inside his mouth, the acid chemicals stinging his eyes. It invaded his pores, his mind, but still he crept forward on hands and knees because he could not leave the girl there, a girl who had been kind to his son.

At the lip of the rim he paused and leaned over. He saw greenish-gray mire, bubbling sludge the color of rotting pea soup, the empty come-along wire floating on the surface, but no sign of her.

And then he heard footsteps pounding behind him. "Hey," someone shouted, and Grizz turned to see a figure bearing down on him.

"Stop!" he said, wobbly on his knees from the fumes, just getting his hand up, but the other man bulled right into him, his shoulder catching Grizz under the chin, and then he was falling backward.

He landed with a sickening smack in the manure, the shock knocking the breath from his lungs. For several seconds he went under, before his toes found bottom and he fought his way back to the surface. Gasping, Grizz spread his arms on the surface to keep from sinking again and tried to keep his head above the putrid liquid. He had never learned to swim, but the stuff was thick enough that he buoyed on top of it. He struggled with every last fiber against the panic spreading through him. They called him here to die, drowned in hog shit, the last of the Fallons in the valley, and with his death his last hope of redeeming what his son had done.

The footsteps went away. "Come back!" he pleaded weakly, trying not to swallow any more shit. In the distance he heard the sound of his truck gunning. He tilted his head back to keep his face out of the poison. The aluminum siding of the pit shone silver, slick and wet, safe ground an impossible eight feet above him. With his head tilted, he saw sky. A snowflake drifted down out of the clouds, pure and white, and caught in his eyelashes. He sent his mind up into those clouds, drew in his last breath, trying to stave off his own terror, a useless rage running through his blood as the pit sucked him down.

Home at the parsonage, Clara waited to hear the sound of sirens howling past on the road leading out of town, but none came. When she tried calling the emergency number, the operator patched her through to a roiling static on the other line that smoothed into silence and then a busy signal before she hung up the phone. She went upstairs to get ready for bed, changing into a nightgown with a robe thrown over it to keep warm. Her hair still reeked of smoke from her visit to the Fallon place, but she didn't want to draw a bath, in case the phone rang or Logan came home early.

Ever since she'd returned, cramping jolted her breath, as if the baby had hold of his umbilical cord and tugged on the other end. She pictured a chubby little monk yanking on a rope leading to a bell tower in her head.

Five weeks remained until her due date. Clara sat in the rocking chair up in the nursery, hoping the motion would ease the cramping. The day's events had exhausted her, yet when she shut her eyes and tried to focus on her breathing, a throbbing pressure in her lower back pierced any sense of calm. Her breath came easier, a lightness in her head and under her ribs, yet her baby manuals said lower-back pain was likely the baby stepping on her sciatic nerve, not some augur of birth. She timed the Braxton Hicks contractions, if that's what this cramping was, knowing that if they grew shorter or intensified that this was not false labor. A suitcase packed with essentials waited by the front door in case she needed to go to the hospital tonight.

She stood and paced the room, her hands on her hips, which also hurt. Logan had assembled a plain pinewood crib, and they'd put fresh sheets on the mattress. A windup mobile of a manger scene, circled by stable animals and a winking crystal star, attached to the railing. The mobile had been hand carved and painted by someone from the church. Clara wound it and listened to it play a tinny version of "Silent Night." Every time she saw the barn animals she thought of Thomas Hardy's poem about the legend of oxen kneeling at midnight each Christmas Eve in memory of the Christ Child. *I should*

349

go with him in the gloom, she remembered the final lines of the poem, the speaker's longing to return to a childhood faith he had lost, *Hoping it might be so.*

Outside snow spilled from low clouds as dark came on. Logan was at the hospital in Sioux Falls, more than a hundred miles away. He hadn't wanted to go after he'd heard the weather predictions, he explained in a note she found on the dining room table. There had been an accident, a car on an icy road sliding through a stop sign to strike a semi. The accident left the parishioner driving the car, a young father of three named Morgan, in a vegetative state. Logan had to be there with the family when the doctors removed Morgan from life support. Clara pictured Logan with his black communion kit, the red velvet lining and its vial of wine and canister of stale crackers. His quiet voice speaking promises of eternity. Unbidden, she thought of Leah down at the bottom of that pit, of her own mother trying to come home through such a storm. Dizzying thoughts whirred in her head like the thickening haze of snow whirring outside in the lamplight.

The doorbell rang.

Clara froze in place. How much time had passed since Grizz hurried off to the Gunderson farm? It must be him, returned with news about what happened. The doorbell rang again, but she remained where she was. All through her body her blood hummed right down to her fingertips, the nubs of her left hand quickening. The ringing went on and on until the sound hived in her mind. This is how you survive: stay still until the shadow passes over you.

Downstairs the door opened and slammed shut. She heard footsteps in her kitchen and only then did she move. Clara slid open the desk drawer where she kept her writing supplies, groping for any sort of weapon, a letter opener, scissors, anything. All she had was the Meisterstrück fountain pen she'd been using to set down her wolf child stories. She touched the tip with one finger, a sobering bite of sharpness.

The stairs creaked. There was no place to hide in this old room, not even a closet. Whoever had come in knew she was here, knew to follow the light upstairs. When he stepped into the nursery, he brought the cold from the outside in with him, a smell like methane. Cold and methane poured from his clothes into the warmth of the yellow room. He wore the same dirty tennis shoes and oilcloth coat she had seen months before. A black-haired boy with a pretty, curving mouth. Kelan.

He held a double-barrel shotgun in the nook of his arm, the gun loose and bobbing with each step. Snow dripped from his hair and coat to the hardwood floor, and he was shivering, breathing hard. When he spoke, his Adam's apple danced in his throat. "Clara, I need you to come with me."

Clara opened her mouth, but nothing came out. The line sounded practiced, obsessive, like he'd been rehearsing it in front of a mirror. "Is this about Leah?" she said, knowing it wasn't. She didn't ask about the gun.

Kelan nodded, his eyes glassy and vacant. Seth. This is what his ghost had been trying to tell her. All along she had known the truth. Two of them that day.

"In the corn. That was you."

"We have to hurry," he said, not looking at her.

It had not been Seth she had seen going back into that corn. It had been Kelan trailing him. It had not been Seth's ghost she had seen emerge from the corn, but Kelan biding his time. And the town, reeling in shock over Will Gunderson's death hadn't considered that there might be something else out there, someone worse. "It must be so hard for you," she said. "I can't imagine."

"Please, you got to help me, Mrs. Warren." In his face she read some inner struggle, a tic pulsing violently in his cheek.

His voice, the pleading. It sounded so much like Seth, like he was channeling his dead friend. She felt the same icy fingers running up and down her spine as the night she thought she heard Seth's spirit under the stairwell. Her grip tightened on the pen she held behind her back. *Focus.* The minute she let him take her elsewhere, she would die; she was sure of it. *Use your voice.* "I'm not going anywhere," she said, sounding as soothing as she could. "Not until I understand what's going on."

Kelan drew in a hissing breath through clenched teeth as though he'd been struck. When he raised his head, he glared at her, his nostrils flaring. She had said the wrong thing. Kelan lifted the gun and walked toward her until she was backed up against the wall.

She got out one word, "Don't," and then he shoved the barrel so hard into her belly that the pain bent her over. Steel met watery membrane, pushed against the tight drum of her stomach. Something wet and warm leaked down her leg. Clara screamed.

"Shut up," he screamed back. "You don't get to decide." He cocked both barrels and pressed deeper, and her gorge rose in her throat. Then he must have seen the urine pooling underneath her because he stepped back. "Gross."

While stooped over, Clara stroked her stomach when she could breathe again, felt pressure shifting from her back to her pelvis, the baby searching for a way out. Somewhere, she'd dropped the pen she had been hoping to use for a weapon. So stupid. Squeezing her eyes shut, trying to steady her breathing. Her heartbeat, the child's heartbeat, thumping in her ears. *Think.*

"Filthy," Kelan said. His voice deeper now. A man's voice, angry. His father?

Clara opened her eyes and studied him. The same gleam, opaque as smoked glass, as she'd seen in that old woman's eyes. Bynthia. Cold and hostile. "I can be clean again," she said. She felt tears warm on her face. Her nose running hot. As though she were a witch, melting. "If you show me how."

"Stop it!" he shouted at her. The gun shaking in his grasp. "Stop crying!"

Clara wiped her nose on her sleeve, wiped away the tears.

The voice, the fatherly baritone, came into him. He drew himself up, circling her, careful not to step in the mess she had made.

"Do you want to live forever?" It sounded like something he'd been asked many times himself, a question beaten into him.

No, she thought. The most important thing was to go on living right now. For her, for the baby inside her. "Yes," she said. Heaven. *Heofon.* The sky, the firmament.

"Forever with me?" Softly spoken now, a slackness sliding over his face.

"Yes," she said, keeping her voice firm. *Lull him into trusting you.*

His face contorted, lips peeling back to show his teeth. "Liar!" he shouted. "You lie! Why do you have to lie to me all the goddamn time?"

Her legs gave way. She was sitting in the puddle of cold urine. Dizzied by a sudden contraction squeezing her middle, by the force of his anger. Kelan stomping up and down the room, ranting. "I've seen you! I've watched you!" She hoped his words carried out into the street. To Nora's, to neighboring houses. "You thought you had me fooled. You fool all the rest of them, but not me. I know what you've been doing. I see everything. I know, I fucking know what you are."

He was reenacting something, some familiar drama. He didn't really see her in that moment, Clara realized. She was an it, an object, and they were both playing parts. A terrible sense of helplessness swept over her, Clara pulling her knees up to her chest, her vision narrowing to a single vanishing point.

Then a sharp pain drew her up to her feet, Kelan dragging her by her hair. "Get up. Not here."

"Let go of me," Clara cried, and he did. His face drained of color, he bid her take off the soiled robe, and she let it drop to the floor, and he stood looking at her in her damp gown, her one shoulder bare, exposed. Whatever happened she was not going to let him push that gun into her belly again.

Kelan pointed toward the door with his gun. Clara brushed past him and stepped into the hallway. Midway down the stairs another contraction halted her, and she had to grab hold of the banister to keep from falling. Kelan prodded at her back with the barrel. Somehow she made it down the stairs, and midway through the kitchen she saw her own shimmery reflection in the window, her hair wildly askew, the boy behind her in a coat too large for him, the sleeves rolled up, his mouth muttering. The images pale and blurring, like they were both already dead, walking together in some other afterlife. "I need shoes," she said when they reached the door. "They're in the other room." Where was he taking her? Next door, to the church? The graveyard?

"Keep going," he said in the low voice.

Outside the snow felt good under her bare soles, woke her up from her dreamy disconnect, but when she spotted Grizz Fallon's truck under the yard lamp, all hope fled. Kelan absently opened the door for her and shut it once she climbed in. He went around to the passenger side and swung himself up. The gun lay in his lap as he passed her the keys. "Don't flood the engine. You do anything stupid, I'll blow your face off."

After what she had been through, the threat sounded weak, pathetic. Her cheeks flushed as sudden anger coursed inside her. "Like Seth did your father?" The words left her before she even knew what she was saying.

"Shut up. Start the engine."

"You asked him to meet you that day in the corn, but he didn't follow your instructions, did he? He wasn't supposed to stop at the parsonage. Your dad wasn't supposed to be there."

The winter storm sweeping down from the prairies, the wind blasting. Full dark and the rest of the town huddled in their homes with televisions turned up loud. In answer Kelan pressed the barrel of his shotgun up under her jawbone, shutting her mouth. "Please," he said. "Just start the truck."

Once they left the driveway, she knew without being told to take the road heading out of town. Clara knew where they were going, though she had never been there. The place where they kept hell. *Helle. Hellir.* Infernal. A cave. A hidden region. Kelan, dazed, was talking to her the whole time. He was sorry, but Seth didn't have the stomach for it. Seth was a chickenshit. And Clara, she was a witness. He needed her to see. Once she saw she would understand. Through the thin nightgown Clara felt the itchy wool blanket Grizz had thrown over the seat. The cab smelled of manure, an earthy, pungent scent.

Thick wet snowflakes clung to the wipers, icing over the windows. Soon it would freeze solid, and they would be driving blind. Clara found the defroster, but when she looked up again her headlights illuminated a huge dog. Not a dog, a coyote. Clara tapped the brakes, and the vehicle skated, a thousand pounds of steel drifting unmoored on the ice.

"What the fuck?" Kelan said. "Run it over." Her hand pressed the horn, but no sound came out. The gray, its muzzle bearded with ice, stayed planted in the road.

She jammed on the brakes and the truck wheeled into a full spin.

Kelan reached across and tried to yank the wheel in the same direction as the spin. His shotgun slipped to the cab's floor. She heard the blast, smelled acrid gunpowder. They were turning, spinning in circles as the truck whipped around on a patch of ice before slipping backward toward one of the steep ditches bordering either side of the road. It caught, held on the lip, and then the snowbank gave way, and they plunged down the ditch. Dimly, Clara heard her own voice, high and shrill, before the roof caved in, and her face slammed the steering wheel.

When Clara woke, her heartbeat pulsed in her forehead, and she realized she was upside down, clamped in by the steering wheel, her scalp torn and bleeding. Her side cramped, the baby pressing on her internal organs. Alive, the baby was alive inside her. The backwash of the headlights against the snowbank illuminated the cab. Beside her Kelan stirred, his face a red smear, one eye crusted shut. Clara touched her ribs. Bruised or broken, she didn't know.

She found she could move her legs, wedged under the steering wheel, and she wormed her way out. Clara pushed at her door, but it was jammed shut. The rear window had shattered, snow sweeping in to fill the cab. Clara crawled under the over-hanging seats to the opening. Just as she reached it, Kelan grasped her ankle. She lashed out with her other leg, kicked him in the face, and kept crawling. Halfway through the window, she cried out. The snow had hidden serrated glass teeth, and these bit deeply into her shoulder and back. She forced her way out, a sound like a ripped sheet inside her as she dropped into the dark cave beneath the upturned truck bed, her arms sinking elbow deep in the snow. Clara dived headlong into a drift, and squeezed her body out from under the truck.

Before she could catch her breath, the passenger-side door crunched open into the other side of the ditch as Kelan struggled to get out. Clara scrambled up the steep slope, grabbing hold of long grasses poking through the snow.

When she reached the top the road lay empty in either direction. Run. She had to run before shock settled in. Under her skin, the lanugo, the long ago. Her wolf self. If she stopped even once, she would not be able to get going again.

Across the road she spotted a small drop

down to the frozen river and across it a span of woods that led to the opposite hill. Home and the promise of safety lay no more than a half mile away. Earth and sky one in the swirling storm light.

Clara set off, crossing the iced-over river as wind skirred snow along the glassy surface. She could hear him behind her, screaming words the wind tore from his mouth, but she forced herself to keep moving. She had lost all sensation in her feet, the numbness spreading into the rest of her body as she waded through deeper drifts where pale, thin birch trees thrust from the snow. There was something human about their peeling skin, their upraised arms. Her mother, urging her on. In the wind she heard another sound as well, an echoing call. They were here, the coyotes, bounding through high drifts, fluid as phantoms among the trees. *Run with us.*

When she turned, she saw her own bloody footprints in the dark; Kelan had closed the distance, lugging the shotgun from the cab.

Clara pushed on through the bramble into a clearing. In the midst stood a run-down cabin leaning crookedly on its foundation. It was lit from within, warm and beckoning, the door banging open and shut in the wind. The sheriff's cruiser parked behind it, the roof humped with snow.

She shouted, not knowing what or why.

When no answer came, Clara limped toward the cabin, crossed the clearing. She climbed up on the stoop, recovering her breath, caught the swinging door, and stepped inside. The smell in the room so strong it burned in her nose, stung her eyes. Something chemical. She wiped her eyes and looked for a weapon.

She spotted the soiled mattress first, centered on the wood floor, a menagerie of impossible animals around it. What looked like red paint splashed underneath it, an uneven pentagram. A kerosene lantern, hissing quietly, cast flickering light over the scene. The sheriff himself slumped in the corner, his uniform soaked with dried black blood. An eyeless boar's head topped where his skull should have been, the jaws wrenched open to show the terrible teeth. BEHOLD THE NEW CREATION scrawled in the same red paint on the wooden boards behind him.

Clara reeled away. The place had been made for her. This bed. This was where Kelan wanted to take her all along, the tableau he made for her. *Please, God.* But with the prayer, the thought that there was no God here. She was in a place where God would not come.

Her leg muscles had stiffened, but Clara managed to limp outside. Kelan stood waiting in the clearing, not more than fifteen feet away, his breath smoking. "Look at me. Look at what you did." He grimaced, fingered the glistening open flap of skin on his cheek.

"I can fix it," she promised. "Let me help you."

"Go back inside," he said. He stood in the center of the meadow, shuddering. He looked near collapse himself, but he had the strength to raise his gun, cut off her only path of escape.

"No," she said. If she was going to die, it might as well be here, where she could feel the snow on her skin. Out in the open, among the trees where her spirit might run free. Not in there.

Kelan cursed. "I can tell you things," he said. He wove back and forth as he came closer. His voice rising and then falling, pleading with her and then berating. "About the devil. I knew him. I lived with him." He told her about the woman in the woods. An adulterer. A slut. Filthy like all women. His father and Sheriff Steve killed her and her lover and took the baby. Didn't Clara know that? Didn't she know who she was? The whole world was going to know. "Go inside. This is where you belong."

When he lifted the shotgun, something roared off in the woods, a cry so utterly inhuman it raised the hackles on Clara's neck.

Kelan pivoted and they were here, the coyotes surging from the woods all around him. Their ears peeled back, their yellow eyes huge and rolling. The gray pounced and snagged the edge of Kelan's coat in his teeth. Off balance, Kelan spun and fired, and the unbraced shotgun leaped in the looseness of his hold and smashed into his face. He toppled backward into the snow. But instead of falling on him, the coyotes fled, scared off by the blast, the gunpowder smell, his high-pitched screams.

The two were alone again in the clearing. Clara limped off the stoop, hoping he wouldn't notice her creeping up on him. Kelan, bleeding freely from his forehead, squatted as he levered open the shotgun, fumbling shells from his coat pockets. He blew on his fingers, numb from the cold, and looked up at Clara as if expected her to try rushing him. She approached, her palms upraised, when it came again, the primal bellow of something immense and wounded.

"No," Kelan said, seeing it first. "It's not possible." The thing entered into the clearing, and Clara retreated, unsure which way to run, caught between the cabin and Kelan and what had come from the woods. It looked like Seth, risen from his shallow grave. Seth's revenant here for vengeance. A thing massive and dark, as though it had formed from the fertile black soils of the farmlands stretching all around. A giant from under the earth, deep in the mountain. Her father's giant, dripping something wet as though disintegrating with each step. HeWhoSleeps. A demon summoned.

Kelan crammed in two shells and clanked shut the chambers. The giant stepped into the clearing, black and seething. It grabbed Kelan from the ground before he could fire, lifted him in a huge hug that left Kelan's feet windmilling above the ground. Kelan wheezed, dropping the gun, his fists flailing, knocking off wet dark earth. His screaming ended when the embrace tightened and all breath squeezed from his body. His rib cage collapsed, bones snapping brittle, an almost delicate sound, like icicles breaking on stones. Then the giant flung him away, the boy's body folding as he fell.

Later she would wonder why she did this, how she had such presence of mind. Clara went over and crouched beside Kelan, crumpled in the snow. He blinked up at her, his pupils darkening, the color of falling ashes. He tried to speak through a mouth filling with blood. She lay her hand on his icy cheek, saying, "It's okay, it's okay," until he shuddered and was still.

The giant swayed above them, black circles ringing his eyes, and when he opened his mouth what came out was an animal's cry of pain.

She was burning up under her skin. Somewhere off in the woods one of the coyotes howled, a question in the night, the others joining in. Clara's own pain washed over her, splitting her strange calm. It came in waves, in beats. "Grizz," she said to the giant. "Seth Fallon." She called by his full name, his baptized name. She needed him to come back to his human self. "I think my water just broke."

ADVENT

Under the door she saw the shadow of his passage in a bar of moonlight. The night stretched long and silent before she heard the scream, a wet gurgle of something being eaten alive, and then nothingness. She waited for it to return to the cabin, press again at the door. What had been killed out there? The girl lay awake with the rifle her father had left her and didn't sleep until sometime before dawn.

The next morning she carried the half-stock rifle with her when she went to gather eggs. One of the hens was gone, the only thing left of her a few feathers drifting down in the dusty light. That was what she heard screaming. But it was not an ordinary fox that had done this. The thing outside her cabin had been heavy, big as a man. She didn't bother to fix the latch. If it came back, what use was a thin strip of leather? How could it possibly bar a monster? She looked at the blue gleaming metal of the gun her father had given her for protection. And what use was this gun? Her father had gone out on the prairies to save her, and he had not returned.

Draw blood from the *loup garou,* he had told her, and he will change to his human form. He will tell you the secret he has brought for you.

Drowsy from a lack of sleep, she went about her errands, out in the sugar maples, moving from spigot to spigot to collect the syrup the cold nights had forced from the trees. Syrup clear as blood, the trees bleeding in a time of change between the winter and spring. The girl herself bled, not understanding why. There were no other women she could turn to and ask about it. The smell of her blood, she knew somehow, had drawn this thing.

There under the trees, goose bumps rippled up and down her arms, and when she turned, she saw the *loup garou* watching her from the shadows. It growled, displaying a mouth of long teeth, and loped toward her. Her feet felt riven to the earth, as if stakes had been driven through them. The growling was a softer sound than she expected, almost a purr. When the *loup garou* raised up on two legs, the matted hair fell away from its face. Its nostrils were flaring, and the large amber eyes held her again. She saw the lean ropy arms, the thick muscles of its thighs, the privates coiled in their dark nest. She shut her eyes, ashamed for looking. It smelled of leaves and sweat and grass. The claws were as sharp as she remembered, but here in the daylight, in the shadows of the woods, it was less a fearful thing. A boy only, she realized. A wild child. It circled her warily, still growling.

Afraid, not knowing what else to do, she opened her mouth, and what poured out was a song, a hymn her mother used to sing to her before bed.

Abide with me, fast falls the eventide.

The darkness deepens — Lord with me abide.

Her voice caught and warbled, but the sound stopped the thing in its path. A boy, then. Her father, she knew in that moment, had killed its wolf mother, the only mother it had known. The boy had struck back in confusion. A boy from the War with Indians. A boy her own age.

She had been alone for a long time. Wherever her father had been, he was not coming back. The wolf child came closer, entranced by the song, the shape of her mouth. She sang on, luring it in, not knowing if it came to save or devour.

The Holden Evening Prayer service Logan introduced at the beginning of Advent season would not have gone well a few months before. This song of light and darkness in the world, which required the congregation to sit up close and sing in rounds, would have been resisted. His German American congregation was not a singing people, unless it was the old, old hymns from the brown book of worship. They had specific places where each must sit when they came inside. The men sat mostly on the north side, the women on the south. Once Logan had roped off the back pews and balcony, and mild old ladies had responded with defiance and torn down the barriers. Once he had tried to coax them to change, and they met him with stony resistance.

All that had passed now. For a short time, they would not complain. They came to be near one another, for the shelter the church offered from the ravenous winter world outside. They needed the promises more than ever. And they came to see the baby, Dena. Clara had made sure the child had a strong birth name. Dena, from the Old English. Dena, which meant "from the valley." The news stations and journalists from around the country had come and gone. It was morning, the nightmare over, and they had to learn to live with one another once more.

They all came for Dena, even Grizz, who sat at the back of the church, not far from the Gunderson family, the boy Lee and his mother, Laura. They were all here. Grizz had scars on his hands, a stigmata. Down in that pit, in the moment of his surrender, he had spotted sharp metal spurs jutting from the aluminum sides. He had impaled his palms into these, lifted himself from the mire. A nylon rope lowered down, looping toward him. He heard a boy's voice, Lee shouting from above that he should tie it around his waist. With the boy pulling from above and Grizz grabbing at the sharp spurs, he had climbed out of that killing pit.

Lee had come for him in his last moment. Lee had pulled him up and stood there shivering, waiting for a punishment that never arrived.

"Where is your brother?" Grizz gasped for breath.

"He's going to take her into the woods. Where they always take them."

Logan, dressed in layers of liturgical clothing, the alb, the stole, the big square cross around his throat, sang the Holden Evening Prayer:

Now as evening falls around us,
We shall raise our songs to you.
God of daybreak, God of shadows.
Come to light our hearts anew.

By Advent the snows were already knee deep. It would be April before they saw the bare ground again. A season of long-lasting darkness this far north with the roads leading out of town glazed with impassible ice. The widows heard voices out in the snow. They heard the voices of those who had gone on before, husbands and children. The widows with their sparrow bones and porous skin listened in the snow and heard someone calling. "Come, the way is soft. Those you love are waiting." They listened; they followed. At the beginning of December, the congregation buried two of them and Clara struggled to remember their faces after they were gone, the shape of their small hands within her own.

After Grizz had killed Kelan, he leaned against a tree and sank in the snow. He went into shock or something like it. Clara had no choice but to go back inside the cabin and search the sheriff's corpse for the keys to his cruiser. It had to be done. She was not going to have the baby out here. Clara had driven both of them home, passing the overturned truck in the ditch, and she made it as far as Nora's house, before the pain of the contractions halted her and she could go no further.

Dena was born in Nora's living room, among the spider ferns and umbrella trees.

Now, Nora was trying to join those other widows. She had a seizure shortly before Christmas. When Clara heard about it she took Baby Dena and went to see her. She carried in Dena, still buckled in her car seat and fast asleep, to Nora's room, which was awash in white, wintry light. Nora's pale hair was mummified in a bandage, and she snored quietly. She'd struck her head on the kitchen floor during the seizure and she had lain there for a day and half before her daughter-in-law, visiting from the farm, had found her. Her hazy blue eyes opened, focused on Clara. "Hello, dear," she said, smiling. "You look well."

Clara herself had been in the hospital for two weeks after her near-death experience, and it was not a place she was eager to return to. Hypothermic, having lost two pints of blood from the accident, Clara's recovery went on even after she was allowed to go home with the baby. Her hair newly shorn in a boyish bob, she did not feel well. "Thank you."

Clara brought over the baby so Nora could cluck and coo over her. "It's too bad they rescued me. I think I was dreaming of Charlie when I had the seizure." She paused, and Clara thought for a moment she might start crying.

"I'm going to need you," Clara said. "This baby is going to need you."

"Nonsense. You'll be fine."

"But I won't." Her throat thickened. "You would think I would have nightmares, but I don't. I don't even know what I dream when I do. I'm not afraid, not for myself, but I'm exhausted all the time. I have to keep checking on the baby every hour. Make sure she's breathing."

"I was the same with my first. It gets better."

"I would die for her. I almost did." Clara went on to talk about how Logan had changed, how well he took care of her, nursing her, but also how he still seemed ambivalent toward the baby. She described her uncertainty about what would happen to her fragile family, her fears about her marriage.

Nora sighed when she was done, "In my day we didn't have any choice, but I'm glad Charlie stuck with me through the bad times. Every couple reaches some kind of turning point. They either break or find a way to go on."

"Do you think we're going to make it?"

"Who the hell knows?" Nora said. She laughed, but it was short-lived when Clara didn't join her. Nora waved her left hand in the air around her. "Reach in that drawer there and fetch me out what you find."

Clara opened the nightstand drawer. Nothing was in there but a Bible and a Baggie that looked like it was filled with dark loam, moist chunks like bits of chewed brownie. Clara held it up to light. "This?"

"You know what it is?"

"A bit of land from your family farm?"

"No, it's from Chimayo. My son brought it from home, but I don't have any use for the stuff."

"Chimayo?"

"It's like the Lourdes of the West or something. People go there seeking healing. Charlie made sure we stopped there on our big trip. His prostate cancer had been spreading. He'd read about the place in *Reader's Digest* and was determined to try anything. Dug that soil from the church basement where pictures were pasted on a wall, stories and letters of the miraculous, candles glowing all around. They say the dirt was holy to the Indians long before the

Catholics built a mission."

"I thought Charlie died of a heart attack."

"Yes, but not cancer. His cancer was cured by the dirt. If there is anything a farmer knows, it's the power dirt has to heal."

"Why are you showing it to me?"

"I'm giving it to you, dear."

"I don't know. It sounds a little pagan."

Nora smiled. "There are some like me who think that it's God's will when a new pastor comes. He is the one God chose for us. But I also believe God sent you here."

Clara shook her head. "What I am supposed to do with this?"

For their first Christmas together, Logan brought home a living tree from a farm ten miles out in the country. He put away his boxed, artificial tree, said he wouldn't mind needles on the floor for once. The smell of the balsam fir filled the room with piney sweetness. It stood eight feet tall and seemed nearly as wide. "What do you think?" Logan asked.

"Much better than that aluminum-foil tree you had at seminary."

"That's antique, you know, made by Mirro. One of a kind." Every Christmas Logan had decorated that tree with his mother, hung bulbs from the pink frosted metal branches, but this year he said was a time for making new traditions.

While the baby napped in her swing, Clara sipped from her mug and helped Logan string up the lights. They both were drinking cocoa that Clara laced with a pinch of dirt. Miracle dirt, if you believed in such things. Pica, that was the name the ancients had for how a woman craved earth when pregnant or nursing. Just a pinch, so Logan wouldn't know. What he didn't know wouldn't hurt him.

Logan had on a Santa hat as he hummed along with Elvis's "Blue Christmas." Together, they put on the ornaments, Clara pretending not to notice when he rehung the ones she had put in place. After the ornaments, Logan hung the tinsel one strand at a time, but Clara tossed hers up in clumps.

Outside the wind sculpted a bare moonscape from the snow, and low clouds sifted down their artic spindrift. Logan finished and dimmed the lights so he could turn on the tree. He liked the big colored lights, the ones that painted a flickering pattern on the walls and ceiling. From out by the graveyard, a familiar sound arose, a few trailing barks rising in pitch, then one, long low howl. Clara went to window to watch them bound in the snow, playfully chasing one another. Logan came behind her and wrapped his arms around her. "They're beautiful," he said. He ran one hand through her hair. "What are you thinking about?"

He kissed the back of her neck, the sweet place where her shoulder met her throat. She thought of a boy being tormented by his own father. Kelan had not been buried in the suicide section. He was buried with the saints. Saints and sinners, all of us, Logan said, convincing the council that in death we were one. There might be suicides in the future, but no longer would they be outcasts in death. *Such a nice boy,* the old ones said. *So handsome. Wasn't Lucifer the most beautiful of the angels?* The story of what had happened went on reverberating in the words and gestures of everything people in town said, migrating in the whispering of teenagers in the hallways of the high school, the low gossip of old people at the pool hall and grocery store, the hushed way parents tried to explain it to their children before bedtime, all of them knowing there was no language large enough to take the awfulness away. They blamed it on the devil. They blamed his father and the man who trained his father, Steve Krieger. And the more they talked and talked, the more they made him into some Other so they could go on. Clara knew. She had set her hand on his skin and knew the monster was as fully human as any of them, even if she did not understand and knew she never would. "I was thinking about heaven," she said. "What if it's not a place? Not somewhere we go, but somewhere inside us."

Logan kissed her cheek, cupped her face. She thought of those widows hearing voices out in the snow, of her mother fighting to get home. Here was the place that made her, the place they belonged for a time. She had healed her family in coming home. She had grounded her own far-ranging mind.

From the swing, Baby Dena began to cry. Dena had large round dark eyes, a widow's brow that crinkled up when she was upset. A colicky baby, crying at all hours of the night. Now that they were home from the hospital, it all fell to her, since Logan avoided holding the baby. Clara tensed at the piercing sound. Each cry meant something different, and she couldn't always tell the "I'm hungry" sob from the "change me now" lament. This cry sounded somewhere in between. Dena wanted to be held.

Logan froze as well, stopped his kissing. The crying bothered him even worse than her, sent him scurrying for cover next door at his church. He seemed still frightened of the baby, born weighing only six pounds, but he followed Clara about, watched her while she bathed Dena, sat beside her during the feedings. The baby, his baby, which he had never expected. His arms were still wrapped around her waist, but they went slack. His breath warm against her neck. "I'll go get her," he said, leaving Clara at the window.

Haying Season

After two weeks of working at the farm, few outward signs showed in Lee. His face had tanned, but his plump cheeks and flabby stomach looked undaunted by all the hard work. Near the scar on his left arm, the skin was prickled by hundreds of small scratches and gashes he'd picked up baling hay.

Late afternoon found them in the hayfields once more, Grizz driving a lumbering International tractor that was trailed by a baler and Lee standing on the hayrack. The tractor glinted silver; the baler licked up lumps of hay from the green ground and spat them out in neatly roped twenty-pound bales that Lee caught and stacked on the hayrack beside him. He had to keep his balance as the rack swayed over the uneven ground and the bales came without ceasing. Each bale had to be wedged in tight, a mountain of hay that might come tumbling down if Lee's aim was not quick and true.

Grizz saw all this, saw the changes in the child. Lee did not hate farmwork the way Seth had, even hard moments like this, and there was plenty of work any given season. Grizz had sold the property around the mountain to the county on the condition that the limestone never be excavated, the burial mounds left undisturbed. In perpetuity, the last of the tallgrass would not be cut. The land would remain as it was, a beautiful portrait of another time. No one would ever disturb Seth's grave.

The funds allowed Grizz to purchase another semi, and he went to work for co-ops in neighboring counties full-time, driving loads. He still only just scraped by each season, and after a wet spring the crops went in late this year. Grizz was, as always, nervous about the harvest. He still awaited the perfect season. He still lived in the land of next year, but he was alive and doing what he loved. And there was one boy, at least, whom he had reclaimed from hell.

Haying was hot, dirty work. Sharp straws poked out from the bales to jab and claw his skin. By the end of the day his body was furred in a fine green dust. But Lee was no longer the tenderfoot, not the foolish boy who showed up in short sleeves to bale hay and left with aching, bleeding arms. His skin was tougher, his balance even and confident. His back no longer ached in the morning. When the ancient baler choked on too large a lump of hay, Lee could hop down and fix the jam. He had learned to handle the far more complicated gearing of the International and could guide the big tractor over the uneven ground on days Grizz let him drive a load of hay up from the fields. Hay stuck to his sweat-streaked skin. Blades of it probed for tender places to make fresh wounds. He breathed in the tractor's exhaust and dust and bugs kicked up from the fields.

And yet it was beautiful to be together in the hot sundown. Swallows dipped and dived around them, hunting insects the tractor stirred up from the soil. The fields shone emerald in the fading light. From this upper pasture, the two had a view of the river valley, and Grizz turned now to point toward the west where thunderheads piled up. They would have to hurry before the rain came. If the hay got soaked, it would mold and rot, and all their hard work would be for nothing. The wind already carried the sweet smell of wet. A shadow from a chicken hawk riding on a thermal passed over the field and chased away the swallows. Lee took the bales and formed neat square stacks while Grizz kicked the tractor into higher gear. They worked in a wordless rhythm, moving faster to beat the rain, his focus on maneuvering the tractor in tight turns, Lee yanking out bales and tossing and stacking.

Then the work was done, and Lee rode down the hill standing atop his lurching hay mound, sapped but triumphant. From his perch, twenty feet above the mowed ground, he could likely see the old landing on the other side of the valley, the silver glinting of the river, and beyond it the rim of the world itself, turning black now with storm.

Lightning rippled from boiling clouds, followed a few seconds later by grumbles of thunder. Grizz heard the cattle moan out in the yard. One large drop of rain splashed his cheek. "Hurry," he called to him, grinding the tractor to a halt outside the barn. Lee scrambled down from the pile of stacked bales, chunks of loose hay spraying down along with him.

A minute later, Grizz emerged from the barn with an immense blue tarp and a coil of rope and motioned for Lee to climb up again. Back atop the hay, Lee took the end of the tarp just as the rain began to lash down. Lee balanced along the flat surface, the tarp fanning out behind him. Wind lifted the sheet and nearly tore it from his grasp. Grizz was shouting from below while he clutched a rope that held it from the other end. Rain blinded him. Grizz imagined the tarp filling up like a sail, lifting the boy and carrying him straight into the thunderheads. But Lee got down on his knees to keep his balance and crawled, still dragging the flapping tarp behind him. Then he was climbing down the other side, the billowing plastic stretching and then lying flat across the bales. Wind and rain battered both of them. Lee was drenched by the time Grizz came around the side with another rope to secure it. "You can let go now," he told him. "Let's get you inside."

On a normal day they would sit out on the white sagging porch and sip tea with fresh mint pulled from the weedy garden Jo had once tended. Sometimes they were joined by the pastor's wife with her baby girl. Seth's old girlfriend had moved back to the Cities along with her father.

On this day, Grizz left him alone to undress in the mudroom, stripping off his soaked socks and the very same ragged shoes he had worn during his tumble down the mountain. After a few minutes he carried to him a bundle of musty-smelling clothes and an old towel. "You can shower down here. I have some shoes that might fit you as well." Lee frowned and said nothing, but when he came back upstairs he was wearing the Judas Priest shirt from Seth and his son's jeans and shoes. "These clothes?" he said.

"Yeah. They were his."

Lee said nothing.

"I'll drive you home."

"That's okay. The rain's stopped outside." They both listened in the new quiet. The faint sound of a radio crooning trickled in from the next room. "I don't hear it anymore." What they heard was the cattle crying out in their pens, and then above it a single, solitary howl.

"Maybe I should drive you."

"No. Let me do this. You said they were afraid of you."

"They won't let me get near."

"And the town may hunt them again next year, if they keep going there."

"It may be that they already have a taste for killing, for housecats and such."

Lee walked outside. Deep ruts in the gravel driveway had become small ponds where the moon's face came and went. When the moon appeared the fields turned luminous. The little wolves were in the meadow, under the cliffs Lee had fallen from. The sound of rain still dripping through the trees filled up the dark woods.

The coyotes romped in the grasses, scaring up mice, their spines arched. They cackled when they caught one and lapped it up with their long tongues. Then they turned, the wind having carried the scents of Grizz and Lee out to them. They smelled Seth on his clothes and the gray loped toward him, his tail bristling. A warm breeze from the mountain washed over them, rippling the clothing they wore, like the sweet breathing of some benevolent giant. Lee didn't hesitate to go forward, and Grizz shut his eyes and whispered a prayer that no harm would come to the boy. He had to let him go, for both their sakes. Lee was among them now, the coyotes circling him as he walked in the meadow. They passed from the waving tallgrasses into the dark trees where the shadows were dancing, a boy and three little wolves who came to him when he held out his hand.

AUTHOR'S NOTE

The murder story that sparked this novel is based on true events in the town of Morgan, Minnesota. I heard only the barest details — a boy with a shotgun tucked into his coat going to his teacher's house and then killing the sheriff by shooting through the car door. In my original draft, I had not intended to write anything about it, but I woke up one morning hearing the voice of a father wondering over his son and what he has done. I had to set it down, and when I did, his voice took over this story. Jessamyn West once wrote, "Fiction reveals truths that reality obscures." While writing *Little Wolves* I intentionally avoided finding out any more details about the actual case. New to parenthood myself, I had to follow this father's voice, and this novel is where he led me.

As I wrote, other stories came to me. A Lutheran pastor who had just finished serving a congregation out on the prairie told me about her church's strict rules regarding the burial of the dead and her struggles with these customs. In the cemetery behind the church, suicides were not allowed to be buried with the saints and instead went into a separate corner. As far as I know, the congregation continues this practice to this day.

These stories form the skeleton, and they are both true, but all else is purely a work of the imagination.

ACKNOWLEDGMENTS

No writer I know of is able to function without a supportive community. With two young children at home, I would not be able to find time and energy to write without the loving support of my wife, Melissa. Years spent visiting and sometimes living at my in-laws' farm has taught me time and time again the vital connection between land and families. For the stories and knowledge they have shared with me I am grateful, as I am grateful to my own parents for raising me with the freedom to take risks, for forgiving me when I fail, and for teaching me how to go on.

As a graduate of the creative writing MFA program at Mankato, I've been fortunate to have stayed in touch with many friends. Nick Healy, who read this story when it was just a kernel, is one such wise voice who guided me along the way. Nick also introduced me to the Wednesday Writers in

Mankato: Nate Leboutillier, Nicole Helget, Tom Flynn, Aaron Frisch, Rick Robbins, and Gordon Pueschner all provided inspiration and help. Here at Normandale Community College, where I'm part of a thriving AFA program in creative writing, I've been able to work with other fiction writers like John Reimringer, Alicia Conroy, and Charlotte Sullivan and many others, gifted writers who understand the importance for teachers of writing to stay active in the craft. They've read various chapters, giving encouragement at just the right times.

I'm grateful to the state of Minnesota for an Artist's Initiative Grant that allowed me to travel to Southwest Minnesota and see the places featured in this novel as well as mentor with accomplished writers like Caroline Leavitt.

Along the way I've also made friends with good people like novelist Peter Geye, whose exciting feedback about the novel this summer gave me the courage I needed to send it out. Peter also introduced me to agent Laura Langlie, who has been wonderful every step of the way.

Editor Mark Doten at Soho Press believed in this book enough to take a chance on it. Read this work knowing that his keen insights and brilliant edits helped make this what it became. If it shines, it's because Mark saw the raw material and helped polish it into the present form.

Invariably, this will go out into the world and I will realize that I have forgotten someone here. There are too many to list. I knew a long time ago that I wanted to be a writer. I was only able to become so because of the great teachers and books and friends and family and students who've inspired me.

I'm grateful. Thank you one and all.

ABOUT THE AUTHOR

Thomas Maltman's essays, poetry, and fiction have been published in many literary journals. He has an MFA from Minnesota State University, Mankato. His first novel, *The Night Birds,* won an Alex Award, a Spur Award, and the Friends of American Writers Literary Award. In 2009 the American Library Association chose *The Night Birds* as an "Outstanding Book for the College Bound." He's taught for four years at Normandale Community College and lives in the Twin Cities area. *Little Wolves* is his second novel.

The employees of Thorndike Press hope you have enjoyed this Large Print book. All our Thorndike, Wheeler, and Kennebec Large Print titles are designed for easy reading, and all our books are made to last. Other Thorndike Press Large Print books are available at your library, through selected bookstores, or directly from us.

For information about titles, please call:
(800) 223-1244

or visit our Web site at:
http://gale.cengage.com/thorndike

To share your comments, please write:
Publisher
Thorndike Press
10 Water St., Suite 310
Waterville, ME 04901